hello world

by

Murray Ewing

Published by Bookship, 2017.

ISBN 978-0-9934239-2-5

Copyright © Murray Ewing 2017.

Cover design by Murray Ewing.

Murray Ewing asserts the moral right to be identified as the author of this work.

This novel is a work of fiction. The names, characters, incidents and locations portrayed in the story are entirely imaginary. Any resemblance to actual persons, living or dead, or events, organisations, companies and other bodies, is coincidental.

hello world

BOOKSHIP

```
10 PRINT "hello world"
20 GOTO 10
```

1

Hi, Mum.

It's me, Tim.

I'm on the school roof. How are you?

I don't know if you keep up with these things, but it's 1984.

1984 is the year they used to think would be the future. You know, in that book, was it by Orson Welles, or H G Wells, or someone? (Can't think of anyone to ask but you. Dad doesn't read books, Joe only knows about motorbikes and heavy metal, and I only know about computers.) Now, of course, we know the future's going to be the year 2000. This time they named a comic after it, not a book. (2000A.D. with Tharg the Mighty!)

Most likely, we won't get there.

It's flat up here on the school roof. I don't want you thinking I'm clinging onto tiles or hanging off a gutter. It's flat, with puddles, and there's a manky old pair of football boots in one corner, and a hairy-looking tennis ball in the other, and apart from that it's just me and the world.

Oh, and a pigeon.

I'm going to tell you about Penny, but first I need to think about nuclear war for a bit. I quite often think about nuclear war. (I don't know, do you listen in?) I haven't been

7

thinking about it as much recently, though, so you could say I've got some catching up to do.

The thing about nuclear weapons is, they're not just big bad things that go bang. They do go bang, but they do it on such a massive scale they have all sorts of side-effects and complications. Some are as bad as the bang itself.

Say they dropped a one megaton bomb on London right now.

(No one's going to bother dropping a bomb on a little town like Eastead.)

There it is, hurtling down from the sky. All those people milling about in the streets below, minding their own business. Someone sees it and points. Others look up and see it too, but they can't do anything. It's too late. Faster and faster it falls, and then—

London is 29 miles away.

Lying here, looking at the sky, the first thing I'd know would be a shocking white flash, brighter than the sun at midday. I wouldn't be totally blinded (you'd have to be within ten miles of the blast for that), but I'd probably end up blinking some pretty serious purple blotches. I might get a bit sunburnt, too.

I wouldn't hear the bang that went with the flash straightaway. What would reach me next would be the Electro-Magnetic Pulse. This is a shockwave of pure electrical force that travels at 90% the speed of light. It sends a jolt of electricity through everything it can. TVs, hi-fi's, fridges, computers, and Patrick's dad's brand new home video recorder would all go fizz-whizz. Aeroplanes might have their controls zapped and come plunging to the ground. It would even electrify things that weren't electrical, like the metal pipes in the plumbing at home. Turn the taps on, you might get fried. Tzzd!

Up here, the only thing to feel the Electro-Magnetic Pulse would be my digital watch. (Which is a pity, because

I like my digital watch. It's got a calculator built in.) I don't know what would happen to it. It might go blank and never work again, or it might fast-forward to the year 2000, which would be sort of funny.

But who'd need to know the time after a nuclear war?

The bang would come a whole 2 minutes 53 seconds after the flash. (I worked that out on my calculator watch.) It would sound like a hundred thousand thunder claps going BOOM! all at once, and might make me deaf for a bit. In fact (I was told by Mr Brow, our Physics teacher), sound travels faster through solids and liquids than air, so I'd probably feel a rumble in the ground before I heard the bang, like a mini-earthquake.

That would be scary.

The blast itself would be scarier.

If I was one of those people in the streets right below it, or if I was within six miles of where it went off, I'd be gone in an instant. Vaporised, like a popsicle beamed into the heart of the sun. There might be a shadow burned into the ground where I'd been, but not much else. Not even a pair of smoking school shoes.

A little outside that, I might not get totally vaped, but I'd still be hurt as bad as if I'd stepped into a burning building. And there'd be a lot of burning buildings about. Cars would explode, so would petrol stations and gasometers. The blast would shatter every window for miles around, and fragments of glass would be flying about in super strong winds. You'd get cut to pieces if you weren't in some sort of shelter. If you were in some sort of shelter, it'd probably fall on you.

Here, it would be different. There'd be strong winds, which might be carrying some pretty dangerous debris, like bits of broken glass or the occasional radioactive sparrow. Telegraph poles and electrical cables might get blown down. I'd have to cling to the roof not to be swept off.

But the worst thing would be what happens after.

When things calmed down, I'd get up, and I'd see it. The mushroom cloud on the horizon. It would be ten miles high and ten miles wide, like a great grey tombstone.

It would be deadly radioactive.

And after that, there'd be snowfalls of radioactive ash, and when it rained, it would be black rain, full of radioactive dust. You wouldn't be able to see it, but radioactivity would be in the air, and it would get into the water, poisoning it. Soon, it would get into everything. The whole world would turn deadly dangerous. There'd be a nuclear winter, which is what happens when dust thrown into the air blocks out the sun for months or even years. Nothing would grow. We'd have no food once the tinned stuff ran out. Those of us who didn't die of radiation would starve, or just give up. Society would collapse. There'd be no electricity or gas, no telephones. Governments would be of no use. (Dad says they aren't any use now.) People would kill each other for food. Martial law would have to be brought in. We'd all be forced to work on special farms, harvesting the occasional glowing potato only to have it snatched off us by some bloke with a gun. Or, if we could, we'd retreat into our own little bunkers, safe from the world, but totally cut off from it. Till the radiation went away. Which might be, you know, a million years.

And of course they wouldn't just drop a single bomb on London. I read (in The Radio Times) that if they launched every nuclear missile in the world right now, it would kill, instantly, half the world's population.

(I don't know, does that include Wombles?)

One thing would be sure. Nothing in the world would ever be the same again.

Life would become nothing but a relentless, pointless struggle to survive.

Anyway, that's what I think about sometimes.

I was thirteen on June 12th. I first spoke to Penny on September 24th. Today is October 25th, and I may never see her, ever again. Even if there isn't a nuclear war.

2

But you'll be wanting to hear how things are at home.

Well, Dad's worse than ever, and Joe's getting more like him every day.

That's the back-of-a-postcard version.

But you'll want the long version, so—

Remember how Dad used to be when he got back from work each day? Snarly for ten minutes, grumpy for half an hour, then slowly simmering down to something a bit more likeable in time for dinner, like a mad scientist with the potion wearing off? And at weekends, he could even be a bit cheerful?

Well, he's like that now, only the ten minutes is an hour, the half an hour is till-nine-o'clock, the likeable is, at best, sitting there making grumpy comments in front of the TV, and the highlight of weekends is when he goes down the pub on a Sunday afternoon and stays there.

For a while he was worse than that.

I mean, at first all he did was sit around, not even going to work. His boss came by to say he understood and all, but... And still he sat around, so he got the sack.

It seemed he was like that for ages, but it was probably only four or five months.

Then I remember coming home from school one day to find Gramps — your dad, not Dad's — in the living room, talking to him. I was really surprised, because Gramps lives miles away, doesn't he? But now I come to think of it, he *had* phoned a few days before, and I'd answered because Dad never answers, and he'd asked how things were, and I'd said okay, but that he'd probably have to write letters in future because the phone was going to be cut off, and did he know how I could get a supply of 50p's for the gas meter because it was getting cold in the mornings and Joe and me were starting to feel the lack of hot water.

Gramps took us (me and Joe, not Dad) to the Happy Eater down the London Road (which was nice, because we'd had nothing but baked beans and tinned peas all week), and had a word with us about how he'd had a word with Dad. Then he took us home but Dad refused to let him back in the house, shouting at him and calling him names, saying he was trying to turn his own kids against him and things like that. So Gramps said goodbye to us, but to me (in a low voice) said that Dad shouting was at least better than Dad sitting around doing nothing.

And he was right, because shortly after that, Dad got a job again.

He's still got it. He works for Acme Printers off the High Street. (They really are called Acme, just like in the Road Runner cartoons.) Quite often he has to work late, and he has to work some Saturdays too, but he's better than he was before.

We don't see Gramps anymore though.

Now to Joe. Joe left school as soon as he could, and at the moment he's on a YTS.

YTS is a government thing. It stands for Youth Training Scheme. (I joke it means Joe is training to be a youth. Joe then hits me. I guess that's why they call it a punchline.)

Joe's training to be a post-room assistant. Of course, what he most wants to be is a Hell's Angel, but he's not old enough so they won't let him in.

Okay, that's another joke. What Joe really, really wants to be is a motorbike mechanic or something like that.

I just realised you wouldn't know about Joe's motorbike. It's odd to think, the last you knew, Joe was fourteen, and now he's seventeen. He's probably grown a foot taller, and a foot thinner, too. Standing there sometimes, he's like a rake with a stoop. If he doesn't shave, he gets this ghost of a Ming the Merciless moustache at the corners of his mouth, which he's always stroking, like he's trying to encourage it to grow, or he's checking it hasn't blown away. That, or he's working on his next evil plot to make my life miserable.

Joe eats, sleeps, and breathes motorbikes. He buys motorbike magazines, listens to heavy metal music about motorbikes, wears his creaky leather biker jacket while we're eating dinner (and Dad doesn't say anything, because Dad wears his work overalls — honestly, sometimes I think every meal I eat tastes of motor oil and printer's ink). He has motorbike dreams. Every spare moment, he's out in the back garden, taking his bike apart and putting it together again, adjusting this or tweaking that, clanking spanners and swearing. Sometimes he even rides the silly thing.

What I should tell you about is how Joe got his motorbike, because that leads on to how I got my computer.

Last year, after ages of not hearing from him, Gramps phoned. He timed it just right, so Joe and me were home but Dad wasn't. I answered. (Joe heard the phone ringing, but shouted at me to answer it. That's how things are done at home. Dad's the brigadier who gives the orders, Joe's the sergeant major who passes them down — plus a few of his own — and I'm the troops. I get to carry the orders out.)

Anyway, Gramps asked how things were and I said okay, and he said, 'Is that okay as in the phone's going to be cut off tomorrow, or really okay?' So I said *really* okay. Then he told me what he wanted to do. He said he'd been thinking about this for a while, but as it was Joe's sixteenth birthday in a couple of weeks, he was going to use that as an excuse. He wanted to buy us a present each, Joe and me. He wanted it to be something really special. He said partly it was to make up for the fact that he hadn't been able to see us for our last couple of birthdays (since the whole shouting thing with Dad), but also he wanted to do it because we were both of us having to grow up without a mum (or 'mam', as he says), and it was the only thing he could think of to try and make up for that. So he told me to really think about it, then asked me to put Joe on the line, so he could explain it to him.

Joe and me really thought about it. Gramps said not to think how much things cost, just what we wanted. Joe was back on the phone first, saying what he wanted was a motorbike. I went next and said I wanted a Sinclair ZX Spectrum 48k. (Which is actually a lot cheaper than a motorbike.) I spelled it out for him. We were both expecting Gramps to say he was hoping we'd pick something less expensive, but he didn't. What he said was he'd phone back tomorrow.

(I don't want you thinking, Mum, that by asking for a computer I was asking for a great big clunky machine as big as a room, all glowing valves and flashing lights and whirling spools of magnetic tape, the kind of thing baddies have in underground bases in James Bond films. What I'm talking about is a new thing called a home computer. It's also called a microcomputer, or micro for short. The ZX Spectrum is an excellent example of just how compact and neat all that old computing power has been made now we've got silicon chips instead of valves. It doesn't fill a room. It's about the size of a book, weighs half a kilo, and you couldn't take over the world with one if you loaded it into a cannon and shot it at people.)

The next day, Gramps phoned again. He spoke to Joe for a bit about what sort of motorbike he wanted. Joe knew exactly what he wanted, because he'd been drooling over biking magazines for months. He said, 'I don't want nothing foreign. No Kawasaki this or Yamaha that. I want a Honda SuperDream.'

I didn't hear what Gramps said, but Joe looked kind of surprised, or winded, and handed me the phone.

I looked at Joe, still trying to work out what his expression meant, while Gramps said he'd been looking into what

I wanted, and had talked to the computer salesman at Rumbelows. At this point my heart fell because I just knew he was going to say the 48k Spectrum was a bit expensive and more than I really needed, so he was going to get me the 16k version instead (which is cheaper, but miles worse). Or maybe he was going to get me an ancient ZX80, which comes as a kit, because I might enjoy putting it together! (I'd have preferred an abacus made of twigs.) But no, what he said next made me look, I know, exactly as Joe had when he'd handed me the phone.

Gramps said, 'I found out that the Spectrum itself isn't enough, and that you need a TV to go with it. So I'm going to get you one of those too. Just a small one, mind. And it's to be for your own use only. I'll not have Joe ferreting it off to his bedroom to watch late night horror films. And I'm getting what they call a printer, too. Seems those are important if you're to be using it for your schoolwork.'

Then Gramps told us we weren't to tell Dad. He was going to do that. By letter.

A week later, Joe had his motorbike and I had my Spectrum and Dad was in a right huff.

What an awkward time that was. Joe creeping out to the back garden, which is where he keeps his bike, too scared to start it and give it a good rev. Me creeping up to my room, which is where I keep my Spectrum, too scared to touch a key in case it beeped. Dad sitting in the living room, watching TV and smouldering like a just-landed meteorite.

He didn't say anything, though.

That's how things are, you see, Mum. None of us says anything. And I don't just mean about Joe's motorbike or my computer. I mean loads of things.

We don't mention you.

I don't know if I can explain it, but, after you weren't there anymore, it was just us three blokes, having to get on with it on our own. And it was like we had to pretend it had always been like that, so it didn't seem something was missing, you know? And that spread to include everything. Because you were so much part of everything. Talking about anything makes it seem we're getting too close to mentioning you so, you know, we just don't. Even when Joe's mouth's going like a windsock in a gale, he's not saying anything. Most days, Dad barely grunts.

Back to my computer, though!

I love my ZX Spectrum.

There's nothing I like more than being up in my room, the door shut, the whole of the rest of the world *out there* and me *in here*, and I'm doing stuff on my computer.

It's my own little world-proof bunker.

Some of the time I play games. The best game in the world is Manic Miner. In it, you play Miner Willy, who's gone down a mine to mine some gold or something, but instead finds all these weird creatures, like giant penguins, mutant telephones, and man-eating toilets. Your job is to get through the mine before the air runs out, without being eaten. Thanks to some nifty programming, Manic Miner is the first ever game to have music while you play. It gets a bit annoying after a while, and for hours after, I can't get its bippy tune out of my head. But it's great all the same. Another game I like is The Pyramid, where you have to guide astro-explorer Ziggy from the top of a giant space pyramid to the bottom, zapping mutant eyeballs, killer trashcans, extraterrestrial tweezers and galactic strawberries to get the energy crystals you need to unlock the various chambers. I sort of like The Hobbit, too, which is an adventure game (which means it's about solving puzzles, not shooting aliens), but I've been stuck in the goblin dungeon for about a year now and it's very difficult to get out.

I don't just play games, I also write programs in BASIC. BASIC stands for Beginner's All-purpose Symbolic Instruction Code, but it's not just for beginners. You can do some pretty advanced stuff with it. I'm learning Machine Code, too, which is what you need to know to do the *really* advanced stuff.

Like Joe does with bikes, I buy all the computer magazines I can, and watch all the TV programmes to do with computers, and talk about almost nothing but computers to Patrick at school (or I used to, but I'll explain more about that later, because I just realised you don't know anything about Patrick, either).

Computers are like this whole separate world, where everything makes sense. You know, they don't always do what you want them to at first, but you can always find out why, and solve it, and then they work.

And they're simple. I don't mean you can't do anything complicated with them, because you can, that's what they're for. What I mean is, I understand them.

That's what I mean.

I understand them.

Which is great because, really, I don't understand anything else.

3

Now to what I was going to tell you about.

Penny, who's this girl.

The thing is, it's complicated.

'If it seems complicated, go back to when it wasn't, and start from there.' That's what you always used to say, isn't it? Like the time I got Joe's Action Man stuck in the toilet. That *was* complicated.

In this case it means going back to the day Penny asked me her big dumb question.

Penny and me have been in the same class since I started secondary school (which is just over three years, now), but we'd never said anything to each other before she asked me her big dumb question, unless it was maybe 'Pass the potassium permanganate' or 'Did you know your Bunsen burner's gone out?' in Science. I don't talk much to girls, and girls don't talk much to me. Sorry, Mum, but I'm not exactly James Bond. (If it makes any difference, I don't talk much to the boys in class, either. They're like a separate species, into football instead of computers. And they're the dominant species, too.)

Anyway, I know exactly which day it was Penny asked me her big dumb question, because it was the day after they showed Threads on BBC2.

I shouldn't have watched Threads. Apart from the fact it started at 9:30 p.m. and went on till 11:25 p.m. and the next day was school, Threads was a serious drama about what happens to ordinary people in a nuclear war. It might have been shown to make politicians see what it would really be like if they started World War Three, but all it did for me was confirm everything I already knew about how awful it would be, and add loads of extra details I was going to have to remember whenever I thought about nuclear war in the future. (It was from Threads I learned about nuclear winter, which is one of the worst things I've ever learned.)

I didn't sleep at all that night. Joe of course loved it, and even stuck the cover of that week's Radio Times, which shows a scene from Threads, on his bedroom door, so now I'm reminded of it every time I go upstairs.

But at least it means I remember the date. I first spoke to Penny on Monday the 24th of September.

It all started with me and Patrick walking home from school, discussing the future of computers. We were doing this partly because the last lesson of the day had been Computer Science, and Scruffy Clyde (sorry, *Mr* Clyde) had set us an essay on the future, and how computers would feature in it. But we were also doing it because, if you're into computers, you generally spend a lot of time thinking about how computers are going to be in the future. This is because computers, though they're great now (at least, to those of us who are into them like me and Patrick), are going to be absolutely mega in the future. So mega, in fact, that even people who aren't into computers are going to have to admit how great they are.

What will computers be like in the future?

They'll be miles more powerful for a start. They may be networked, too, over the telephone lines, though I can't see that being useful for much. I mean, one of the best things about computers is you're not being bothered by other people while you're using them, so why would you want to plug in a phone line? One thing we can be sure of is computers will use floppy discs instead of tapes for storage. Floppy discs are the future!

The biggest thing in the future of computers is artificial intelligence. This mostly means computers that can beat Gary Kasparov at chess. What computers have achieved at the moment is best described as artificial stupidity. They're stupid because they do exactly what you tell them to, even if it's totally pointless. If you say to a computer, 'Start with zero, double it, and keep doing that till you reach minus one', it will do exactly that never-ending task forever. (Or at least till Dad tells you to turn that bloody thing off and go to bed.) Really, this is the whole point about computers. They're designed to do the boring stuff, leaving us to do the interesting stuff.

Like programming computers!

That's how I think it's going to be, anyway.

(If we don't all get zapped in a nuclear war.)

Patrick, as usual, had only one thing to say on the subject. 'It's obvious any future computers will be based on the BBC Model B, which is clearly superior to all other micros. I mean, we can't be using ZX Spectrums with their little rubber keyboards in the future, can we? We need serious machines.'

'And a computer named after a TV channel counts as a serious machine, does it?' I said. (The BBC Micro is named after the British Broadcasting Corporation. They helped develop it, and even use it sometimes for special effects on Doctor Who.)

'The BBC is a highly-respected commercial entity with specific computing needs.'

'Yeah, they needed a computer named after them.'

'The *best* computer,' Patrick said.

'The best computer in the world is the Cray X-MP,' I said. 'It costs fifteen million dollars. Or is the BBC Model B, at three hundred and ninety-nine pounds, suddenly better than that?'

'Best *micro*-computer,' Patrick said, eyes rolling as though I was being deliberately stupid.

Which I was. The Cray X-MP weighs more than five tons.

'The BBC Micro,' Patrick continued, 'has eight distinct graphics modes. How many has the Spectrum got? Four, is it? Two? No, wait, it's *one* isn't it?'

'It only needs one,' I said. 'It's good enough for everything.'

'Eight graphics modes means you can balance functionality with memory usage, as required.'

'Which you have to if you've only got 32k memory,' I said. 'Spectrum's got 48k.'

'Uh, 32k expandable by 64k. So that's 96k, which is a *bit* more than 48. Hmm, even twice as much, I think? It also has a built-in assembly language interpreter, a far better implementation of both Standard *and* Extended BASIC, *four* sound channels...'

And then I give up listening and let him drone on. Patrick could drone for England.

You see, Mum, back when I didn't have a computer, Patrick had a ZX Spectrum. That's how I knew I wanted one. He was always telling me how great it was. As soon as I got mine, though, *his* disappeared into the attic, never to be used again, and his dad bought him a BBC Model B. And ever since, by some twisted process known only to the living brain that is Patrick Luffley, every conversation we've ever had on the way home from school (which is every day, because we always walk home together) manages to find its way round to the subject of why the BBC Model B (i.e., his computer) is so much better than the ZX Spectrum (i.e., mine).

The fact is, everything Patrick owns is better than anything I could ever own. He lives in a lovely house, which his mum (who practically worships him) keeps so clean and neat that any germs who even *think* of entering it die of despair. Specks of dust can't land anywhere, because everything's covered in a force-field of spray-on polish. His dad works in London for some big city company, and is always getting Patrick everything he wants. Not only has Patrick got a BBC Model B micro, he's got a proper computer monitor, a dot matrix *and* a daisy wheel printer, a floppy disc drive, a joystick, and a modem. Plus so much software, there's some games he owns that he's only played once!

None of this would be annoying if Patrick wasn't always reminding me of it.

When it comes down to it, me and Patrick are friends because we're the only two boys in our form (4PU) who are into computers. We sit next to each other in class, we spend break times together, we both go up to the computer room at lunchtime, and we walk home from school together. But if we talk about anything other than computers, I usually end up wondering if the two of us live on the same planet.

'...sub-procedures, the AUTO command, the RENUM-BER command...'

He's still at it.

When we walk home from school, we of course get to Patrick's house first. Sometimes he invites me in for a SodaStream and an hour of watching him play his latest games. Sometimes I even get the honour of watching him program. (I love programming my ZX Spectrum, Mum, but there's nothing more boring that watching someone else do it. It's like being hungry and watching someone else eat.)

The thing is, he never lets me know if he's going to invite me in till we actually get to his house. Sometimes, when we've been in the middle of an involved discussion, I've followed him down his drive to his front door, only to have him look at me as if to say, 'What are you following me down my drive for? Your home's *that* way!'

So then I cross the London Road (yes, Mum, using the Green Cross Code) to Pritchard Lane, down that to King George Way, up that to Pritchard Gardens and our little council house, all the while lost in my own little world.

Usually.

But this Monday, there was Penny.

4

You can't be in the same class as someone for three and a bit years without getting to know a few things about them. If you're me, it'll probably only ever be a few. In fact, if she hadn't asked me her big dumb question, I'd most likely have gone through the whole of school knowing only two things about Penny Poundley.

The first was, she lived somewhere near me. I knew this because after school I'd often see her walking home ahead of me. She'd go down Pritchard Lane, then King George Way, then Pritchard Gardens, just like I do. But then she'd go round the corner to Fallow Lane (the tarmacked part, not the bumpy part), and I had no idea where she went after that. She'd be walking on her own, singing pop songs, and I'd dawdle so as not to catch up with her. I mean, I couldn't talk to her about computers, could I?

I certainly couldn't talk to her about pop music.

It's obvious Penny's into pop music, not just because she sings it to herself on the way home from school, but because of her badges. She wears a black Harrington jacket, and seems to be working hard to cover it with badges. She's got all sorts: Ban the Bomb, Big Brother is Watching You, Solidarity with the miners, Don't blame me I voted Labour!, several sizes of CND symbol, Guide Dogs Golden Jubilee, Buzby on the phone saying 'Make someone happy', Checkout at Tesco, Bejam: Join the freezer people, Currys are electric, I'm a stamp bug, 'If you know what's good for you, OK?', a whole load of TV ones, including Crackerjack, Top of the Pops, Jigsaw, and even a Captain Zep Space Detective one, which you can usually only get if you write in with the clues Captain Zep used to solve one of his cases. But most of all, she's got pop badges. I'm not going to list them all. It would take too long, and anyway, I don't know who most of them are. Altogether, they make a lot of tinny clacky sounds, like a low-budget suit of armour.

Now I've told you about her jacket, I suppose I should describe the rest of her, so you can picture her as she ambles home swinging her schoolbag, singing her pop songs. The main thing you see from the back, of course, is her hair. So what can I say about her hair? Well, I now know Penny calls it 'mousey', but always with a look that seems to be hoping you'll tell her it's not mousey at all but some far more wonderful colour. The ZX Spectrum is capable of producing eight colours: black, blue, red, magenta, green, cyan, yellow, and white. Penny's hair is none of those. A far better description would be somewhere between Shreddies and Shredded Wheat, but I think a comparison to breakfast cereals isn't what she has in mind.

Now to her face.

Okay. Penny's face.

I don't know, how do you describe a face? I mean, I could say she hasn't got a huge nose or a carbuncle or anything, but saying that just makes you think of a huge nose or a carbuncle, doesn't it? (*Stop* thinking about a huge nose and a carbuncle.)

She, you know, looks like a girl. Only, her own sort of girl, not some standard girl. Not that there *are* standard girls, I don't think. Are there, Mum? No, that would be silly.

I'm obviously getting nowhere with this. I'll just have to invent a word or two.

Penny looks Pennyicious, with some unique Pennycularities of her own.

You can fill in the gaps yourself.

So that's enough description. I'm not going to bother with her hands or her elbows or anything, other than to say she's got them. Two of each.

(I haven't seen her elbows, so I'm assuming. But it's a safe assumption because, you know, her arms bend.)

Right, so the other thing I knew about Penny before she asked me her big dumb question is something everyone in our year would have known some version of, because when it happened it went round the school like a playground craze.

What happened was this. At the beginning of secondary school, some people in our class already knew each other, and some (like me) didn't know anyone, so some started out with friends, and some had to make them. I made friends with Patrick because he had this little handheld LCD Game & Watch game and he let me have a go on it for 10p. Penny didn't know anyone either, but seemed happy enough taking her time. She claimed a desk at the front of the class, on the furthest side from the door, like she wanted her own little corner. It was away from the main group of girls, who sat at the back, gossiping. Sometimes their gossiping got noisy, and if they were in a bullying mood, they'd make loud comments about other people in the room. Neither Patrick nor me escaped their notice, but all you had to do was pretend you were too deep in conversation to hear what they were saying and they'd get fed up. Penny seemed pretty good at ignoring them totally, which is quite a skill, because it means you not only have to look like you haven't heard what they're saying, but you have to look like you're not *trying* to look like you haven't heard what they're saying, which isn't as easy as it sounds.

(I tend to blush all the way to my ears, which gives it away.)

Anyway, there was this other girl called Steph. Several times, Steph tried to be part of the girls at the back, but they'd tell her she had to pass a test first, and come up with something ludicrous, like she had to come into school wearing black lipstick, or she had to run past the headmaster's office waving her knickers in the air. Patrick, who'd been to the same primary school as both Steph and the girls at the back, said they all knew each other, but had had a falling out at the end of primary school, so that was probably what was going on.

By the end of the first week, everyone in class had made at least one friend, apart from Penny and Steph. It was at this point Penny started talking to Steph, and after a day or so, the two would be seen together at break times, and eating lunch together in the dining hall, and then they started sitting next to each other in class. So, for a while, it seemed everyone was happy. Then, the second weekend after the start of school, one of the girls at the back, Laura, had a birthday, and gave out invites. Steph got an invite. I saw her look of surprise as Laura gave her a card with a, 'Here you go, then.' Penny wasn't there at the time.

The Monday following, everything changed. Steph came in and, completely ignoring Penny, sat with her new/old chums at the back of the class, and in moments was gossiping with the rest of them like things had never been different. Penny looked a bit puzzled, and at one point went over to try and have a talk with Steph, but couldn't get her on her own. So she went back to being the lone girl at the front, and that might have been that if Steph hadn't started making comments about her.

It was Friday of the third week. Penny was at her desk, and the girls at the back were obviously bored. With five minutes to go before the start of school, they began ranging around for people to have a go at, but everyone was ignoring them. Then Steph piped up and said, in that loud, pointed way bullies do when they're getting warmed up, 'What I want to know is, if your mum's barmy, does that mean you'll go barmy too?'

The only reason I knew this was directed at Penny was because Steph was fixing her with a look as she said it.

Penny ignored her.

So Steph said, 'Course, she may be barmy already. I

mean, sitting on your own at the front of class, that's a bit barmy in't it?'

Penny looked round, and gave Steph what I can only call a was-that-really-necessary look. But she was obviously hurt.

Steph, though, wanted more than that. She got to her feet and walked to the front of the class to stand before Penny's desk.

'Can't you hear me, Pen? Deafness run in the family too?'

Penny got to her feet. She was shorter than Steph, but didn't seem intimidated. She just seemed angry. She said something I couldn't quite catch, but there was definitely an 'I thought we were friends' involved.

Whatever she said, though, didn't have any effect on Steph, who had gone well over to the dark side. It was like she was trying to prove to her new friends how little she needed her old one.

'That just proves you're barmy, Pen. Deluded. It's the first sign. Like your mum, eh? Bats in the belfry.'

Penny's face went this very deep shade, almost purple. Steph just gave her a mocking, 'So what?' look in return.

So Penny punched her. Full in the face.

I'd never seen a girl punch anyone before, and if you'd have asked, I wasn't even sure it was possible. But Penny did it, and Steph fell over, and when she got up she was clutching her nose, with blood seeping between her fingers in sticky red lines.

Everyone went totally silent. If Penny had taken out a gun and shot her, it couldn't have shocked us more. Mr Slaughter chose that moment to turn up to take the register, beaming his usual placid smile, which turned sickly as soon as he saw the blood. The girls at the back, of course, were only too pleased to tell him what had happened — their version of it, anyway, because Penny wasn't saying anything.

Mr Slaughter took Penny and Steph to the headmaster's office, and I don't know what happened because of it. What I do know is, some time later, a new girl came to class, and Penny volunteered to show her around, and to have her sit next to her. It was like she'd decided to grab this girl as a friend, and no one was getting in her way. A few months after that, Steph's family moved and she went to another school, and Penny and the new girl, Kash, have been best friends ever since.

(Penny's best friend really is called Kash. Her proper full name is Kashmira. She's from India.)

So that's what happened, Mum. I'm not saying Penny was right to do what she did, I'm just saying she did it.

Now back to that Monday after school, and Penny and her big dumb question.

As I walked down Pritchard Lane after leaving Patrick, I was first of all thinking about the future of computers, then about how there wasn't going to be a future of computers because of nuclear war, then about Threads on TV last night and how horrible it had been, so I didn't notice I was walk-ing on one side of the road while Penny was on the other. Pritchard Lane isn't a busy road, so there weren't any cars whizzing between us. It's quite shady, with a lot of trees, and the main danger is you might get hit on the head by a conker falling from a tree (or perhaps thrown by a mali-cious squirrel).

It was only when we'd got far enough from the main road and I could hear her footsteps that I looked up.

'Hi Tim,' she said, with a little smile.

'Hello,' I said, wondering why she was talking to me.

There was a short silence so I thought, phew, that's over with.

Then she said, 'You've got a computer, haven't you?'

Which is a dumb question, but it wasn't her *big* dumb

question.

So I said, 'Yes,' meaning it to sound laden with *obviously*, but at that moment my voice did a little Aled Jones warble, so it was more like I was about to burst into song.

Penny either didn't notice or pretended not to, which is very polite of her. Then she asked her big dumb question.

'Could I borrow it?'

5

Could I borrow it?

Could I *borrow* it?

I felt like saying, 'Yeah, can I borrow your arms, legs and head?'

My *computer*.

Some of this must have shown on my face, because Penny looked a bit taken aback, like a girl who'd chucked a sweet wrapper down a dormant volcano only to have it rumble threateningly in return.

'Maybe not,' she said.

We walked on in awkward silence, till I realised I was either going to have to speed up to get rid of her, or say something. Speeding up would have been a tad rude, so I said, 'Why?'

She pepped up. 'Well, I bought this magazine called Computer & Video Games. Have you heard of it?'

'Yeah,' I said, resisting the impulse to say, 'There's this thing called the moon, have you heard of *that*?' Computer & Video Games, or C&VG as we readers like to call it, is the second best computer magazine there is. (The best is Crash!, which is better because (a) it's got a cool name, and (b) is specifically for the ZX Spectrum. Computer & Video Games, on the other hand, tries to cover all the more popular home computers, including the BBC Micro, Dragon 32, Vic 20, Atari 400, Commodore 64, Sharp MZ, and so on, which means a lot of the magazine is wasted as far as I'm concerned. But still, it's great.) I couldn't imagine why Penny would have bought it though, as she obviously didn't have a computer.

'It had the Thompson Twins on the cover,' she said, and when I looked blank, added, 'You *know*, the Thompson Twins!'

'Um...'

Without a moment's notice, she started singing.

I glanced back down the lane, scared someone might hear.

'They're a *pop* group,' she said.

'Oh.'

'You mean you haven't heard of them?'

'Sort of.' The truth was, I *had* heard, vaguely, of the Thompson Twins, it's just I couldn't admit it. The reason for this is silly, but it basically comes down to Dad. Whenever Top of the Pops is on TV, he spends the entire show making comments about how bad the music is, how 'namby-pamby' or 'weird' the singers look, and how no sane human being could ever like any of it. 'Call that music?', with a disgusted look on his face, is his verdict on everything in the top forty. (Apart from whatever's at number one. In that case it's 'Number one? More like a number two.' Which he thinks is so witty, he says it every week.) Because of this, in our house, it's vital to pretend to know nothing about pop music. Get caught singing a chorus or two while doing the dishes, and you give up all hope of a quiet week. (Joe, of course, is allowed to belt out as much heavy metal as he likes. Heavy metal groups are just as weird as pop groups, but because they're leather-spiky weird instead of namby-pamby weird, and because they're almost never on Top of the Pops, Dad doesn't hate them like he hates pop groups.) It was obvious, though, that the opposite was true for Penny. From the look on her face, saying I didn't know who the Thompson Twins were was like saying I was unfamiliar with the concept of breathing. Still, I couldn't break the habit. It was like Dad had put a padlock through my jaw when it came to pop music.

'What's all this got to do with computers?' I said, to get back to safer ground.

'Well, the Thompson Twins were on the cover, so I bought it thinking it was a pop magazine. And it had a free flexi-disc, too, so I thought it might be a new single. But when I got it home and played it, what came out was this eee-krr-eee sound, which isn't anything like the Thompson Twins. It was more like a cat being strangled. That's when I checked, and realised it was a computer magazine.'

'Oh,' I said, feeling I had to say something, but not wanting to commit myself.

'So I looked into it, and it said this flexi-disc had a computer game on it. But not just any computer game. It's a Thompson Twins computer game.'

'Oh,' I said, again.

'Thing is, I haven't got a computer. But you, apparently, have.'

'Mm,' I said. It was getting more and more difficult saying something without actually saying anything, so I thought a change from 'oh' to 'mm' might work.

Penny stared at the wet autumn leaves plastering the pavement and kicked one or two.

'What kind of computer have you got?' she said.

'A ZX Spectrum. 48k.' No oh-ing or mm-ing my way out of that one.

'I think that's what they said it was for,' she said.

We carried on walking, both turning up King George Way. I stayed on my side of the road, Penny stayed on hers. We were out from under the trees now, so no more danger of falling conkers. Unless there was a really determined squirrel with a catapult.

I was starting to remember. The latest C&VG did have a pop group on the cover. In fact, I'd felt a bit nervous bringing it home, in case Dad saw it and thought I'd bought a pop magazine. And it'd had a free flexi-disc attached. A flexi-disc, Mum, isn't a computer disk (which is floppy, not flexi — it's a key difference). A flexi-disc is a record just like a top forty single, but made really thin so it's mega cheap, and can be given away free with magazines. To prove to Joe I hadn't bought the magazine for the record on the cover, I took it off and skimmed it at him. He skimmed it back. After a bit of skimming to and fro, it had been too battered to fly anymore, so Joe whanged it in the bin.

'There was a competition,' Penny said, sounding a bit forlorn. 'To meet the Twins backstage. But you have to play the game to enter.'

I sort of waggled my head in sympathy, and wished this conversation would go away.

Penny looked at me.

I looked away.

I kept looking away as long as I could. When I looked back, she was still looking at me.

'The Thompson Twins,' she said, 'are my favourite group in the whole world.'

I have no explanation for what happened next.

I had this sudden burst of bright, heroic feeling in my chest. It was like I'd realised Penny was the damsel in distress, and I was the knight in shining armour, and I knew exactly how to slay the dragon. Best of all, I wouldn't have to do any actual fighting.

'I suppose you could use my computer,' I said. 'It'd have to be in my room, but, anyway, I'd need to show you how to use it, so...'

And then, just as suddenly, the heroic feeling was gone and I was left with what I'd said. How had *that* happened? I felt tricked. I'd been possessed, moonstruck, hexed, cursed, hypnotised. My bedroom, my computer, were my one refuge from the world, and now I'd invited this strange girl into it. I might as well have invited Genghis Kahn or Dracula. Or both.

But it was too late to do anything.

Penny's face lit up. 'Really?'

'Yeah,' I said, but only because I couldn't say, 'No, of course not, I was temporarily insane!'

She did a little dance in the leaves in the kerbside gutter, kicking them into the air and singing something about having the time of her life.

I felt like my shoes had turned to lead.

As we carried on up King George Way (Penny now in the middle of the road, chasing leaves like a puppy), she said she'd rush home and get the flexi-disc, then meet me at my house.

'It's number 93 isn't it?' she said.

'Yeah,' I said, still partly stunned, and now thinking, 'How come she knows where I live?'

Mum, why didn't you tell me girls have special powers?

6

Penny dashed off towards Fallow Lane with a 'See you in five minutes!'

I stood frozen for a moment, thinking this is what it must feel like to have been buzzed by a UFO. Something so strange has happened it's threatening to turn your whole world upside down, but now it's over you can't be sure you didn't imagine it.

Only, it wasn't over. Penny was going to come back. As I let myself into the familiar gloom of our cramped little hallway, though, I had an idea. When she came back, I could just not answer the door. I could pretend to be out. I could even pin up a note: 'I've had to go to town to meet my dad at work… For, um, some reason that's far too com-plicated to explain in a note pinned to a door.' And then I could do my utmost to avoid her for the rest of both of our lives.

I kicked off my shoes, adding them to the pile at the bottom of the stairs, a sorry-looking mess of plimsoles, trainers and slippers that was slowly becoming less and less wearable, more and more archeological.

In four minutes, Penny would come running round the corner from Fallow Lane, all grinning and eager. She'd dash up to the door, knock and wait. Then knock again. Then she'd peer through the letterbox, perhaps call my name. Then she'd see the note, and read it, and then I'd hear the sad plod of her footsteps — not running now, or dancing — as she turned and walked away, perhaps letting the precious flexi-disc slip among the dead leaves and conker shells on the ground, forgotten, lost, abandoned.

I suddenly felt really, really bad.

What was I so worried about anyway? She couldn't really be worse than Dracula or Genghis Khan. She was only a girl.

A girl.

That was it. A girl. I had no idea what to expect. It was all a bit unknown and worrying. But either I pretended to be out and spent the rest of the evening (and no doubt most of the next day) feeling bad about disappointing her, or I put up with it for an hour or two and then it would all be over.

It couldn't be *that* bad, could it?

I might even learn something. Like, who the Thompson Twins were, or what girls are really like.

So I hung up my parka and did my best to get ready.

How to get ready?

Make sure things were tidy. I took a quick look at the living room. It was tidy. Ish. Then I ran upstairs (trying not to look at the picture from Threads on Joe's door, but of course looking at it anyway) and into my room.

Hey, this was pretty tidy, too.

Then I reminded myself this was an unknown quantity, a *girl*, coming up here. I closed my eyes, reset myself, and opened them again.

What a mess!

And only three minutes to go.

The first thing I did was hide my copy of the latest Computer & Video Games, with Penny's precious Thompson Twins on the cover (who couldn't be twins, because there were three of them, and they didn't look anything like each other), just to avoid the need for any explanations about where my copy of the free flexi-disc had gone. Then I did a quick skim for yesterday's socks, and any other lingering laundry items. I gave the blankets on the bed a shake to unrumple them, then flipped my pillow so it looked a bit more fresh and clean. My pyjamas I stuffed under the bed. I realised I had no idea what sort of home Penny came from. It might be even worse than Patrick's. I'd heard rumours of homes where they changed the bedclothes *every day*, where they always squeezed the toothpaste from the bottom of the tube, and where specks of dust were interrogated, classified, analysed and disinfected before being individually swept into specially treated black sacks. Such houses were, I was sure, more likely to occur where girls were found. Our beds were changed on a more irregular schedule, mostly relating to Dad's sudden household purges, where everything but the curtains and carpets got shoved into the washing machine, and we were all enlisted in vacuuming, dusting, and wiping things down with bleach.

Thinking of bleach made me think of smells. Did my room smell nice and clean?

I sniffed. I couldn't smell anything. I sniffed harder. Still nothing. For all I knew, it smelled entirely of farts and feet but I was too used to it to tell. I tried not breathing for a few seconds, then did a mega-sniff. All that happened was I got dizzy.

I realised how hopeless it was. This was a house lived in by three males who didn't care too much for the finer points of housekeeping. Used to it as I was, for all I knew it stank like a swamp and looked, to the trained eye, like Dr Frankenstein's oubliette. (I learned what an oubliette is from Blue Peter on telly.)

It was now five seconds after Penny had said she'd be here.

I stood there paralysed for another twenty, and was just thinking some critical thoughts about girls and their sense of time when there was a light double tap at the door.

I didn't know a door knocker could be tapped so lightly and still be heard.

'Hi.'

'Hello.'

Penny held up the flexi-disc with a muted little 'ta-da!', and I did my best not to snatch it from her hands and send it zinging down the road.

'Come in then,' I said. There was an awkward bit while I held the door open against the pressure of the coats hung on the wall behind it, at the same time trying to get out of the way enough in our tiny hall to give her some room to actually come into. In the end, I had to open the living room door and let her step into that so I could close the front door. I'm sure it wasn't usually this awkward, letting someone into our house. Mind you, when was the last time I'd let someone into our house?

Then we stood in the hall while I thought what to do next.

I knew I ought to offer her a drink, and perhaps a biscuit, but there was part of me that didn't want to be that welcoming. This was her thing, so she should have brought drinks and biscuits if she wanted them. What was bothering me was setting some sort of limit, so I said, 'My dad and brother get back about half five.'

'I'll be gone by then,' she said.

That still gave us an hour and three quarters. I wish I'd said five. Or would half four have been believable?

'Will that give us enough time to do it?' Penny said.

'Eh?'

'There's a question you've got to answer to enter the competition, and to do that you've got to finish the game.'

'Oh, um, dunno,' I said, making clear it was no concern of mine.

We lingered in the hall till I realised I couldn't put it off anymore.

'We'd better go upstairs, then.'

I clomped on up, feeling gloomier by the minute.

'Nice,' Penny said, as she came into my room, and I checked to make sure she wasn't being sarcastic. She didn't seem to be, but I wasn't entirely sure how to tell, with a girl.

'Is that your computer?' she asked.

'Yeah,' I said. Though what I wanted to say was, 'Well, it's attached to a TV and a Sinclair power supply isn't it?'

She peered at it. 'Dinky.'

'The Spectrum's the most popular home computer around,' I said. 'And it's amazingly compact, considering the amount of computing power they've packed into it.'

'Oh, I mean I like it,' she said. 'That rainbow in the corner. Nice.'

Nice, nice. Was everything nice to this girl? She probably thought nuclear war was nice, too.

'So,' she said, holding up the flexi-disc, 'how do we — what do we — where does this go?'

'Well, obviously, we've got to transfer it to tape, first,' I said.

She gave a little wiggle of the head. 'Obviously.'

I went to my shelf of computer tapes and made as much fuss as I could of choosing one with some blank space on it. Actually, I'd bought a pack of five new C60s from Woolies last Saturday, but I wanted to make sure she knew the difficulty she was putting me to.

When I'd chosen one, I found Penny looking round my room, puzzled.

'You haven't got a record player,' she said.

'I only buy tapes.'

She looked around again, doing a three-sixty-degree turn, so I pointed them out to her. My collection of music tapes. Oxygene by Jean Michel Jarre, and Equinoxe by Jean Michel Jarre.

She stared hard at them. 'Two? You've got two?'

'Plus this one,' I said, quickly.

She took the other cassette off me. 'Doctor Who Sound Effects? Okay, you've got two and a half.'

'I don't listen to much music,' I said. 'It's not a crime.'

'Okay, but how are we going to get this flexi-disc onto

tape, as we so obviously need to?'

'My brother's got a record player. In his room.'

'Is that the door with the radiation warning on it?'

'Yeah.' I didn't move. 'The thing is, if Joe finds out I've been in his room, he'll kill me.'

'Okay.'

'And if he finds I've let anyone else into his room, he'll kill me even more.'

'Okay.'

'So don't touch anything.'

'Okay.'

'And don't tell anyone you've been in his room. Ever. Even your Aunt Mabel's pet cat. Joe's got this way of finding things out.'

Penny pulled a face. 'Not nice.'

I led the way.

Joe's door is covered in pictures of heavy metal bands, buxom women sitting on motorbikes, and various Do Not Enter signs and hazard warnings. Pride of place went to the recent Threads cover to The Radio Times, which showed a battered-looking traffic warden, his face half covered in bandages, a rifle up against his shoulder. This was the grim face of post-nuclear law enforcement, the state society would fall into.

I gave a light knock. 'Just in case,' I whispered.

Penny widened her eyes and listened.

No sound.

'It's no guarantee he isn't in there,' I said. 'If we go in and anything moves, run for it. I'll say you were a burglar and I managed to fight you off. Most likely, he's at work.'

I opened the door to Joe's room.

It was dark. The curtains were still closed from this morning.

'Joe?' I said.

No reply.

I moved forward slowly. 'Joe?'

Still no reply.

I'd reached the light switch. The moment of truth. If I turned it on and he was there, life, as I knew it, would be over.

Click.

It took a few seconds of staring at the mess of rumpled blankets and sheets that was Joe's bed to be sure it was, in fact, empty.

'Phew,' I said.

'Phew,' Penny echoed, so close to my ear I jumped.

We moved further in, treading carefully.

Joe's hi-fi was on the far side of the room. To reach it, I had to cross a carpet strewn with socks, T-shirts, and the occasional hint of what I hoped (for Penny's sake) weren't Y-fronts. Once I got there, I took a moment to memorise the exact state he'd left his hi-fi in. The record player lid was up, and Iron Maiden's latest album, Powerslave, was lying on the turntable like a coiled, sated (and very flat) shiny black serpent. The stylus was in its cradle, but the clip to hold it there hadn't been flipped into place. Right, I had the state of the record player memorised.

'Why are all the women in these magazines wearing so little?'

I whipped round. Penny was flipping through a stack of magazines at the foot of Joe's bed, mostly made up of Metal Hammer, Back Street Heroes and Amateur Photographer (which Joe sometimes buys, even though he doesn't have a camera — odd, that).

'Some of them aren't wearing anything at all,' she said.

'I thought I said—'

'Sorry, sorry.' She patted the stack into a neat pile.

'Not too neat, or he'll know.'

She skewed a few magazines, then stepped back, hands

held up as if she was being ultra-careful not to disturb anything.

I turned to Joe's tape player. It was shut, and there was a tape inside. I pressed the eject button and removed the tape, carefully laying it down with the side that had been playing face up. I checked my tape was past the non-recording leader and carefully slotted it into place.

'Conan the Adventurer! Conan the Buccaneer! Conan the Usurper!'

I almost dropped my tape. Penny had discovered Joe's cache of sword and sorcery, and before I could say anything, was taking books down, one by one.

'Weird of the White Wolf by Michael Moorcock. Is that a real name, do you think? And why is the white wolf weird?'

'Will you leave it—'

'Sorry, sorry,' she said, and put them back. Then, re-membering, carefully disarranged them.

'Don't touch anything else,' I hissed, as though the room might be bugged. (I wouldn't put it past Joe.)

'I touch nothing! I step where you step!'

I rolled my eyes. 'Just give me the flexi-disc.'

She reached it toward me on tiptoes, not wanting to come any closer as the underwear was a bit more frequent where I was standing.

I laid the disc on top of Iron Maiden, checked the rpm, put the tape on pause-record, and lifted the stylus arm. The turntable began to rotate. I moved the stylus over carefully, and set it down as gently as possible on the flexi-disc's outermost groove. The speakers gave a little static-sounding pop, then snicked lightly at each revolution of the disc. There was a short spoken intro, explaining what the disc was, then a gap. I unpaused the tape, and a second later the room filled with the grate, screech and warble of ZX Spectrum data.

7

Back in my room, I put the C60 cassette into my tape player, and while it was rewinding, checked the EAR and MIC connections to my Spectrum, doing my best to make it seem this was a complicated operation requiring precision and expertise, though in fact I used it everyday and knew it was set up fine. Then I turned on the Spectrum and my TV.

Penny, perched on the corner of my bed, watched intently, like she was expecting the answer to her competition to flash up any second, and perhaps only for a second.

Once the TV showed the standard Sinclair Research copyright message, I typed LOAD "", pressed enter, and started my tape player. The border of the TV screen alternated red and blue for a few seconds, then went crazy with blue and yellow stripes as the data began to come in.

I sat back.

'Is this the game?' Penny said worriedly.

'It's loading,' I said.

This obviously meant nothing to her. Which is the trouble with talking about computers to non-computer people, Mum. There's loads of everyday words (like 'load' itself) that have special meanings for computers, and you can get so used to using them in their computer sense you forget other people might interpret them in a completely different way. For instance, I once told Dad I was debugging a computer program and he said we had some fly spray in the cupboard under the sink, if I needed it. So you're stuck with two options. One is, you explain everything in detail, which can end up with you going right down to the basics, like what a computer is (nothing but a machine that jiggles ones and zeroes), and risk confusing them even more. The other is, you give them a short, simple version and they go away not appreciating how ingenious it all is. So I said, 'It's converting the audio signal on the tape to digital data and putting it into its memory. When it's finished, it'll automatically run it as a program.' That was the option one version.

'Oh,' Penny said. 'Clear as daisies.'

I rolled my eyes and gave her option two. 'It's working. We just have to wait a bit.'

After a couple of minutes, the screen went black and said `THE THOMPSON TWINS ADVENTURE bY DAVID SHER © 1984 QUICKSILVA`.

'Ah, Quicksilva,' I said. 'They did Ant Attack. You wandered round this abandoned city being attacked by giant ants. It was a real advance in 3D graphics.'

Why was I saying this? Penny had no interest in killing giant ants, or the evolution of 3D graphics.

I stopped the tape and the game started, taking a few seconds to draw its first screen.

I read out the text as it appeared. 'The Twins are in the middle of a long beach stretching out to the east and west. There is deep sea to the north. Exits lead north, south, east and west. What shall we do?'

Penny looked blank. 'What *do* we do?'

'We have to tell the computer what we want it to do.'

'Can it hear us?'

'We type it in.'

'Ask it for the answer to the competition.'

'I think it's going to be a bit more complicated than that. It's an adventure game. You know, the computer describes where we are, and if there are any useful objects about, and we say things like GO NORTH or TAKE SPATULA, stuff like that.' Seeing how none of this was getting through to her, I felt a deep, sinking weariness as I realised how long the next hour and a half was going to be. I took in a breath for a really deep sigh.

Her face suddenly brightened. 'Oh, you mean it's like those Choose Your Own Adventure books? The Werewolf of Firetop Mountain, or whatever?'

I almost fell off my chair. 'Yeah.' I was too amazed she'd even heard of The Warlock of Firetop Mountain to correct her. (I've got all the Fighting Fantasy game books from Firetop Mountain to the latest, Island of the Lizard King, and have finished every one. Sometimes even without cheating.)

'I get it,' she said.

And she did. A moment later, she was telling me what to type, and we were zinging along. We only drowned the Thompson Twins half a dozen times.

Girls are funny things. I know you're not going to agree with me, Mum, because you were one, obviously, but that's what I found myself thinking, sitting in my room with Penny right next to me. It seemed both normal and strange at the same time.

The thing is, since you, there's been nothing but males in this house. We don't go on family visits anymore, and no one comes here (not since Gramps, and he's of course a bloke). At school I really only talk to Patrick, or the occasional other boy in the computer room. So, while we have women teachers and cheery dinner ladies and as many girls in class as boys, I really haven't had much to do with them. In fact, Penny's the first girl to be in our house since you, Mum, which is over three years.

(Which is why she had to be gone before Dad and Joe got back. I'm not saying we've got a rule or anything. We couldn't have, because we never discuss things like that. As I said before, we never discuss *anything*. If the house caught fire, Dad would sit there scratching his armpit, daring the rest of us to be un-man enough to mention it. But still, I had no idea what would happen if they got back and she was there, and I didn't want to find out.)

As Penny sat there, leaning forward to read off the TV, I

found myself secretly studying her. The side of her head, for instance. Her ear. She had a little dash-like dimple in the lobe that must have meant she'd had it pierced. Her hair looked quite silky and shiny, like in those ads for hairspray. (The ones that go 'Is she, or isn't she?' I still have no idea what that means.) I wondered what would happen if I touched her shoulder, whether it would feel exactly the same as prodding Joe in the shoulder (without the layer of biker leather, of course), or whether it would be subtly different, somehow more girlish. I even wondered if I might get a spark off her, the way negative and positive terminals in an electrical circuit do, if you hold them close enough.

I know all this sounds silly, Mum, but it was what was going through my head at the time.

Sitting there, being herself, being so different from anything else I knew, Penny was like a whole new world.

We didn't finish the game. It got to five fifteen and she said she'd better go, and I knew I couldn't have her there when Dad and Joe got back, so I shrugged and said, 'Okay.' Like a computer. Computers say okay to everything.

Then I sat there while she went downstairs.

She called out 'Bye' and 'Thanks', then closed the front door behind her ever so quietly. Once I'd heard her footsteps pass the window I looked out, but she was already round the corner. I went downstairs and ambled about, enjoying the last few minutes of having the house to myself before Dad and Joe got back.

Everything felt different. Sort of good, but also sort of empty.

I found myself thinking of you, Mum. There isn't much of yours left in the house. We don't have a picture of you, because you were always around and we didn't need one, and no one's put one up now. Dad got rid of all your clothes and things, and sent your jewellery to your sister. There's the old photo albums, but they're at the bottom of a box that's way off in a corner of the attic. (No one takes photos anymore.) In fact, there's only one thing in our house that reminds me of you. You'll laugh, but right at the back of a shelf in the pantry, there's a little plastic tub of hundreds and thousands, which you used to sprinkle on the cakes you made. None of us makes cakes, but no one's bothered to throw it away. Every so often, I take it down and give it a little shake, to make sure it doesn't turn into a solid lump. Then I put it as far back on the shelf as I can, so Dad won't notice it and throw it away. That's the only thing of yours in the house I can think of.

So I did that, then I did a quick check to make sure there weren't any signs of Penny's visit. I examined the hall for mousey-coloured hairs, and even put on my shoes and scrubbed them on the doormat, to make sure there weren't any girl-sized shoe marks for Joe or Dad to find.

Then I went back upstairs, where the Thompson Twins adventure was still waiting for its next command. Say what you like about computers, they're patient.

The front door opened then slammed as Joe came home.

'Oy! Computer boy! Get the kettle on!'

Thud thump as he kicked off his boots.

I pulled out the Spectrum's power supply, turned off my TV, and went downstairs.

'Hi Joe,' I said.

He just sniffed loudly and turned on Ask the Family on BBC1. I went into the kitchen and filled the kettle.

Dad came home a moment later.

'Bloody bastards,' he muttered on his way through the kitchen to the toilet, not meaning Joe and me, but the world in general.

I thought a bit about nuclear war, then the kettle boiled.

8

When everyone had finished their dinner but me, and I was on my last two chips, I said, 'Dad? What do you think the future's going to be like?'

Joe huffed, like a contemptuous horse.

Dad didn't say anything. We had the news on, and he was watching that.

I pushed a chip round my plate, gathering up salt crystals and ketchup. 'Cos, we've got to write this essay. For homework.'

Dad said nothing.

I watched the news for a bit. President Reagan was telling the UN he wanted to have talks with the Russians about the arms race. He was saying it like he knew it ought to be the Russians asking to have talks him with him, but he'd decided to be generous and stoop to their level.

'Never happen,' Joe said.

Dad gave a grunt.

I finished my last chip but kept my knife and fork in my hand, because the moment I put them on my plate, that would let Dad and Joe know I'd finished, then dinner would be over and someone would have to start doing the dishes. And that someone would be me, because I'd finished last. (At least, that's the rule whenever it's me who finishes last. Otherwise, it's still me, just for some other reason.) But I wanted to sit there with all three of us watching TV for a bit longer.

'I mean,' I said, 'if the Americans and Russians *did* have talks, and we didn't have a nuclear war—'

'Ain't going to happen,' Joe said.

'But if they *did*—'

'Don't be such a wazzock.' Joe flung a hand at Reagan on the telly. 'He only wants talks with the Russians to put them off their guard. Make them get rid of some of their nukes, then bam! Hit 'em. Eh, Dad?'

Dad's face gave a twitch, the visual equivalent of a grunt.

'But unless the Russians get rid of *all* their weapons,' I said, 'they'll still bomb them back.'

'But not as much. The Americans will lose half their population, yeah, but the Russians'll lose all theirs.'

'And the whole world will be a radioactive cinder,' I said.

Joe shrugged. 'Price of freedom.'

I tried balancing my fork on the back of two fingers, then one, and just caught it before it clattered onto my plate.

'But what if that didn't happen,' I said. (Joe tutted.) 'What would the future be like then?'

No one answered.

I said, 'If I write this essay and say there won't be a future cos we're all going to die in a nuclear war, I'll lose marks, cos they'll think I'm trying to get out of writing it properly.'

'So make something up,' Joe said.

'But what?'

No one answered.

I said, 'I just thought, you know, what if the future *wasn't* nasty because of nuclear war but, instead, it was nice?'

As soon as it left my lips, I knew I shouldn't have used that Penny word. I had this sudden, horrible thought that, despite all my efforts earlier, they'd know a girl had been in the house because I'd used the word 'nice'.

'Nice,' said Dad, pushing the word into the world like a geyser glolloping mud. He didn't even look at me as he said it.

And then of course Joe took it up, knowing he'd got Dad's support. 'Ooh, nice, ooh, nicey-nice,' he said, twiddling his fingers and wobbling his head like I was being so la-de-dah.

I know when to give up. I plonked my knife and fork on my plate, and instantly Joe and Dad passed me theirs. I took them into the kitchen and started filling the washing-up bowl with hot water and a squirt of Fairy Liquid. This time, I gave it an extra-long squirt, so the water was really soapy, and I could make a mound of bubbles in my hands. When Joe came in, I blew it at him, and said it was radioactive fallout.

'Look at it like this,' Joe said. He picked up a plate to dry but, discovering some microscopic bit I hadn't washed properly, put it back on the washing-up side so I had to do it again. 'Say you're Russia and I'm America, right? And we've both got, like, a hundred thousand nuclear missiles each, right?' He poked me in the shoulder. 'Right?'

'Right,' I said, wondering why I had to be the Russians.

'So then I say, let's get rid of half of them each, yeah?'

'Okay.'

'So what would you do?'

'Get rid of half my nuclear missiles,' I said.

'Which is what makes you such a pillock. Because as soon as you get rid of them, I'd bomb the crap out of you.'

'Why?' I said.

'Because it's the only way to win, isn't it?'

'You don't win a nuclear war,' I said, trying my best to do Dad's sarcasm, but getting nowhere near it. 'You survive it, or you don't. And mostly you don't. And even if you do, it's horrible.'

'Look,' Joe said, 'once you've got nuclear weapons, you've got to use them, haven't you?'

'No,' I said, but Joe just punched me in the shoulder.

'You have to. No use having them otherwise. Because if you don't use them, the other bloke — you, the Russians — will. But the only safe way to use them is if the other bloke

— you, the Russians — don't have as many. You know you're going to get nuked, no matter what. So the only thing to do is, make it so you get *less* nuked than the other guy — you, the Russians.'

'Or not use them at all,' I said.

'What, and know the other bloke *is* going to? You may be a computer wiz, Tim, but you don't know anything about anything, do you?' And he punctuated this with a sharp prod in the exact spot on my shoulder where he'd punched me.

This time it was my turn to tut. But I did it quietly, knowing there was no point arguing with Joe. He was probably right. I mean, it didn't matter what I'd do if I was the Russians and had loads of nuclear weapons, because the first thing I'd do is get rid of them. But the Russians hadn't done that. Nor had the Americans. (Nor had the British, not that we count, much. I mean, we can probably only blow up the world once over. *Real* superpowers can do the entire solar system, several times.) So it was obvious the grownups, or maybe just the politicians, or the ones at the top anyway, thought like Joe, not me. So, whether I was right or wrong didn't matter. It was the Joes of the world who had their fingers on the button, and eventually we'd all go up in smoke.

Even Penny.

I hadn't meant to think of her, but as soon as I did, it made me stop.

I'd got used to the idea of me going up in smoke, but it didn't seem fair she should, too. I thought back to her being in my room, playing the Thompson Twins adventure game. If the four minute warning had gone off at that moment—

Joe poked me in the shoulder again, hard.

'Know what I'd do, the moment they dropped the bomb?'

'Sizzle,' I said, but he ignored me.

'First thing I'd do, I'd go to the gun shop on Kings Road, right?'

'But we'd all be dead,' I said. 'If they dropped a bomb, we'd be dead.'

'They'd only bomb London and the military bases, Timbo. Greenham Common. Get rid of those lesboes. Rest of us would be left to fend for ourselves.'

'And die of radiation poisoning.'

'Only the weak,' Joe said, with a prod in my shoulder that meant he was talking about me. 'Me and my mates would be on our bikes. We'd secure the area. Set up a new regime. We'd be like Judge Dredd in Mega City One. Judge, jury and executioner, all in one. First thing we'd do, we'd go to the gun shop on King Street, break in, and get all the guns.'

I rolled my eyes. 'What if someone else got there first?'

'They wouldn't. And if they did, we'd tell them about our plan, and get them to join us. Then, once they'd handed over the guns, we'd shoot them. No room for looters in the new world order, see?'

'But you'd be looters, too.'

'Not when *we* have the guns,' he said, like I'd totally missed the most obvious point.

I carried on washing.

'Then we'd round up the women. The healthy ones. Good looking ones, anyway. Put 'em in one place so we can protect them. Make them work on a farm. I'd be leader, so I'd have my pick. Might have to have more than one wife, just to keep the population up.'

'What if the only healthy women were ugly?'

'Wouldn't happen,' he said.

'What if there were more men than women?'

'Shoot the sods, wouldn't I?'

'What if—'

'What if, what if, what if! Bloody what-if machine, you

are.' Then, with half the washing still undried, he chucked the dish-towel over my head and said, 'Going for a ciggie.' A moment later, he was fiddling with his motorbike in the back yard.

I finished the washing and started the drying.

At 7 o'clock it was the Krypton Factor on ITV, which Joe loves because he can sit there saying how much better he'd be than any of the contestants, but we only got to watch the first twenty minutes, because the darts started on BBC2.

Dad said, 'Darts.' Joe gave me a 'What are you waiting for?' look, so I got up and changed the channel.

After a bit (because you don't have to listen to darts, just watch it), I said, 'They might have hover cars.'

No one said anything.

'In the future, I mean.'

Silence.

'And you might have computers controlling the cars, so you just typed in where you wanted to go, and they'd take you there.' I must admit, it seems unlikely you'll ever get a computer to find its way round Britain's windy road system, but the hover cars were a dead cert.

I waited a bit.

'And, doing the weekly shop, you might just type it all into a computer, and a robot would get it for you, and deliver it to your house.' (Most likely, we'd all be eating futuristic pill-meals, so no need for shops.)

I was determined to get at least one idea from them.

'And hospitals—'

'Shut up,' Joe said.

I thought this was just Joe being Joe, so I said, 'Hospitals might have computers—'

'Shut up, Tim,' Joe said.

I still didn't see why he was saying it, so I said, 'And the computers could make, like, the initial diagnosises—'

And then Dad said, 'Bloody useless.'

It was only then I realised what I'd said.

If I said sorry it would have been going on about it, so I shut up.

9

At 9:30 BBC2 started showing yet another program about the dangers of nuclear weapons, this time a documentary, which of course Joe insisted on watching, so I feigned a yawn and said I was off to bed.

'Coward,' Joe said, as I got up to go and brush my teeth. On my way back through the living room to go upstairs, I deliberately didn't look at the TV, and heard Joe sniggering because he knew I was doing it.

Dad said, 'Don't spend all night on that computer.' He never tells Joe not to spend all evening tinkering with his motorbike.

Upstairs, I browsed through my game tapes, but couldn't find one I felt like playing. I picked up the latest Computer & Video Games, thinking I might type in one of the program listings, but instead found myself staring at the cover, wondering what it was made the Thompson Twins Penny's favourite pop group. As I didn't know anything about girls *or* pop music, it was a case of trying to fit one unknown to another, which was two unknowns too many. Like trying to juggle jelly with rubber hands. I looked at the corner of the bed where Penny had been sitting, wondering if she might appear, like a genie, and provide the answer.

The C60 I'd recorded the Thompson Twins game on was still in my tape player. I realised what I most felt like doing was playing that. I mean, what if I did, and finished it, and went to school next day and said to Penny, 'I've got the answer you need for your competition. It was easy, once I put my mind to it'?

But I wasn't about to do that, was I?

How about, I could finish the game, do a print-out of the final screen with the competition answer on it, and slip it into her school bag while she wasn't looking? She'd know who it came from, but I wouldn't have to say anything.

But that would be silly. I might get caught.

If there *was* a nuclear war, and we were forced to live in small communities, I suppose Penny, living nearby, might be part of the one I was in. We might find ourselves working together on the same post-holocaust food farm. And as we were both young, we'd be more likely to survive radiation poisoning and starvation and so on, so it might even end with only the two of us left in all Eastead. And if a group of mutant bikers came to town, circling our farm with its precious patch of scraggly vegetables, I'd grab a pitchfork — no, make that a shotgun — and stand between them and her, and they'd have to ride off and find some easier prey.

But that was silly, too. I was starting to sound like Joe.

No, the whole episode with Penny was done with, sealed in its own special watertight canister and buried a thousand feet down (which is what they do with radioactive waste). So I'd better forget it. Better, in fact, pretend it had never happened, so I never got tempted to think anything like it would ever happen again.

So I played a bit of Manic Miner then went to bed.

I was wrong, though.

I only realised *how* wrong at the start of school next day, when I was sitting at my desk beside Patrick, waiting for the bell to go off, and Penny came in.

As she walked past me to her desk she started to give a little smile like she was going to say hello. I panicked and turned to Patrick and started talking about the first thing that came into my head.

'Sunny intervals with scattered showers today. And did you know it's a new moon tonight?'

Penny passed by.

Patrick pulled a what-do-I-care face and shrugged, a typical conversation ender from him.

I felt bad for a moment, but at least it was over with. It was like a necessary but painful operation had been performed, and life was back to normal.

The bell went and Mr Slaughter came in with the register to find out who was skiving off today.

But the operation hadn't been successful.

It's like when people have an arm or a leg amputated, but still get bothered by it itching. They've had the limb removed, but the ghost limb remains. Well, I spent the day being bothered by a ghost Penny. Only, in my case, she was a girl not a severed limb.

Suddenly she was everywhere. Not just in our form room, and not just sitting somewhere near me in Maths and English and virtually every other lesson I took (apart from Computers, she did Music instead), but she was everywhere in the corridors, too, and in the canteen at break. I tried not to look at her, but I kept needing to check she wasn't looking at me, and if it turned out she was, there'd be this awkward moment where it seemed I'd been caught staring at her. Which I suppose I had been.

I felt sorry for her. I mean, here she was, this normal girl. With her pop songs and her badges, she could go around saying hello to anyone she liked. But for some of us it was more complicated. I mean, what if they dropped the bomb? Yeah, things were nice and normal *now*, but any moment it could all get flipped into the most horrible world imaginable, with everything in ruins, and people struggling to survive, and dying of radiation poisoning. She hadn't thought of that, had she?

By the end of the school day I had my evening planned. I was going to go home, load up Manic Miner, and see how far I could get with this cheat code I knew for infinite lives. And Star Trek was on at 5:10, so I could watch that afterwards.

On the way home Patrick and me popped into the newsagents. Patrick bought himself a Wispa, but I, as usual, didn't have any money on me.

I said, 'Lend us a bit for a Curly Wurly?'

'Get your own drogna,' he said, then went outside to nosh his down before I could ask for a bit. (Patrick calls all money drogna because of this TV programme called The Adventure Game. It's set on the planet Arg, and people from Earth go there to solve puzzles. The money on Arg is called drogna. But I think really it's because he's saying, 'I don't have to worry about money, so I can call it what I like.')

I slowed down by the computer magazines on the way out, checking to see if there were any new ones. Then, as I turned to leave the shop, I almost bumped into someone.

'Sorry,' I said, then saw it was Penny.

She gave me a smile, and for a second I was so totally flummoxed, all I could do was stand there. Then I saw she had her purse out, and something told me exactly what was going to happen next. I don't know how I knew, but suddenly I was sure she'd heard me asking Patrick for money and she was going to offer to lend me it herself.

It was like the four minute warning was sounding in my head. At first, I couldn't do anything, then it was all I could do to stop myself bowling her over in the rush to get away.

It was all getting too complicated.

As Patrick and me walked up the London Road, Patrick as usual going on about the superiority of the BBC Model B over the ZX Spectrum, this time with specific reference to its Teletext capabilities, I hardly listened. All I could think of was Penny, and the strange effect she was having on my brain. It was only twenty four hours since she'd spoken to me for the first time, and already it was like trying to deal with a bucketful of monkeys in my head.

Then I realised what it was. We hadn't finished the game. She didn't have the answer to her competition. That was why she kept popping up. It couldn't be for any other reason.

I looked across the London Road, and there she was, dawdling up towards Pritchard Lane, a little behind me and Patrick, though on the opposite pavement. I waited till Patrick came to the end of one of his endlessly self-satisfied sentences, then said, 'See you tomorrow.'

'Don't you want to come in for a—'

'Nah, bye.' And I took advantage of a gap in the traffic to dash across.

Penny was still behind me, but I pretended not to see her, and went at my usual pace down Pritchard Lane. As soon as I was under the trees and out of sight of Patrick, I crouched down to undo, then do up, my shoelaces. When I'd finished, Penny was on the path on the other side of the lane.

'So, do you want to finish that game, then?' I said.

She grinned, and pulled a couple of Curly Wurlies from her bag.

10

'So you really like computers?' Penny said.

She was sitting on the corner of my bed again, drinking Tizer. We'd finished the Thompson Twins game, Penny had her competition answer, and she was gazing at the stuff in my room.

'Yeah,' I said, looking at my stuff too, trying to see it through her eyes. There were computer game cassettes on one shelf, computer books on another, a stack of computer magazines on the floor, and I even had a picture of Sir Clive Sinclair, inventor of the ZX Spectrum and head of Sinclair Research, on the wall. I had other stuff, too, like Doctor Who books and Fighting Fantasy books, but if you took a quick look and blinked, the afterimage you'd get would most definitely be 'computers'.

'What do you like about them?'

'I dunno. You can do loads of stuff with them.'

This was beginning to sound dangerously like a conversation I often had with Dad. He didn't buy the idea that computers would be a lot more useful in the future, and in fact thought they were just a fad that would be replaced this time next year by some other 'toy' (as he *insisted* on calling them), like the Rubik's Cube or Cabbage Patch Dolls. To prove they were so much more I'd say, 'You can do the household accounts on them,' and he'd say, 'Show me this thing doing the household accounts, then.' So I'd try to explain it was more complicated than that, because you had to write a program first, and he'd take that to mean you couldn't do the household accounts at all. (I have no idea what it means to do the household accounts. It's just an example they give in computer books when saying what computers are good for.) Usually things end with him saying, 'What about this printer thing, then. Let's see what it can do.' So I'd print something out on my Sinclair Printer,

which only works with this special four inch wide shiny
thermal paper that looks and feels like the sort of toilet
paper they put in public loos to stop you using too much of
it, and Dad would say, 'Well, you're not going to be putting
Acme out of business for a while yet, are you?' Then he'd
have a good laugh and leave.

I decided to try a different tack with Penny.

'Look,' I said, and typed:

```
10 PRINT "Hello Penny!";
20 GOTO 10
```

Then I pressed RUN and ENTER, and the screen filled up
with 'Hello Penny! Hello Penny!' over and over again.

'Wow! It's saying hello to me.' She seemed genuinely
touched.

'Only because I told it to,' I said. 'Computers just do
what you tell them to.'

I added a few lines to make the 'Hello Penny!'s come
out in different colours.

She liked that even more.

She said, 'Make it say "Hello Tim and Penny".'

So I did that. The screen filled up with 'Hello Tim &
Penny! Hello Tim & Penny!'

'Aah,' she said.

I wondered what that 'Aah' meant.

I got rid of that program and typed this one instead:

```
10 PRINT "Nuclear War!"
20 PRINT "Press any key to launch
        missiles..."
30 PAUSE 0
40 NEW
```

I pressed RUN and ENTER and told Penny to have a go.

She read the instructions, then pressed a key.

The screen went black, with red spark-like flashes at the

bottom, like it was all going up in smoke and flames, then it went white and showed the Sinclair Research copyright message. It was just the usual Spectrum reset, but it did look a bit like a nuclear bomb going off, if you pretended.

'What happens next?' Penny said.

'Nothing. It's a nuclear war. Everything's gone.'

'Oh.' She downed her last mouthful of Tizer. 'I liked the Tim and Penny one better.'

I felt a bit stupid, and couldn't think of anything to say.

Penny, meanwhile, had gone back to looking round my room. She looked thoughtful for a moment, then said, 'What you need, Tim, are more music tapes.'

Before I could think of a reply — like, 'And you need more computer tapes!', which I'm glad I didn't say because that would have been totally utterly stupid, as she didn't have a computer — she got to her feet. 'I'd better get this competition entry in, if I'm going to stand a chance.'

And after another 'Thanks, Tim!' from the bottom of the stairs, she let herself out the front door. She gave a little wave when I peered through the window, then disappeared round the corner to Fallow Lane. I took our empty Tizer glasses downstairs and washed and dried them and put them away, so Joe and Dad wouldn't wonder why I'd used two, then turned on the TV in time for Star Trek.

This week, Captain Kirk had to track down and destroy a Romulan spaceship that had crossed the Neutral Zone. The Romulans and humans are a bit like the Russians and Americans, two huge superpowers on the brink of terrible war, where the slightest thing could set them off. This time, Captain Kirk didn't get to kiss any exotic alien beauties, which is a pity. He deserves a break every now and then.

11

After double Maths first thing the next day, we had Computer Science, which, as always, did its best to address the eternal question: Mr Clyde, man or Spitting Image puppet?

You might think that because I like computers, Computer Science ought to be my favourite lesson, or Mr Clyde my favourite teacher. This is wrong, to the power of about twelve zillion. It's wrong partly because Mr Clyde is a trumped-up scruffy pillock, but mainly it's wrong because he doesn't actually teach us anything about computers.

There are two reasons for this.

The first is that Mr Clyde is an English teacher who wasn't very good at teaching English, and when the vacancy came up for Computer Science he thought, 'Hey, I've got a ZX80 at home and can make it add two numbers together, I'll become a Computer Science teacher instead.' (The ZX80 is an ancient version of the ZX Spectrum, Mum, from as far back as 1980.) And because our headmaster, Mr Corking, is about a hundred years old and thinks anyone who can plug a computer in must be pretty hot stuff, he was impressed by Mr Clyde dropping a few computery phrases, like 'power supply' and 'user manual', into his conversation, and gave him the job.

Once, when Mr Clyde had to leave the room to sort out a ruckus in the corridor outside, and take the two boys involved to the headmaster's office, we discovered his secret. He's got a copy of The Penguin Computing Book in his top drawer. All the important bits have been underlined in red ink, and he basically teaches us from that. Which is why, whenever any of us asks a question about something we really want to know, he tells us to stick to the topic, and if any of us asks something that's part of the topic but isn't in The Penguin Computing Book, he shakes his head wearily and says, 'I tell you, you guys have a *lot* to learn about computers in the real world.'

But it's Mr Clyde who has a lot to learn about computers in the real world.

This is the second reason Mr Clyde doesn't teach us anything. There's no one in the entire Computer Science class who isn't obsessed with computers. We read about them, we talk about them, we use them every day. If there's a new thing to know about computers, we know it. We're *hungry* for everything there is to know about computers, and we're way ahead of Mr Clyde.

I'm not being big-headed, Mum. It's a simple fact. Nobody over the age of sixteen knows anything about computers. Okay, there may be a few exceptions like Sir Clive Sinclair and Lesley Judd, but mostly they don't. They may use computers at work, they may have read every page in every manual there is, but they don't *get* computers like we do. To them, computers are just a thing they use, no different from a washing machine or a hover mower. To us, they're the promise of what life's all about. It's what I said before. Computers are all about the future. And we're kids, we're all about the future, too. We're made of future-stuff, like polystyrene foam or Space Dust. And we know that if we wait just a little bit longer, the world will be ours, the future-world, all shiny and full of nifty gadgets.

(If it doesn't get blown to a radioactive cinder first.)

Anyway, from the looks of it, Mr Clyde's *tie* is about fifty years old, so I don't know what that makes the rest of him. He doesn't shave properly, he's got bags under his eyes the size of pillowcases, and he looks like he's dressed in the leftovers from a Blue Peter Bring and Buy Sale. He's always got this world-weary tone, like he's seen it all before, done it all before, and we kids don't know nothing. And that may work for any other subject, but it doesn't work for computers. And not with us.

That Wednesday morning, for instance, we spent the

entire lesson learning about punched cards. Punched cards are a method used to store computer data. They're pieces of card with lots of little squares printed on them, and the way you show this or that piece of data is you punch out a square so it leaves a hole, which can be detected by a punched-card reader.

About a thousand years ago.

Nobody uses punched cards now. And it's not like we're ever going to go back to using them. We've got tapes, and floppy discs, and bubble memory. So what's the point spending a whole lesson learning about punched cards?

Computer Science isn't like any other lesson. In Chemistry or Biology or Maths if something was true in the past, it's still true now. In Computers, if something was true in the past, it's old hat.

Anyway, that's the last time I call him Mr Clyde. He's Scruffy Clyde from now on, and that's if I'm feeling nice. Otherwise he's just plain Scruff. He thinks he knows stuff, but he doesn't.

Or maybe I'm just in a mood because he had a go at me in class.

The thing is, Mum, my mind was a bit wandery that morning. It had been mostly okay in Maths, because in Maths there's always plenty to keep me concentrating. A quadratic equation to solve, or a cosine to calculate. I did find my attention drifting on the odd occasion. Penny and Kash sit next to each other one row ahead of me and two desks to the left, and once or twice I glanced up to see them talking in that low-voiced, heads-together way girls sometimes do. I wondered what they might be talking about. They might have been discussing the proper way to expand a polynomial, but I did find myself wondering if Penny was telling Kash about coming round to my house and finishing the Thompson Twins game. Would she tell her that sort of thing? If not, was it because it was too uninteresting to mention? Once, I looked over and saw Penny looking at me. She just raised her eyebrows in a way that could have meant 'hello', or could have meant 'what are *you* looking at?', or could have just meant 'hmm'. I couldn't work it out. I don't understand girls generally, Mum, but Penny suddenly seemed far more difficult to understand than all the rest of them combined.

So that was Maths. In Computer Science, it was far worse. My mind didn't just wander, it detached from reality like an untethered balloon and went off into the stratosphere. Scruffy Clyde was droning on about the Jacquard Loom, and Hollerith's solution to the US census problem — both classic examples of the use of punched cards, one from 1801, the other from 1880! — and I just fuzzed away in a world of rambliness.

It wasn't all about Penny. At one point I wondered what would happen if a Mutant Telephone from Manic Miner came through the door and gobbled up Scruffy Clyde. That was a happy thought. But some of it *was* about Penny.

Penny didn't do Computers, she did Music instead.

She probably thought that, apart from using them to play Thompson Twins adventure games, computers were boring. She probably thought boys who were into computers were boring, too. Most likely, it was only politeness that had stopped her from yawning all the way through yesterday at my house, particularly whenever I explained something about my ZX Spectrum. Which, now I came to think of it, I'd done rather a lot.

I wish I hadn't. I wish I'd shut up.

She probably thought I was a real div. A real twit. A real berk and a duh-brain and a—

'—the name of that company was?'

I gawped up at Scruffy Clyde, and realised I had, for an instant, no idea what lesson this was, let alone what topic the question related to.

'Uh,' I said, seeing some sort of sound was demanded of me.

'Uh?' he mimicked.

'Um.'

'Um?'

I thought, 'Just give me a blast of sarcasm and go away!' But he didn't. He kept standing there, waiting.

'Sir, it's I—'

'I don't want to hear what you think it is, Patrick. I want to hear what this young man thinks it is. You are a young man, aren't you? Not a fish? Gawping like that, it's hard to—'

'IBM,' I said. It was a guess, but a pretty safe one, considering Patrick had given me the first letter, and IBM is the biggest computer company in the world.

Scruff stood there a full five seconds, giving me a look and a half. Then he turned away, missing only the swirl of a Darth Vader cloak to make the movement complete, and carried on describing how Herman Hollerith's devising a means of quickly counting the population of the USA using punched cards ultimately led to the formation of International Business Machines, or IBM, as they're better known.

(A fact about IBM: When intercontinental ballistic missiles, which are used to launch nuclear weapons at countries far away, were first invented, they were referred to as IBMs, and it was only when people started getting them mixed up with the computer firm that they were called ICBMs instead. Computers and nuclear weapons have a lot of funny little connections like that.)

As soon as I could, I gave a thank you thumbs-up to Patrick.

(Patrick, though, gave me a blank look. Which made me realise he hadn't been helping me out, he'd been too bursting to let Scruff know he knew the answer to keep quiet.)

I really did my best to concentrate for the rest of the

lesson, but it was hard. Scruff kept droning on, and somewhere in the distance I could hear the occasional clunk of a piano being played. Perhaps in a Music lesson, somewhere else in school. Perhaps in the very Music lesson Penny was having right now. Perhaps, for all I knew, it was Penny herself playing the piano. I had no idea if she could, I had no idea if she couldn't.

Why should it matter?

It shouldn't. It didn't.

Computers were what mattered. Computers, and the threat of nuclear war.

There wasn't *room* for anything else.

I just wished I could reset my head and get back to how I usually was. I liked how I usually was. Or, at least, I knew how to get by with it. I mean, how I usually was had been carefully developed to keep all the various difficult areas in my life finely balanced. Dad, Joe, Patrick, and nuclear war — all held back just far enough that I had a little bit of room for myself. But this thing with not being able to get Penny out of my head was a whole new problem I'd never encountered before. Like developing a craving for toothpaste sandwiches.

Maybe it would go away after a while.

It was bound to, wasn't it?

Scruff finished the lesson with a ten-minute lecture on how useless we all were at writing essays. We chalked that up as a victory for us, because whenever he starts teaching us English instead of Computer Science it means he's getting defensive about how little he knows and how much we do.

And we just ignore him anyway.

12

The bell for lunch break went, and me and Patrick headed up to the computer room. Time for the *real* computer lesson of the day.

The computer room is at the top of the science block, and it's our own little ivory tower. It's got eight BBC Micros (six Model B's, two Model A's), two ZX Spectrums, and a ZX81, which only gets used if you're so desperate for a computer fix you'll stoop to 1k of memory, a mono-chrome display, and a hard flat keyboard that feels like you're typing on vulcanised bubble wrap. There's an enormous, ancient printer that uses this special 15-inch-wide fanfold paper, though it hasn't been used for years because there isn't a computer old enough to plug it into. There's also about twenty boxes of the paper that goes with it. (We use it for scrap, and for scrunching up and throwing at each other.) In one cupboard, there's an old LOGO turtle, which isn't a hibernating reptile, Mum, it's a small, wheeled robot housed in a clear plastic dome, which you plug into a computer and tell how to move using a simple program-ming language called LOGO. It's got a pen, and you can tell it to PEN UP or PEN DOWN and draw mathematical shapes. The thing is, one of its wheels isn't working, so it can only do left turns. And somebody nicked the pen. There's two cupboards full of well-thumbed manuals, and another one full of interesting-looking electronic junk that we think might be the innards of a mainframe computer, donated by some company that thought kids might want to marvel at the sight of burnt-out valves and spaghetti wiring.

Which we do.

Basically, the computer room is the TARDIS and the Starship Enterprise rolled into one. It's even got its own Doctor Who/Mr Spock, called Chip.

Chip isn't a teacher. He should be, because he knows

more about computers than anyone in the entire school, and probably the whole of Eastead, too. And I don't just mean the stuff we're taught in Computer Science. Chip knows about computers in the real world, because unlike Scruffy Clyde, he's actually had a job using them. And not just using them, I'm talking about the ultimate — writing games. So, there are about a thousand reasons Chip should be our Computer Science teacher. The two reasons he isn't are: he's only sixteen, and he hasn't passed his exams yet.

Chip's real name is Simon. When he used to be a pupil here, people started calling him Silicon Simon because he was so into computers. (At the time, there were even fewer people into computers than there are now, so he was pretty unique.) Then, after a while, they dropped the Simon and just called him Chip (as in silicon chip, not the sort you eat with fish).

There's a whole story about how he was the perfect pupil till he discovered computers. One day he was top of the class in everything from Physics to History (they didn't have computer lessons back then), the next he was skiving off to spend all his time tinkering and programming. His mum said she couldn't get him out of his room even to eat meals, but had to leave food outside on the landing, and even then, the only suff that got taken in was what could be eaten with one hand while he typed with the other. (His dad, a GP, wasn't around, because his parents had just got divorced. Chip said his dad had been recruited by a secret government organisation called the Nuclear Police, to conduct research into how the human race — and the UK government in particular — could survive a Third World War, and it was so top secret he wasn't allowed a family life anymore. But I also heard he ran off with his receptionist, which sounds a bit more likely.)

Anyway, Chip totally failed in all his lessons and didn't even turn up for his O level exams. But that didn't matter, because he'd written a game called I Am An Egg, and he took it to a trendy new software company called Imagimakers, and they not only bought the game, they hired Chip full-time. And so, at the age of sixteen, he left school to become one of Imagimakers' top games programmers, with full licence to spend all his time working on whatever project he came up with. He started on a massive, three-game epic called This Madhouse Planet, which was going to have the most advanced sprite-handling and artificial intelligence routines ever, not to mention true story-telling gameplay. Then Imagimakers went bust and all of Chip's code was impounded as company property. You'd have thought that, for a genius programmer like Chip, it wouldn't have been hard to find a new job, but loads of software houses were going bust, and no one was hiring. People were saying the home computing bubble had burst. (They're still saying it now, but it's only adults who think computers are a fad. The rest of us know they're here to stay.)

Chip found himself wandering the streets of Eastead, nothing to do, pretty much devastated by the loss of all the work he'd put into his three-game epic. Then he bumped into one of his old teachers, Miss Pye, who teaches Maths. She got him a part-time job supervising the computer room at lunchtimes and after school. It was only meant to be for a few hours a week, but from that point Chip spent all his time in the computer room. He's supposed to be studying to retake his O levels and go into the sixth form, but what he's actually doing is working on a new mega-epic game (as yet unnamed), while teaching us kids everything there is to know about computers in the *real* real world.

Chip knows how to pirate a computer game like nobody. (Not because he wants to make money off the back of the software industry that gobbled him up and spat him out. It's just to see if he can do it. And he can.) He's also the one to go to for how to get infinite lives in games, and how to solve difficult adventure game puzzles. And no one, absolutely no one, is better at programming. BASIC or Machine Code, ZX Spectrum or BBC Micro, he not only knows how to do everything, but how to do it using as little memory or as little processing time as possible, so it's either quick or compact, whichever you need. Sometimes he can do both quick *and* compact, and that's when a look of real satisfaction spreads across his twisted face.

I'm not being nasty, Mum. Chip really has got this funny, twisted-looking face, and it only gets more twisted when he's pleased with himself. You couldn't call it a smile. The entire right half scrunches up and tries to pull as much of the left with it as it can. His eyes bulge even when he isn't pleased with himself, and he's scrawny thin from the greasy flop of his hair (which grows down to his shoulders, almost as long as a girl's) to his scuffed suede pixie boots. I've heard it said that the girls in his year voted him the ugliest creature in school, and that's over the ancient yellow lab-rat that gets wheeled out for dissection every year in Biology. (After which Mrs Flock puts its internal organs back into place, closes it up, and soaks it in preservative fluid for another year.)

But Chip is the coolest bloke there is, and he's king of the computer room.

The great thing about the computer room is it's *ours*. Teachers hardly ever go there, and if they do, you can tell they don't feel right. They open the door to find umpteen pairs of eyes, all glazed computer monitor green, staring back at them, and they instantly know the usual classroom power structure no longer applies. They deliver their message, or get what they were looking for, and back out. And boys who are into football and only like computers for playing games lose all their clout the moment they step through that door. They know it, too, so they keep away.

(That's not to say we don't play games in the computer room. But mostly it will be because someone's trying to map Atic Atac, or find the code to get infinite lives in Terror-Daktil 4D, or figure out how the sprite routines in Lunar Jetman work.)

I feel safe, high up there in the computer room. As safe as it's possible to feel in a world that any moment could be wiped out by three thousand megatons of nuclear-powered radioactive death, anyway.

Well, I *did* feel safe in it, till that Wednesday, when Penny showed up.

13

By the time me and Patrick got to the computer room, all but one of the good computers was taken, so Patrick (of course) took that, and I had to either give myself a ZX81 lobotomy, or watch him work on his graphics compression routine. I pulled up a chair and sat beside him. Next to us, a couple of third years were getting all excited over one of those programs where a line bounces round a screen, leaving a pretty pattern behind it, and next to them a spectacled second year with a sniffle was hex-dumping system variables on a ZX Spectrum. Chip sat at his usual desk with his back to the door, twiddling a pen between the fingers of his right hand while his left pattered out bursts of code on a BBC Model B.

A pair of first years came in and huddled behind him for a moment before summing up the courage to ask, 'Chip? How d'you get infinite lives in Hunchback?'

While his left hand kept up its tap-dancing spider act, Chip said, 'POKE 26254 comma zero, chaps.'

'Cor, thanks, Chip.'

'Say, "I am but an egg".'

'I am but an egg,' the first years said in unison, and Chip's face scrunched lopsidedly while his right hand, which had been twiddling the pen faster and faster, dumped the pen and joined its partner for an extended bout.

The first years left, but as the door closed behind them, I caught a glimpse of a face in the corridor beyond. Someone was trying to peer into the computer room.

No, not someone. Penny.

What was she doing here?

My first impulse was to shift my chair closer to the wall so I couldn't be seen through the little window in the computer room door.

Patrick glanced over his shoulder. 'What are you doing?'

I was now sitting directly behind him, so couldn't appreciate the full magnificence of his programming skills.

'I was going to look through these manuals,' I said, and slid open one of the low cupboard doors, only to be greeted by two shelves of thick, spiral-bound dullness. I'd forgotten this was where they put the documentation for the monitors, floppy drives and other hardware, full of nothing but escape codes and circuit diagrams.

Anyway, Penny should have given up by now, so I shifted my chair back.

A flicker of movement caught my eye. A face had just pressed against the window in the computer room door, then disappeared, and I heard someone in the corridor saying, 'I can't just—'

A girl's voice.

Chip looked round, frowning thoughtfully, then went back to pecking at the keys.

A moment later, the face appeared again.

Obviously she wasn't going to go away. And it was too much of a coincidence to hope she was here to talk to someone else, or had got the wrong room. Perhaps she'd just discovered she didn't have the full competition answer, or maybe this was some especially shortsighted girlish plot to thank me, and so embarrass me in front of everyone in the computer room. Either way, if she came in and spoke to me, Patrick would listen in like a hungry cat at a mouse hole, and as soon as he knew I'd invited Penny Poundley to my house and hadn't told him about it, he'd spend the rest of the day alternately interrogating me and making fun of me. And the worst part of it would be having to explain why I hadn't told him about it. Which I hadn't, because if I had, he'd only have spent the rest of the day interrogating me and making fun of me.

He had no right to be jealous, Mum. I've invited him to my house loads of times. It's not my fault he only came once. This was shortly after we first became friends, and he'd just reduced the amount I had to pay him for a go on his Game & Watch game from 10p to 5p. He'd invited me to his house after school (or, his mum had), so in return, the next day, I invited him to mine, and he tagged along happily enough down Pritchard Lane, but once we got to King George Way and Pritchard Gardens, he started looking more and more worriedly at our surroundings, like he was expecting a gang of skinheads to jump out and mug us. He even said, 'Do you have to walk past these council houses every day?' Then of course we got to my house, which is a council house, and he didn't say anything more about it, but he did ask to use our phone to get his mum to pick him up afterwards so he didn't have to walk back through such dangerous territory on his own. After that he always had an excuse whenever I suggested coming to mine, so I gave up asking.

But there'd be no explaining this to Patrick. He'd just latch on to the fact I'd invited a *girl*, not once but twice, to my house. I'd never hear the end of it. I'd say, 'All she wanted was the answer to a competition. I couldn't say no, could I?' And he'd say, all luvvy-dovey, 'And when are you going round your *girl*-friend's house for tea and cakes?'

I had to do something.

I got up and pretended to wander, bored, over to the monstrous printer in the corner. I fiddled with its platen roller while looking out the window at the playground below. Then I pretended to have only just noticed someone peering through the window in the computer room door, so I went over and opened it, though only wide enough to let my head through.

Penny jumped back a bit, then smiled brightly. 'Hi Tim.'

She wasn't alone. Kash was by her side, giving me a long level look that, if I had to put it into words, would have said something like, 'I'm only here because Penny's my friend and she asked me to come along, but as long as I'm here I'm going to make sure you fully appreciate the effort it took her to come to this far-away corner of the science block to speak to you. Be polite, or else.'

Kash has a very penetrating look.

'Um, hello,' I said, trying to will Penny into speaking as quietly and quickly as possible.

'Sorry for, you know, coming up here and, um, disturbing you,' Penny said. 'It's just, I thought, well, I ought to, you know, say thank you for, you know, yesterday and the day before, letting me use your computer and so on, um...' At this point she sighed, and pulled a face, as if all this was taking a lot of effort, and though I couldn't believe anyone would actually be nervous talking to me, that did seem to be what she was. (Kash, meanwhile, continued to stare at me, as un-nervous as a stone tiger.) 'Anyway,' Penny said, catching her thread again, 'I thought I might, to say thank you, invite you round, um, my house, after school, today? You know, for a cup of tea, and, um, I thought I could play you some Thompson Twins, so you'd know what the fuss is all about?'

Then she looked at me wide-eyed, waiting for a reply.

My brain froze, like my head was stuck in an infinite loop and there was no one to press reset.

Penny's look turned a bit concerned, and she said, 'Um, what do you think?'

'Uh, yeah,' I managed. Then I panicked and added, 'But—'

Penny bit her lip. Kash, meanwhile, narrowed her eyes the tiniest, most threatening, amount, like she was going to squeeze me to death with her eyelids (which I wasn't totally sure she couldn't do).

But—? But what? But nuclear war? No, that was silly. I don't mean nuclear war is silly, it's deadly serious. I mean I couldn't *say* it as a reason for not going to Penny's. So —

but what? But Dad and Joe? It wasn't that, either. But Patrick? Aha! It was but Patrick. But Patrick, but Patrick. Um, why was it but Patrick? (And why wasn't my brain working?) *Girl*-friend, *girl*-friend, tea and cakes, tea and cakes. *That* was why it was but Patrick!

Penny and Kash were still staring at me, one increasingly concerned and perhaps a little nervous, the other ever so slightly more murderous.

'Uh, wait for me on Pritchard Lane, yeah?' I blurted.

'Oh, yeah, sure, of course, I mean, yeah,' Penny said, with a relieved-looking grin, like we'd both given a presentation in class, and it hadn't gone badly.

She'd just started to raise her hand for a goodbye wave when Kash said, 'Who is that?'

Kash has this super-correct way of speaking, like she measures each word out with a steel ruler before saying it. It makes you feel you have to be absolutely honest and accurate in whatever you say back, otherwise she might hit you with that very same ruler. There's something a bit scary about her.

I glanced behind me, through the gap in the door I'd kept as small as possible, to see Chip considering the three of us, a look of idle curiosity on his face (and on Chip's face, even idle curiosity has such an uglifying effect, you might mistake it for tummy ache).

'That's Chip,' I said.

'Chip,' Kash said, as though I was obviously lying, because no one on Earth could be called Chip.

'As in silicon chip,' I said. 'As in computers.'

'Oh?' Like a lawyer about to present evidence to the contrary.

'Uh, he used to be called Silicon Simon.' I have no idea why she needed to know that, only that I had to keep saying stuff till I'd satisfied that suspicious look.

Kash narrowed her eyes, then nodded slowly. 'So this is

the famous Silicon Simon.'

'Famous?'

'My sister was in his class. She used to tell me about him. The ugliest boy in the whole year. Then one day he disappeared. But here he is, in the computer room.' She looked at him a bit more, then said, 'She is right. He is *so* ugly!' But the way she said it, it was like a compliment.

Now I had no idea what to say.

'Um, see you, then,' Penny said brightly, and the two of them went off down the stairwell to the normal part of school.

So, that was it. Somehow, I'd agreed to go to Penny's house after school.

How had that happened? What did it *mean*? Was it something that was going to horrendously complicate my whole life and bring all my carefully-balanced ways of dealing with the world crashing to the ground in smouldering ruins? Or was it just, you know, something that was going to be a bit pleasant? A bit nice?

Why did I feel it was going to be both?

I really don't understand anything, Mum. Have I said that?

I arranged my face in its most convincing look of bland ho-hum-ness, then went back to sit behind Patrick.

He watched me all the way, though I pretended not to notice.

'Who was that?' he said.

'No one.'

'They were girls.'

I shrugged. 'Yeah.'

'What did they want?'

'Dunno. Nothing.' And as that meant he either had to turn around and give me the Gestapo treatment or let it go, he let it go.

A moment later, Chip said, ''Ere, Tim m'lad, come and

have a look at this.'

This was unusual. Chip, unlike Patrick, isn't the sort to need to show off what he's doing, certainly not to me.

I went over, and Chip jerked his head sideways at a nearby orange plastic chair, so I pulled it up and sat on it. His monitor was full of raw machine code. I hoped he wasn't going to ask me about that.

'Who was that, then, at the door?' he said in a distracted, unconcerned voice.

'Just some girls.'

'Just some girls, he says. What did they want?'

'Nothing.'

'You mean they came all the way up here, to the top of the science block, to say nothing?'

'Yeah.' The innocent act had got me this far, and I was going to stick to it.

'Took them long enough to say it.' He gave a sniff, like he wasn't bothered, then said, in a slow, casual tone, 'Who was the, er, one with the dark hair?'

'That was Kash.'

'Kash?' he said, eerily similar to the way Kash had said 'Chip?' earlier.

'Kashmira Kumar. She's in my class. She's Indian.'

'Really? I thought she was Martian.' He twiddled a few more keys, smiling to himself (though it took a trained observer to tell it was a smile). 'So, is she the one who came all the way up here to say nothing to you or was it the other one?'

'It was Penny, um, the other one,' I said. Then realised, from the way Chip's smile skewed that little bit more sideways, that I'd given myself away.

'Kumar,' he said, drumming his fingers on his chin. 'Kumar... Got a sister, hasn't she?'

'Think so.'

'In the sixth form?'

I shrugged. I mean, the sixth form. It's a foreign country, to me.

After tapping out a few more lines of code, he said, 'You're a man of hidden depths, Tim, m'lad.'

I wasn't sure what to say to that.

'Alright then, off you hop.'

I went back to Patrick, who again watched me all the way.

'What did he want?'

I shrugged. 'Just wanted my opinion on something.'

Patrick peered around the monitor at Chip, a hurt look on his face. 'Why didn't he want my opinion?'

'Dunno,' I said. Then I stared out the window at a passing aeroplane till Patrick got on with his programming.

Things, though, were getting complicated.

What I needed was a good old think.

14

Last lesson of the day was history with Mr Bosworth.

Like all teachers in school, Mr Bosworth has a nickname. Only, in his case, it's the most inappropriate nickname I've ever heard.

Mr Bosworth belongs to another age, when all teachers wore tweed suits and pupils treated them with instant respect. He's a quiet old man, with fluffy tufts of white whiskers down the sides of his face, a portly belly, and a bit of a flushed look, like he's too hot under all that tweed, but would never consider taking off his jacket or even undoing a waistcoat button, because it's not the done thing. He keeps odd ends of coloured chalk in his pockets as well as a paper bag of toffees, which he'll occasionally offer to a pupil who gives him a good answer, or have one himself while giving us a lecture, making his already mumbly voice incomprehensible. Despite the fact he belongs to the age of the cane, Mr Bosworth has no trouble keeping order in class without one, simply by being so likeable. If anyone makes fun of him, he'll blush and smile, or perhaps laugh and say, 'Very witty. Have a toffee.' (Which of course shuts them up for a bit.) He'll often spend an entire lesson rambling on about this or that event in history (half of which you can't help thinking he must have witnessed himself), and if he does actually set you some work to do, he'll more often than not sit down at his desk and promptly fall asleep, or drift into a daze watching birds out the window. He's quite capable of losing the thread of what he's saying halfway through a sentence, then thinking the reason everyone's so quiet is he must have set us some work, so he'll pop a toffee in his mouth and wander round the class, peering over shoulders, murmuring, 'Good, well done', even though we're not doing anything. You can't help feeling that, when he retires, he'll be taking a bygone age of education with him.

His nickname is Old Bollocksworth. Some people even call him Old Bollocks-warts. I only ever call him Mr Bosworth.

The great thing about history with Mr Bosworth is you can settle into an end-of-day doze, perhaps have a game of hangman (which Mr Bosworth will occasionally suggest an answer to, if he sees you're at it), or just have a good old think about things.

A good old think was what I needed.

This whole thing with Penny. What was going on?

She and me were so different, we might as well come from two alien worlds. But at the same time, I couldn't help feeling there was something about her that was just like me — and like me in a way Patrick, Dad and Joe could never be.

It was such a puzzle.

Not like a programming puzzle. With a programming puzzle, you tinker for a bit, have a think, realise what's wrong, then solve it. Penny, I had the feeling, wasn't the sort of puzzle that ever got solved.

But, in a nice way.

'Nice' is such a Penny word. I feel I'm letting Dad and Joe down again by using it. But it fit. Penny was nice. (Even if capable of punching people.) Just thinking she existed in the world was nice.

The world, though, isn't nice.

The world's got nuclear weapons in it.

So how does that work? How does it all fit together?

It's like Mr Bosworth being called Old Bollocks-warts, when he's this gentle old man. Nice, in a world of not-nice. Like an endangered species. Maybe that was the way to think about it. One day, probably soon, Mr Bosworth would retire and be replaced by some steel-eyed taskmaster, all red ink asterisks and 'See me later!'

And Penny? What would happen to her?

I didn't want to think about it. Because sometimes, it's like the world listens in. It listens in for the things you like, then rubs its hands with glee because it's found another thing to stomp on.

The world's got big feet for stomping.

The world's got nuclear bomb feet.

The bell went, making me jump. Everyone got up with a grinding screech of chair legs, and filed out into the chaos of the corridor. I shuffled along behind Patrick, thinking glum thoughts, and didn't notice Penny behind me till she gave me a tap on the shoulder, then a smile and a see-you-later wave, before being lost in the press.

That tap on the shoulder lingered as I made my way out of the school building. It hadn't produced a spark, as I'd thought it might. But the smile sort of had.

Outside, it was the usual soft explosion of kids released from a day pent up in school. Some ran, some jumped, some made for the trees in the park over the road to light up. (And stood there with those deadly serious expressions smokers have, like they're trying to defuse a bomb, not suck nicotine from a paper tube.) Some kids took off their ties, some loosened them to hang round their necks like hangman's knots. A few girls were putting on makeup. A few boys were kicking a football. There were several clumped queues for the bus, where huddles of girls would burst into screamy laughter, and scuffles of boys would break into fights.

Almost immediately, Patrick started a discussion of the BBC Micro's built-in error handling capabilities. I say a discussion, but as it was him doing all the talking, really it was more of a lecture. Without notes. Also, without any hope of him pausing for breath till we got to his house.

'Is that Chip behind the bushes?' I said.

We stopped and looked. It *was* Chip, half crouching behind the bushes beside the school gate. He seemed to be trying not to be seen. But he was doing it in a way that made him even more obvious than if he'd simply stood there. He had this wide-eyed peeking-out-from-behind-cover look that was, frankly, scary, like a pair of boiled eggs staring out from a leafy salad. He seemed to be spying on the door to the sixth form block.

As soon as he saw me and Patrick he gestured us over.

'Alright, chaps?'

He emerged from behind the bush to talk to us, but positioned himself so he could keep watching the sixth form door, using us as cover.

'What are you doing, Chip?' I said.

'Eh? Can't I get a bit of fresh air every now and then? Very good for you, fresh air, I've been told.'

Oblivious to anything but his own monologue, Patrick asked Chip his opinion on the BBC Micro's error handling capabilities.

'Highly advanced,' Chip said, only half paying attention. 'Bit of a cheat, though, in't it? Structured programming principles and all that. One point of entry, one point of — exit... Aha!' He crouched behind us and proceeded to look even more suspicious as he watched a group of sixth formers leave the building and head for the bus queues.

Then he grinned. (Or it might have been back pain from the way he was crouching, but my guess is a grin.) I hadn't noticed till now, but Kash was in one of the bus queues, and as the sixth formers passed her, one of their number broke away to stand next to her. A tall girl with dark hair. Looking like Kash, only a few years older. Her sister, then. In the sixth form.

I looked back at Chip, who now had a half crazy staring look on his face.

He snapped back to the conversation we'd been having.

'After all, no error-handling in machine code, is there lads? Well, that's enough fresh air for one week. Back to base. Looks like we've all learned something, though, eh?'

And then he was gone.

Patrick started up again, this time explaining how much BBC BASIC supported structured programming principles.

I thought a bit about Chip, and the look he'd got when he saw Kash's sister, but I had no way of interpreting it. Computer problem-solving grins were about as far as my skills in deciphering Chip's facial expressions went. This was something new.

So I puzzled over that for a bit, then about computers for a bit, then I remembered Penny's tap on the shoulder. And the smile. Then I probably got my own half crazy staring look on my face.

15

As me and Penny walked past my house, I risked a look up at Joe's bedroom window. It would have been just my luck for him to have finished early for the day and to be standing there watching. If he had, though, I'd have known about it instantly, because there's a direct link between the part of Joe's brain that spots you doing things he thinks you shouldn't be doing and his mouth. As soon as one's triggered, the other klaxons it out. And Joe has lots of ideas about what I shouldn't be doing.

(Judge Dredd's first name is also Joe. I think this is significant.)

As soon as we got round the corner, I felt this little burst of relief, and wanted to say something, anything, to Penny, because up to now I hadn't said much. She was swinging her bag, ba-ba-bah-ing the synth bit from a pop song I recognised but couldn't put a name to, occasionally surfacing with a breathed-in lyric or two.

'Where is it you live, then?' I said.

'Just up here, at the end of the lane.'

I tried to picture it. Fallow Lane's a meandery road, with Mead Close coming off it at this end, a cluster of bungalows at the other, and not much between but tarmac and trees. The far end makes a T-junction with the Hixfield Road, which is the way I walk into town on Saturdays, so I knew it quite well. Thinking of the bungalows made me remember something Joe once told me.

'Not the mad old woman's house?' I said.

I'd meant it as a joke, but Penny didn't smile. 'What do you mean?'

'There's meant to be this mad old woman who lives in one of the bungalows up there. She doesn't like people looking at her house, and if she catches you at it, she throws roof tiles at you.'

'Oh,' Penny said, still failing to be amused.

I shrugged. 'Just something my brother said. Ages ago. She's probably moved away or something by now.'

Penny went back to singing, a bit louder this time, then broke off and said, 'I can't believe you've only got two music tapes. That's like having nothing but fish fingers for dinner every day. And I didn't see a radio in your room, either. Please tell me you've got a radio.'

'We have, downstairs, in the living room. We don't listen to it much, though, cos...'

'Cos?'

'Well, Dad doesn't really care about music. I put it on, in the mornings, before school. I'm usually the only one in the house by then.'

'You're not beyond all hope, then. Radio One?'

'Radio Two,' I said.

Penny rolled her eyes, like I couldn't have said a worse thing, and I almost said it was what you used to listen to, Mum, but I couldn't say that, could I?

Instead, I said, 'I know that song you're singing, though. That—' (got the title at last!) '—Sweet Dreams one. They play it on Radio Two sometimes.'

Penny went on singing the synth bit.

'It doesn't make sense, though,' I said. 'I mean, it's not exactly about sweet dreams is it?'

She sang a line or two, then shrugged. 'It's about screwed up adults. People start off with sweet dreams but get screwed up and end up wanting screwed up things.'

'Oh,' I said. I'd sort of known that, but hadn't been able to admit to myself it was right. 'Why'd they want to make a song about that, though?'

'What should they make a song about, butterflies and flowers?'

'Isn't that what pop songs are supposed to be about? Happy things?'

'Have you heard Enola Gay by OMD?'

'I think so,' I said, hoping she wasn't going to ask me to sing any of it to prove it.

'Enola Gay's the name of the plane that dropped the bomb on Hiroshima. That's what that song's about.'

'Why'd anyone want to write a song about that? I mean, nuclear war?'

'There's loads of them. Ninety-Nine Red Balloons. Two Tribes by Frankie Goes to Hollywood.'

'Wasn't that banned by the BBC?' I said, dredging my limited pop knowledge for a fact to prove I wasn't a total div.

'That was Relax.'

'Oh.' I remembered now. I'd never got to the bottom of why Relax had been banned. I'd asked Patrick, but he wasn't sure, though he thought it was most likely something to do with drugs. I'd even asked Joe, but he found it so funny I didn't know, he laughed about it for days. I couldn't bring myself to ask Penny.

I glanced up to see her giving me a sidelong, appraising look. Then, coming to a decision, she gave a little smile. 'I'm going to start your education in pop music. You taught me about computers, I'm going to teach you about pop music.'

'Alright then,' I said.

I must have sounded a bit sulky, because she said, 'It'll be fun. Pop music's fun. Even if it's also—' and here, she widened her eyes and leaned in closer '—a bit dark, too.'

I gave a nervous laugh. When she'd leaned in, that had been the closest our faces had ever been.

We came to the bungalows at the end of the lane. Totally unlike the hundred-odd council houses on Pritchard Gardens, these bungalows (or cottages, as they seemed to want to be called, from the names like Pine Cottage and Arbour Cottage on signs outside) were all slightly different from each other. Most had very neatly laid-out gardens in front, bordered by brick walls so low a cat could step over them. One of them, though — the first we came to on the right — had a great tall hedge. This was the one Joe had said was the mad old woman's house, and it fit, because if she didn't like people looking at her house, of course she'd grow the hedge as tall as she could.

It had a low, iron gate, with the name Silversmith Cottage worked into a pattern of curling metal vines. I was about to say this was the house I'd been talking about, and surely Penny must have heard of the mad old woman if she lived in one of these bungalows, when she put a hand on the gate and opened it.

I said, half puzzled, half alarmed, 'What are you doing?' All I could think was she was going to take me to the mad old woman and make me apologise for calling her mad.

'This is where I live,' she said. 'Why?'

'Nothing,' I said, as innocently as I could, and followed her through the gate.

16

The first thing I saw was a stack of roof tiles by the front door. The next was a headless garden gnome with a bunch of dead flowers poking out of its neck. I almost bolted.

Penny was already halfway down the flagstone path that curved across the lawn. The grass was shaggy, a bit more than simply not having been cut since the end of summer, and there were a lot of what looked more like weeds than flowers poking up. A couple of thistles, too. Brambles from the hedge reached toward the flagstones, like they wanted to snag you and drag you under if you strayed from the path.

Penny turned to face me and waved vaguely at the garden. 'Needs a bit of love, I suppose,' she said, walking backwards towards the house, then she turned again and fetched a front door key from her pocket.

I eyed the pile of roof tiles. They were a bit mossy. That didn't mean they hadn't been thrown at anyone recently, or wouldn't be in the near future.

Penny started up another song as she opened the front door and ushered me in. She interrupted herself long enough to call, 'I'm back, Mum. Got someone with me.' She listened for a couple of seconds, then resumed singing, taking off her jacket and hanging it on an old-fashioned hatstand by the door, which immediately tipped against the wall.

Patrick's mum would have appeared as soon as she heard a key in the lock, to ask how we were, offer drinks, and check we weren't treading mud into her carpets. Penny's was obviously less concerned about such things.

The hallway I found myself in was gloomy, with a dark red murkily-patterned carpet, and a lot of strange objects on two little tables in the far corners, including some odd bits of tree root and rock, a door-knocker shaped like a dog's head, a deer's antler, and what I guessed was a badger's skull. Penny started chatting away as she disappeared into the kitchen, through a doorless doorway to the right, but I didn't hear any of it because a monster was staring me in the face. Two monsters, in fact.

They were paintings, on the wall opposite the front door, either side of a passage that led further into the house. Both were large and mostly black. One had a jagged line of sharp teeth curving across it, as though you were staring into the maw of some massively fierce creature. There was a flash of angry eye to one side, and no other details. The other painting had fewer teeth on show, but was no less scary. Here, the creature (if it was the same one) was licking its tusk-like teeth with a warty tongue, like it had just taken a bite out of something. Or someone. The glint in its eyes made it look evilly ready to take another.

Penny poked her head through the kitchen doorway. 'I call them Pinky and Perky. Cheerful, aren't they?'

'What are they doing there?' I said. 'Are they meant to scare burglars away, or something?'

Penny smiled lightly, almost fondly, at the two horrendous paintings. 'Mum'll like that. I'll tell her if she emerges.'

She went back into the kitchen, to give the kettle a thoughtful shake and switch it on.

'Should I take my shoes off?' I said.

'You can if you want, but I wouldn't. Mum, um, dropped a load of staples in the hallway a while back and I still find one stuck in the sole of my shoe every so often.'

'Staples?'

'She makes her own canvases. The staples are from a staple-gun, so they're pretty nasty if you get one in your foot.'

I looked back at those monsters in the hallway.

'Yeah,' Penny said, dropping tea bags into a pair of

mugs, a Union Jack one and a Charles and Di one. 'They're hers.'

'You mean, your mum painted them?'

'Mm.' She got a bottle of milk out of the fridge, lifted the lid and gave it a sniff. 'Why?'

'I've never known anyone who's a painter before.'

'It's nothing special. Anyone can be a painter. You just need some paints. You splat them on a canvas, and you're a painter. Sugar?'

'No,' I said.

'Sweet enough?'

'No,' I said, not really listening because I was still thinking about those paintings. The idea that someone's mum had done them seemed weird. I couldn't imagine a mum painting monsters.

'Twisted and bitter like the rest of us, then?'

'Eh?'

The kettle clicked. Penny poured a gout of steaming water into each mug, then topped it off with a dollop of milk.

'Here.' She turned the Union Jack mug's handle towards me, and took up the other. 'Shall we go to the Bat Cave?'

She led the way back to the hallway, then down the short passage between the monster paintings. The walls in the passage had paintings on them, too. The first was of a couple standing hand-in-hand, dressed like a fairy tale prince and princess. The prince had a lion's head, so this was obviously Beauty and the Beast. The Beast looked proud, but Beauty had her head turned to one side and hanging down, with most of her face hidden by her hair. All that could be seen was one cheek, which had a vivid claw-mark scar down the side of it. Opposite this was a painting of a woman on a chair, brushing her hair, which was so long it grew to the floor, then flowed out of a window in the wall. But the woman — Rapunzel, I suppose — was almost a monster, with her mouth hanging open and a pair of huge tusks poking up from her lower jaw. In the greasy-looking tangles of her hair on the floor were some human bones. Next was Sleeping Beauty, a princess asleep in a bed with a prince standing over her. But the prince was glancing over his shoulder as if to make sure he wasn't been spied on, and had a wicked leer on his face. One hand was reaching for the sleeping girl's thigh. Finally, opposite that, was a painting of a dark woodland, with a wolf. On the ground was a torn red cloak, and the wolf was licking its chops.

I looked at Penny for an explanation, but she just gave a what-can-you-do shrug.

Her room had a name plate saying Penny's Room, with a picture of a teddy bear in bed on it. Next to it, I couldn't help noticing, was a sharp dent in the wood with a faint grey splatter mark and drip-streaks. The only thing I could think was that someone had thrown a pot of black or grey paint at the door pretty hard, and not cleaned it off properly afterwards. Surely that couldn't be right, but it made me think of all the black paint in those fairy-tale and monster paintings in the passage and hall.

Penny was waiting for me to follow her in.

When I did, she closed the door firmly, giving the handle a hefty tug, as if to make doubly sure. Then she threw herself back to sit on her bed.

'So this is my room,' she said. 'What do you think?'

The only thing I could say was, 'There are posters on the ceiling.'

'Yeah. They used to fall on me at night, but I've got the trick of it now. I gave up on Blu-Tack and used Mum's staple gun instead.'

17

The walls and ceiling of Penny's room were covered in pop posters. There wasn't an inch spare.

'When you wake up in the morning,' I said, 'how do you know which way is up?' I looked behind me and saw that the door was covered in posters, too. 'And how do you find the way out?'

'Up,' Penny said, 'is opposite the floor, which I can tell because it's got my school uniform on it. And who needs to know the way out? Most days I'd rather stay in here.'

She gave a little bed-bounce onto her feet, then crossed the room to a ghetto blaster on a table in the corner. Tapes, both bought and copied, either in their cases or out, were strewn over the table, and more were on the shelf just above it.

I was still looking at all those posters. Or they were looking at me. Everywhere I turned, I found myself being smiled at, stared at, pointed at, blank-looked at, by small huddles of people with weird hair. And makeup. Even the blokes had makeup. I don't know what Dad would have said if he'd walked into that room. He'd have probably exploded.

I realised Penny was no longer clattering through her tapes, but studying me.

'You look a bit, I don't know, rabbit in headlights.'

I said, 'Don't you find it a bit strange being stared at by all these, um...'

'Um?'

'Well, my dad would call them weirdoes.' For starters.

'Weirdoes,' she said, dead-pan.

'That's what he calls them when they're on Top of the Pops.'

Penny gave me a flat look. Then, suddenly, she took her school jumper off.

I stepped back, wondering what was about to happen, but all she was doing was swapping it for a big baggy one, black with a few squares of white, yellow and pink at funky angles. She gave her hair a quick ruffle, to get the school day out of it, then said, 'And what would you call them?'

'I don't know.' I was really out of my depth.

She turned to look at all the faces looking at her.

'Weirdoes. I like weirdoes. That's what they are.' She went back to sorting through the tapes around her ghetto blaster. 'I mean, who wants to be normal, if sitting there watching Top of the Pops calling everyone a weirdo is normal? The whole point of pop groups is to be weird. To be not what everyone else is. To get away from all this—' she gave a buzz-off flick of the hand '—*normal*-ness.' She said this like it was the last thing in the world anyone would ever want to be, then added, 'Don't you think?'

'Um...'

'Well, give it a think. Give it a good old compute. And listen to this while you're at it.'

She'd finally found the tape she'd been looking for and snapped it into her player. She pressed play, and a moment later a tickling rhythm began. Then a synth joined it and I realised it was quite loud. Then, when the whole lot kicked in, I realised it was far louder than any music I'd ever heard being played before. My first thought was to look for the door, not to escape (though that was an option), but because I was sure, any moment, Penny's mum would come crashing in, yelling at her to turn that racket down. But she didn't. And when, after a while, I realised that wasn't going to happen, something else did. Standing in the middle of that strange room, being looked at by all those faces, with the music so loud it seemed to have replaced the air itself, I realised it was okay. The music filled the room so much, it was like being underwater. Not drowning, or swimming, but like being a fish immersed in its own proper world. And all of a sudden, those staring weirdo faces seemed to be friendly. I realised why Penny had them up there. They weren't staring like I was different from them, or they were different from me, but like I was *one* of them, and they were all happy for me to be there. A bunch of happy fish, all underwater together, swimming through an ocean of music.

Penny was grinning as much as her face could fit, like she knew exactly what was going on in my head. I was disappointed when she turned the music down.

'What was that?' I said. I'd been aware of singing, but the actual words had been swamped in the dizziness of the moment.

'The one I told you about. Enola Gay.'

'The one about the atom bomb?'

'Yeah.'

I didn't know what to think about that. I said, 'Did you see Threads the other day? On TV?'

'No.'

'It was about nuclear war.'

'I bet it was miserable.'

'It was.'

'Why d'you watch it, then?'

'Why d'you listen to this song if it's about nuclear war?'

'The music's good.'

'But how can it be good, if it's about, you know..?'

She thought about this, then turned the music down a bit more. 'There's this really old song called What a Wonderful World. Have you heard it?'

'I think so.'

'The guy who sings it is this really old black guy, and I always end up thinking, whenever I hear it, how he must have, you know, suffered all sorts of prejudice, and maybe poverty and tragedy and all that, too. But he's singing about the world where all that bad stuff happened, and he's saying it's wonderful. And on the one hand, it seems really sad, because he's not saying *all* of life's wonderful, but just these few things that remind you how wonderful it *could* be, if only there wasn't all the bad stuff. But also, it's really happy, because he's saying, despite all the bad stuff, just being alive is wonderful on its own. You know? And I think music's sort of like being alive, only more. It's like the concentrated orange juice version of life. So even a song about nuclear war is great, because it's much more about being alive than it is about nuclear war.'

The song ended. Penny popped the tape out and put another one in.

'This is the Thompson Twins, who I keep going on about.'

She perched on the edge of the table. I sat on a chair. We both sipped our tea and listened. I realised I knew the songs she was playing, from the radio, and Top of the Pops, and that I'd even found myself singing some of them when I was alone in the house, or in my head on the way to school. I hadn't realised how much pop music I knew, mostly because I always felt I had to pretend not to know it, because of what Dad would say. All of a sudden, that seemed so incredibly stupid, shutting off a part of myself like that.

'Sometimes I think they should have pop lessons in school,' Penny said. 'Then I think, thank God they don't!'

18

All of a sudden it was five o'clock and I said I'd better get home.

Penny had to tug hard on the door handle to open it, then she popped her head out and listened.

'I think Mum's emerged,' she said. The way she said it, it could have been a warning.

I picked up my empty mug and followed her past the paintings in the passage, to the hallway.

Penny's mum was in the kitchen. My first thought was she had only just got out of bed, because she was wearing a dressing gown. Then I saw she had jeans and a top on too, and that both her top and the front of the dressing gown had smudges of paint on them, so this must be her painting get-up. She didn't look as old as Patrick's mum, nor was her hair as done-up. She was smoking a cigarette, staring at the floor, waiting for the kettle to boil.

'Hi, Mum,' Penny said.

Her mum looked up, but didn't say anything straight-away. She took a long drag, then glanced at me.

'Oh, I see,' she said, around her cigarette. 'It's a boy.'

'This is Tim,' Penny said, depositing our tea mugs by the sink.

'Hello,' I said.

Penny's mum ignored me. 'So what have you two been up to in your room?'

'Listening to music.'

'I heard that. I just wondered what else.' She said this with an arch look, which would have made me blush bright crimson if it had been turned on me. I was glad I was still in the gloom of the hallway.

Penny was unfazed. She said, 'Are we going to have dinner tonight?'

Her mum breathed out a cloud of smoke with a weary

sigh, then turned to fill up a chipped mug from the kettle. 'I'm in the middle of things, darling. You'd better fix yourself something.'

Penny pursed her lips, but didn't reply.

Her mother went through the process of making tea. There was a fed-up weariness to her every move. She clattered the teaspoon down almost angrily at the end of it. She took a last drag on her cigarette, stubbed it out in the bin, then picked up her mug and turned to go.

Penny said, 'Tim thinks Pinky and Perky are there to scare away burglars.'

I mumbled, 'No, I just...'

Penny's mum turned. 'Come out of the darkness, young man, and let me have a look at you.'

I stepped into the kitchen.

'So what do you think of my broken fairy tales?'

I wish I could have glanced at Penny for a clue to what I should say, or at least for encouragement, but right then it was like her mum had caught my gaze and wasn't letting it go. I felt this was a test, and had no idea how to answer.

I said, 'Um, are they for a book?'

For a moment, she just observed me, flat-eyed. Then she looked at Penny and smiled at her. It wasn't a one hundred percent nice smile, but I couldn't have said why.

Then, without answering my question, she turned to go.

I suddenly remembered my manners and said, 'Thank you for having me, Mrs Poundley.'

Penny's mum gave more of a cough than a laugh and, as she went out through a door on the far side of the kitchen, said, 'I'm not Mrs Poundley. I'm not Mrs *anything*.'

Then she was gone.

I looked at Penny.

Penny had gone slightly red in the face, though not from embarrassment. She looked more angry. She stayed there for a moment, glaring tight-lipped at the door her mum had gone through, then said, 'Come on,' and led me to the front door.

'Bye, then,' I said, once she'd opened it, but she said, 'Tim...'

'Yeah?'

She still looked annoyed, but made the effort and shrugged it off. 'Sorry about that. She was in a funny mood. She gets like that.'

'Oh,' I said. 'Okay.'

She sighed. 'That mad old woman you said about? That was probably her. She can, you know, go off her rocker sometimes. Even worse than she was now, if you can believe it. She's been known to throw things. Roof tiles, even. But she can be nice, too.'

'Oh.'

'And, that — what she said?'

'Yeah?'

'She *is* my mum, but, well, my parents aren't married.'

'Are they divorced?' I said.

'No. They never were married.'

'Oh,' I said.

I didn't know what else to say to that, and Penny was obviously finding it difficult, too.

'See you, then,' I said.

'Bye.'

I walked down the flagstoned path and turned at the gate. Penny was still there at the door, so I waved, then started back down Fallow Lane. It was gloomy but not yet dark.

What Penny had said.

It didn't matter, but—

I had to stop.

It didn't matter, but it was the fact she'd said it. To me.

If you said that to someone at school, you'd be signing your own death warrant, because the next thing, they'd all be calling you a bastard, and there'd be nothing you could do about it, because it'd be true.

But she'd told me.

I looked back up the lane, and there she was. She'd come to the gate and was watching me. Like she'd been waiting for me to realise.

And now she saw I had, she went back in.

I stared at where she'd been, wishing I'd waved or something.

Then I carried on back home. Inside, I put on the TV and watched Think of a Number, then went upstairs and zapped Myon invaders till Joe and Dad came home.

For tea, we had fish fingers.

19

On Saturday, Dad got up late then had us do one of his cleaning blitzes. I got the bathroom and the stairs, as usual, while Joe went about the living room with a feather duster. (If only. I think he just blew on things.) Dad, meanwhile, operated the washing machine. (I never remember you having to watch it while it worked, Mum.) When we were done, he gave me my pocket money and I went to town, just as the rainy morning started to clear.

I wasn't sure whether to go by my usual route, down Fallow Lane, or not. Not because I didn't want to go past Penny's, but because she might see me walking by and wonder why I hadn't called in to say hello. I wasn't sure if I was supposed to. I wasn't sure exactly what we were. I mean, I was pretty sure we weren't boyfriend-girlfriend, because you have to ask someone if they want to go out with you before you're that. I think. And I didn't know, really, if you could call us friends — in the way Patrick and me were friends, I mean — because we had no interests in common, so what was there to be friends about? But with that thing she'd said about her parents, Penny had bypassed the Patrick stage and moved into a different, difficult-to-think-about stage which didn't have any rules. Not that I knew of, anyway.

(Penny probably knew them. Girls, I think, tend to.)

Besides, I was scared I might be seen by her mum instead.

In the end, I walked on the opposite side of the road (which has the better path to walk on, because it doesn't have Silversmith Cottage's huge hedge sticking out into it, so I had a logical reason), and pretended to be so deep in thought I didn't realise I was walking past Penny's house. Then I felt bad about that, and at the last minute looked up, but couldn't see anyone anyway.

In town, I went to WHSmith's. Chip was there, in the stationery section, stocking up on squared paper and coloured pens. 'For a new project,' he said, in a confidential tone, which made me feel quite special. He picked up a luminous pink felt-tip and gave it a serious, almost tortured look.

I left him to it and moved on to my usual haunt, the computer games section. There, I gave the shelves a quick scan for new games and bargains, but I hadn't come to town to buy a game. The real reason I'd come to town was in a corner of the shop I'd never been to before, and I was only in the computer games section to psych myself up.

I gave a quick look around (for Dad and Joe, who of course were at home, one watching Grandstand, the other fiddling with his motorbike, so this was just me being paranoid), then took a deep breath and made my way to the pop music section.

For a moment, I just stared at this wall of tapes. Music tapes are exactly the same shape and size as computer tapes, but to me, they are alien objects. I don't understand them. I can tell, by looking at a computer game cassette, exactly what sort of game it is, and how good or bad it will be, but with music tapes I have no idea. It's like their covers are written in an entirely different language, from one of those distant countries where people nod their heads for no and shake them for yes. And somehow I'd managed to forget the names of all the bands Penny had mentioned, along with all the songs I half knew and pretended I didn't.

I started thinking this was maybe a bad idea, and retreated somewhere safe, the kids' books section, to spend a moment flipping through the Doctor Who paperbacks to see if there were any new ones. But I wasn't really paying attention. I was just catching my breath and gathering my courage for another go.

I remembered a name. The Thompson Twins. How could

I have forgotten?

Repeating it to myself under my breath so it didn't disappear in a puff of panic, I went back to the pop music section, determined to see this through.

Now there were two older girls there, cooing over a tape with a couple of moody-looking leather-jacketed blokes on the cover, so I couldn't get near. I hung about till they'd finished, then moved in, wanting to get this over with quickly before anyone else arrived. Thompson Twins, Thompson Twins. Why was it so difficult to find the T section? I seemed to be on the verge of forgetting my alphabet, too. Perhaps if I thought in ASCII codes? 'A' was 65, so 'T' was 84, as in 1984, so it ought to be easy to remember—

'Would you be wanting any help, sir?'

I whipped round, about to say 'No thanks' and exit the whole shop, but it was Penny. She was dressed in jeans and a top that was bright yellow and pink, like a fruit salad chew.

'Your face!' she said.

'What about my face?' I said, grumpily.

She shrugged. 'It's on the front of your head.'

While I was trying to work that one out, she picked a tape off the shelf. 'Here,' she said. 'Queen. The Works. I think you'd like it. Radio Ga Ga. You're a bit gaga, aren't you?'

'How can you tell what I'd like?'

She picked up another tape, looked at it, put it back. 'ESP. All girls have telepathic powers. Didn't you know?'

I know it sounds stupid, but for a moment I wasn't sure whether to believe her or not. Because I remember you, Mum, always seeming to know what was going on with me, like when I was upset about something, so it might be true. I said, 'Alright, what am I thinking?'

'You're thinking of pink elephants doing the can-can.'

'No I'm not.'

'But you are *now*, aren't you?'

'You're—'

'—weird,' she joined in, then said, quickly, 'Jinx.'

'That's—'

'Uh!' She held up a finger. 'You can't saying anything till I un-jinx you.'

So I stood there while she looked at a few more tapes, then gave me a wave and walked off to another part of the shop. I looked at the tape she'd handed me. It was true, I did like the Queen songs I'd heard. Plus, Dad couldn't say anything bad about them, because it was sort of like the music Joe liked, too.

I queued up and bought it, every so often casting a glance at Penny, who was in the magazines section. I was waiting for her to give me a told-you-so look, but she kept her back turned. I knew she was smiling, though.

Once I'd bought it, I went to look at the computer magazines. Penny was only a few feet away, nose in a magazine, but looking very pleased with herself.

I lifted the corner of what she was reading to see the cover. 'Just Seventeen?' I said. 'You're not seventeen.'

'Well you read computer magazines and you're not a computer,' she said. 'Not yet, anyway. And I haven't un-jinxed you. You're not allowed to speak.'

I stood there in silence for a bit.

Then I said, 'I bought the tape.'

'I know.'

I waited a bit more.

Then I said, 'What are you going to do now?'

She hummed and hah-ed. 'I think I'm going to buy you a bar of chocolate. A Yorkie. I think you like Yorkies.'

'How do you know that?' I said, because she was right.

'I just think you like a chocolate bar with well-defined corners. You're that sort of person.'

I thought for a bit about what sort of person she was, but couldn't come up with anything. 'What are you going to have?'

'Cadbury's Caramel,' she said, in the breathy voice of the cartoon bunny from the ads.

Which made me blush, so I said, 'I'll buy one for you, then,' and went off.

'I always like it when I get a half-p in my change,' Penny said, examining the coins in the palm of her hand.

We were walking down the hill from Smith's, past Bejam Freezerfoods and Radio Rentals, and I was trying to break my Yorkie into chunks without looking like it was a strain.

Penny broke a segment off her Caramel and ate it.

'I always check the year, to see if it's 1971. The first ones came out in 1971. On the 15th of February, to be exact. Do you know how I know that?'

I'd just managed to snap a chunk of Yorkie off and pop it into my mouth. It was still too much of a brick to let me say anything without spluttering chocolate spit, so I shook my head.

'Me and the half-p coin came out on the same day. It's how I got my name.'

'They're going to take them out of circulation at the end of this year,' I said, as soon as I could, proud to find I knew a relevant fact.

'Yeah. Sad, isn't it?'

I couldn't see why.

She said, 'Don't you feel sorry for them?'

'Who?'

'Half-p coins.'

I sniggered, but she didn't seem to be making a joke.

'I mean,' she said, 'they're like little baby coins. Whenever I get some change and there's a half-p, I think the biggest coin is the daddy, and the next biggest is the mummy, and the half-p is the baby, and I try not to spend them unless I can get rid of all three at once, otherwise it's breaking up a family. But now there won't be any half-p's, there can't be any little families anymore.'

'Can't the one-p's be the babies?'

'No. They'd look weird. Like grown men in nappies.' She turned on me. 'Am I being a bit strange?'

My mouth full of chocolate again, all I could do was hold up a hand with first finger and thumb an inch apart.

She said, 'On a scale of?'

I held up both hands, a foot apart.

She looked unsatisfied.

I moved my hands further apart, but she frowned.

'Come on, I'm stranger than that.'

Then she smiled, making me wonder if it had been a joke after all.

We got to the end of the shops and started crossing the footbridge over the bypass.

Penny said, 'So what does your dad do?'

'Works at a printer's, in town.'

She ate another bit of chocolate and looked at me expectantly. It was my turn to ask her something. The most obvious thing would have been to ask what her dad did, but I didn't know if I could, considering she didn't have one. Or she did, but he wasn't around. I mean, I didn't know if it was like the way we don't mention you, Mum. And I couldn't see how it couldn't be. But I had to say something, so I mumbled, 'What about your, um, yours?'

'He's a sound man for the BBC,' she said, and instantly I knew there was no don't-mention about it. She was quite proud. 'You know those fluffy microphones on poles film people have? He's the one who holds it. It's actually more technical than that, but whenever he explains it, all I want to hear about is the fluffy microphone. I'm always asking him to get me one, but he says they're way too expensive. He gets me badges instead. From TV programmes he's worked on. And some he sneaks into, just to get the badges.'

We left the footbridge and started across the sports field, where some kids were playing football with piles of coats for goalposts. I'd finished my Yorkie while Penny had eaten only two bits of her Caramel. I felt a bit of a pig, and slightly guilty I hadn't offered to swap a chunk of mine for a chunk of hers, which I'd normally have done if it was Joe or Patrick, though Patrick would have worked out some rate of exchange more favourable to him, while Joe would have taken a bit of mine only to tell me he'd finished all of his. Still, it would have been the polite thing to do. I wasn't sure if girls operated by the same rules, though.

Penny said, 'He lives in London.'

'Do you see him?' I said, still feeling any moment I might step on the conversational equivalent of a land mine, but she seemed quite happy. Nothing like us at home and you, Mum. I never thought things could be different from that, but it seems they can.

'Sometimes,' she said. 'Not much. He's always saying, you know, when he's better set up, but...' She shrugged.

A football came rolling to a halt in front of us, and the kid who'd been running after it stopped and looked at us expectantly. I thought, I'm not going to kick it. Whenever I kick a ball it goes off at a totally random angle, and I look a right div. And it'll be even worse in front of Penny. Then, I don't know why, I thought, but what if I *did* kick it and it was a really good kick, what would she think then? And suddenly I felt that heroic surge again, like when I'd said she could use my computer, and before I knew it, I'd done a step, turn and kick, and for a moment, just a moment, I was Pelé in slow-motion. Then the ball went off at a sixty-degree angle and the kid had to jog just as far to get it, only in a different direction. His 'cheers' sounded decidedly limp.

Penny gave me a well-contained look.

I said, 'If I'd been wearing football boots...'

Her look became less well-contained.

I said, 'You can kick the next one.'

Over the sports field, we took the path down by the allotments, which isn't really a short-cut, but does get you away
from the main road. It had the added advantage of not being
the way Patrick would walk to or from town, on the rare
occasion his mum didn't give him a lift. In fact, there wer-
en't many people about at all. It was like we had Eastead to
ourselves. And not in a nasty, post-nuclear, radioactive way.
More Day of the Triffids, though without the triffids. I liked
it.

Penny told me about the TV programmes her dad had
worked on — not Doctor Who, unfortunately — then said,
'It's how they met. My mum and dad. He was part of a
documentary crew making a TV programme about my
grandad.'

'Your grandad?'

'He's sort of famous. But not much. Only if you know
about art and stuff. He's a sculptor.'

'Is he rich?' I said.

'He's got a nice enough house, but not really big. He
bought Silversmith Cottage for Mum when she was preg-
nant with me, though. Meant to be for her and me and Dad,
but she kicked Dad out as soon as she got the cottage. She
once told me that was all she wanted, the cottage.'

'That sounds a bit...' I said, but couldn't think of a polite
way of saying it.

'Yeah, it does,' Penny said, meaning I didn't have to.

We left the allotments and started down the rough road
beside the railway.

'I think that's how my mum and grandad were, though,
when she was growing up,' Penny said. 'He was always off
working in his studio, or in some other part of the country
at some special do or something, some unveiling of his
latest creation. She got to doing things just to get his attention, or to get things off him. Like seducing the sound man
of the TV programme they were making about him. Sort of

funny, if it wasn't so...' She pulled a face, then changed the subject. 'So how did your parents meet?'

'I don't know,' I said.

'You must do.'

I tried to think, knowing it was the sort of thing I ought to, but didn't.

'I know your mum's, um, she died,' Penny said quietly.

I suppose everyone in my class knows that. It's probably the one thing everyone does, if they know anything about me at all. That, and that I'm into computers. It was odd to think of myself like that, the two biggest things in my life just a pair of minor facts to everyone else. So-and-so was who he was because he's got brown hair and scuffed shoes, Tim was Tim because he liked computers and his mum was, you know.

I knew I ought to say something, but my mind was an utter blank.

We walked on a bit, me feeling awkward, and perhaps Penny feeling awkward too.

Then she said, 'So, have you got any not-very-famous grandparents, or is it just me?'

21

We were walking slowly by the time we got to the end of Fallow Lane.

Penny said, 'Want to come in for a cuppa?'

She asked it casually, but I knew it would mean something if I said yes, and it would mean something if I said no. And I wanted to say yes, because I'd liked this walk back from town. It felt like I'd just bought a wonderful new computer game, and could bask in the glow of knowing I'd soon be home playing it, only in this case, I didn't want to get home, I wanted to continue being with Penny. But there was one thing.

'Will your mum be about?'

Penny looked at her shoes. 'Yeah, probably.'

She thought I was saying no, so I said, 'It's just, I don't know what to call her. I can't call her Mrs Poundley. I think we've worked that out.'

'Her name's Rhea,' Penny said. 'Everyone calls her Ree. She wouldn't mind.'

'That'd be weird,' I said. There's something fundamentally wrong calling an adult by their first name. You don't do it with your parents, you don't do it with friends' parents, you don't do it with teachers, and there aren't any other adults you need to talk to.

'You could try "Hey! You! Mad woman!"' Penny said.

I pretended to give it some serious consideration.

'Or how about, if you ever have to get her attention, though I can't think why, give me a look, and I'll say, "Mum!" to get things started, then you can say what you need to say. A two-man operation.'

'What sort of look?'

'How about...' She stuck out her tongue and crossed her eyes.

'Right,' I said. 'And if I do this—' I gurned like a gargoyle '—it means "That went well, perhaps we should have another cup of tea?"'

'I'm glad we've got that sorted,' Penny said, and led the way through the gate of Silversmith Cottage.

Penny's mum was in the kitchen. She was in a dressing gown again, but a different one. This was black silk, that caught little snakes of light off the bulb in the ceiling. She was sorting clothes from a plastic basket into piles on the kitchen table. I saw rather more frilly-edged white things than I was prepared for, so I stayed in the dim-lit hallway.

'Hi Mum,' Penny said, as she made for the kettle. 'Tim's come in for a cuppa.'

I couldn't help glancing up when Penny said my name. It got me a flicker of a look. I also saw, as Penny's mum straightened, that not only was her dressing gown not belted up, but all she had on underneath were more frilly-edged white things.

I got into a hasty study of the badger's skull in the hall-way.

'Mum,' Penny complained quietly, noticing too.

'Darling?' her mum said, in a voice that had no darling about it.

Almost mouthing it, Penny said, 'Can you do your front up?'

Her mum ignored this for a few moments, then said, with a flat casualness that made it all the more hurtful, 'I'll dress how I want in my own house, thank you madam.'

Her mum continued to stare at her, so Penny turned and got the two mugs we'd had the last time, and put a tea bag in each.

'Don't be so prissy,' her mum said, not letting it go.

Penny fiddled with the teaspoon for a bit, twiddling its round end against the counter. It slipped and clattered, and her mum said, 'No need for that.'

'I wasn't...' Penny bit it back. 'Do you want some tea?'

'No, darling, I'm going out.' She picked up the largest pile of clothes and put them in the washing machine, then swept the remainder back into the plastic basket. 'I probably won't be back till tomorrow.'

'Really?'

'Yes, really. No need to sound so whiny.'

Her mum threw the basket on the floor, tutted when it fell over, then ratched the washing machine dial to the right and started it going. 'You can take this lot out and hang it up when it's done, can't you?'

'Yes, Mum,' Penny said quietly.

Her mum, deciding she didn't like the quiet tone, put her hands on her hips and said, 'Or are you going to be too busy?'

'No,' Penny said. 'It's just...'

'Just what?'

'Can't you be polite when I've got someone round?'

'No darling, it seems I can't.'

The kettle boiled. Penny filled the mugs, added milk, squeezed the tea bags and binned them.

She'd just picked up the cups when her mum said, 'Don't give me that look.'

'I didn't—'

'Just go, then!' her mother said.

Penny struggled for a moment, then gave a quiet tut and left the kitchen.

A balled-up T-shirt hit her in the side of the face.

'And don't you tut at me, miss.'

Penny's cheek went red. She shrugged the T-shirt off her shoulder and led the way to her room.

Neither of us said anything for a bit. I wasn't sure if she was going to cry. I hoped she wasn't, because I didn't know what to do if she did, but it almost seemed the best thing she could do.

Then she sighed and looked a bit better.

I realised saying anything was better than saying nothing, so I said, 'Are you alright?'

She pulled a doesn't-really-matter face and shrugged. 'It's like, sometimes she's my mother, sometimes she's my wicked stepmother.' She took a sip of tea and blinked because it was hot. 'Do you want to play your tape?'

I put it into her machine and pressed play. At the end of side one, Penny got up to turn it over, and I heard the front door closing. It wasn't a slam. It might even have been guiltily quiet. Penny paused, as though checking the emptiness of the house, then pressed play.

Queen's The Works turned out to be a perfect album for me. There was one song about computers, and another about nuclear war.

22

We'd both just finished our cups of tea when Penny said, 'Do you want to see my mum's studio?'

'Will she mind?'

'Of course,' Penny said, and grinned.

We took our mugs into the kitchen. Penny righted the basket of clothes her mum had chucked and checked the washing machine, which was sloshing slowly, like it was chewing something it didn't like. Then she led the way through the far door to her mum's studio.

It was a small room, like a conservatory, with a glass roof and two walls nothing but windows. It wasn't quite a mess, but was certainly a jumble. There were a lot of wooden-framed canvases of various sizes leaning loosely against each other, their painted sides turned to the wall. There were three easels, with canvases on them, but the canvases were covered with paint-smeared sheets. There were a couple of old ice-cream tubs full of paint tubes curled up like dead metal bugs, some glass jars of brushes, various tools (including the scary-looking staple gun), rolls of canvas and lengths of wood for the frames, plus a similar assortment of weird objects to what was in the hall — a rock with glittering veins of crystal, a rusty twist of iron, an old chimney pot — and a shelf of books about artists.

Penny lifted the sheet off one canvas and peeked. 'Don't look at that one.' The next, she checked then showed me. It was hardly begun, just some lines in brown paint that looked rather angry. She lifted the sheet off the third.

'Oh,' she said.

I peered over her shoulder. It was almost nothing but murky black-brown swirls, except for two figures facing into the painting, a boy and a girl holding hands. It looked like the fairy tale paintings in the passageway, so perhaps this was Hansel and Gretel about to enter the woods where the witch lived.

Penny said, 'That's a new one.' She glanced at me. 'The boy's got your colour hair.'

I shrugged. 'The girl's got yours.'

Penny dropped the sheet back over it. 'She's probably going to paint a monster about to eat them.'

She started flipping through the paintings leaning against the walls. After a bit, she said, 'Here it is.'

She lifted one and showed me.

'That's you,' I said.

'About a year ago. She still hasn't finished it. None of this lot are finished.'

There must have been thirty canvases against the walls. Penny went through them, occasionally lifting one and showing me. Most were of children or monsters or both. There was a good one of a cat. 'I'm not showing you the naked ones,' she said.

She leaned dangerously over to get at the furthest canvases. 'There used to be one of my grandad, but it seems to have disappeared. Sometimes she gets a bit dramatic and burns them.'

A sound from the kitchen made me check the door. It was only the washing machine going into a spin, but it made me think. 'Your mum might come back,' I said.

'She's gone till tomorrow.'

'She didn't really mean that, did she?'

'Yeah.'

'What, leaving you on your own?'

Penny shrugged. She showed me a small picture of a woman sticking out her tongue. 'Self portrait,' she said. She looked at it. 'She's always doing it. When she gets like this. She's not always like it. But when she is, when it's at its worst, she has to, you know, go away. And she feels guilty leaving me on my own, so she tries to make me want to see the back of her by being like she was, out there. But she's just unhappy.'

She put the painting down, facing into the room.

'She gets growly. She can't paint, which makes her more growly. She goes away. She comes back. She goes to bed for about a week to lick her wounds, then comes out and she's normal again. For a bit.'

'Are you saying she's a werewolf?'

Penny wrinkled her nose. 'More a were-person.'

She headed back towards the kitchen.

I nodded at the picture she'd left facing the room. 'Won't that mean she knows you've been in here?'

'Yeah,' Penny said. She widened her eyes wickedly. 'She might even guess you've been here, too.'

At the front door, Penny said, brightly, maybe-jokily, 'You could stay and I'll cook you dinner.'

I gave a laugh. 'I'd better get back. My dad...'

'Yeah.' Penny kept smiling, as though it had been a joke.

'Thanks for, you know,' I said. 'Bye.'

'See you.'

'Yeah, see you.'

As I walked down Fallow Lane, I felt bad. Penny was going to be all alone, now. But it would have been too weird for me to have stayed and for her to have cooked us dinner. What did I mean by 'too weird'? It took me all the way to Pritchard Gardens to work it out. It would have been too weird because it would have been like we were playing at being grown up. And that was the first time I realised that, really, I was half grown up, because I was thirteen. It was like I was on the borderland, not one side or the other. And that meant there were going to be a lot more moments like this from now on, where I glimpsed the grown-up me giving a wave from the future. I'd never thought about it before because I'd been so sure, what with nuclear war and so on, that there wouldn't be a future. Now I suddenly thought how much I wanted there to be one, just so I could, you know, say yes next time, and stay at Penny's for dinner. As long as her mum was out.

At home, I gave a long look at the scene from Threads on Joe's bedroom door. I realised, for the first time, I didn't just feel scared by it, I felt a bit angry, too.

On Sunday it rained. I kept looking out the window, wondering what Penny was doing, and whether her mum was back.

23

Monday morning, I was doing my usual wait till the last minute before leaving for school when I saw Penny going by. She slowed down, looking up at my bedroom window, so I knocked (on the living room window, I was downstairs), got my shoes on, and joined her.

She told me her mum had phoned to say she'd be gone a few days more.

'Is it for her painting?' I said, still puzzled exactly where she was and why.

Penny gave me a should-I-or-shouldn't-I look, then said, 'She's at her boyfriend's.'

Which I hadn't expected. We turned down King George Way.

'What's he like?' I said, not sure what the appropriate question to ask was.

She shrugged. 'Haven't met him. Not this one.'

And I really didn't know what to say to that.

After school, I walked home with Patrick as usual, but when I crossed the road, Penny was lingering under the trees on Pritchard Lane. We talked about the school day. In Chemistry, Mr Saltz had scalded his hand on a Bunsen burner and we all thought he'd used a swear word, but he insisted he'd started to say, 'For Christ's sake, don't do that yourselves.' Someone said that was taking the Lord's name in vain. 'For Chemistry's sake, then,' Mr Saltz said, then told us to get on with the experiment. In French, Mrs Norman had been reduced to tears when the class got out of hand. Again.

When we got to my house, I asked Penny if she wanted to come in, but she had to go to town and do some food shopping.

'You can come to mine tomorrow, though,' she said. 'I'll buy some cakes.'

Tuesday after school, Patrick invited me in to see his new high score on Elite, which is the first game to use 3D wireframe graphics with hidden-line removal. He'd been going on about nothing else since his dad got it for him at the weekend. I said I had to do something for my dad. At Penny's we watched Star Trek till 6, then I went home and said I'd been at Patrick's.

I didn't think about nuclear war at all. When I went upstairs, I could look at the picture from Threads on Joe's door and wonder why it had bothered me so much. It was a TV programme, not something that was definitely going to happen. Doing the dishes, I sang I Want To Break Free, even when Dad came in and put the kettle on. He went off grumbling, but I didn't care.

On Wednesday after school I invited Penny in, but she thought her mum might be back and she ought to go home. Thursday morning, though, she said her mum still wasn't back, so she'd definitely come to my house after school. She was fed up of thinking she had to do the right thing when her mum obviously didn't care. I spent the day trying to work out which was worse, not having you around, Mum, or having a mum like Penny's, who was gone half the time, and slightly mad the other half. I couldn't decide.

I didn't really listen to Patrick on the way home that Thursday, and almost didn't notice when he stopped, abruptly, outside his house, and narrowed his eyes at Pritchard Lane.

'Is that Penny Poundley?' he said.

She was just in sight, not looking at us.

'She's not waiting for you, is she?' he said, suspiciously.

'Why would she be doing that?'

He pulled a God-knows face, then said, 'See you,' and disappeared inside to blast some Thargons.

At my house, I got Penny and me some Tizer, then showed her a program I'd spent the last few evenings typing in from a book and dealing with the usual bugs before getting it to run.

'It's called ELSIE,' I said. 'It lets you have a conversation with the computer.'

'A conversation with a computer?' Penny said. 'Is that like a conversation with you?'

I ignored that. 'One day, thanks to artificial intelligence, computers will be indistinguishable from people. There's this thing called the Turing Test. You have three people in different rooms. No, two people, and one computer. And they can only communicate through typing on a keyboard, and they see each other's replies on a screen. The idea is for one person to try and work out which of the other two is a person and which is a computer, just by the questions he asks, and the answers they give. And one day, you won't be able to tell one from the other.'

'Sitting in different rooms, typing into keyboards isn't a conversation,' Penny said. 'It's not even a telephone conversation. And those are one step away from Hell.'

I wondered if she meant her mum phoning to say she wouldn't be back for a while.

'Have a go anyway,' I said.

I loaded ELSIE and ran it. Penny sat in front of my ZX Spectrum and read the first line off the TV. It was: 'Hi, I'm Elsie, what's your problem?'

'Sort of rude, isn't it?' Penny said.

'It's supposed to be a psychiatrist,' I said. 'In the future, computers will help people with all sorts of problems.'

'I thought you said computers only do what people tell them to?'

'Yeah.'

'So, if people haven't solved all our problems, how can computers solve them if they only do what people tell them to?'

'Computers are a lot faster,' I said, lamely.

Penny turned to the screen, thought for a bit, then tapped out: 'Tim thinking computers are like people is my problem.'

ELSIE processed this for long enough to prove what I'd said about computers being faster untrue, then came back with: 'Did you come to me because you are thinking computers are like people?'

Penny typed: 'Not me, Tim.'

We sat there for half a minute, then the screen said: '3 Subscript wrong 741:1'.

Penny looked at me.

'It's a bug,' I said.

'Well, people have those too, so I suppose you're half right.'

I had a quick look at the program's line 741, but realised I was going to have to follow the whole thing through to work out what was wrong, and that would take ages.

'Here's a question for you,' Penny said. 'I'm not sure if it's rude or not, but I heard someone talking about something to do with computers, and they mentioned a thing called an ass-key. It sounds like American slang for something indecent, but I just wanted to be sure.'

'It's A-S-C-I-I. It stands for American Standard Code for Information Interchange,' I said, glad to find I had a way to redeem myself after the failure of the program I'd spent so long typing in. (I had the sneaky feeling that was the real reason Penny had asked.) 'It's how computers store letters and character symbols.'

'Well, I was right about it being American, anyway.'

It was starting to look rainy outside, and gloomy enough to give everything that cosy twilight feel.

Penny said, 'So, I suppose you want to work with computers when you grow up?'

'Yeah,' I said. 'But I think everyone will. They'll be used in all walks of life, from schools to shops to, um, hospitals, and things. What do you want to do when you grow up?'

'Get away from home.'

'You mean, away from Eastead?'

'Not... no. I just mean, get a place of my own. Not have to, you know...'

She meant put up with her mum.

I fiddled about with line 741. As the cursor moved along the line, it made its usual bipping sound. Penny said, 'Sounds like an ant with a machine gun.'

A few drops of rain hit the window, like someone tapping to get our attention.

'I bet you miss your mum,' Penny said.

I shrugged.

'I can't imagine what it's like,' she said. 'It's so sad.'

'It's just what happened.'

'But you must feel sad.'

I tried to put into words what I'd never had to before, and came out with, 'It's how the world is. You can't feel sad about it, because then you'd have to feel sad about everything.'

Penny looked out the window. 'But it's not how the world is. You only feel sad because something good is gone. That proves there are good things in the world. Doesn't it?'

'Mm,' I said, unsure.

'I mean, think of all the normal families out there. Don't you feel it's unfair?'

'Don't you?' I said. 'With your mum, and your, you know, dad?'

'Yeah. I feel I'm owed something. Compensation. Don't you?'

'I never thought about it. I just thought, that's how things are.'

Because of the clouds, it was almost as dark as evening, apart from the grey light from my Spectrum's TV.

'Sometimes I think it's all a bad joke,' Penny said. 'Only, some people get to be the ones who laugh, and the rest of us are the ones who get laughed at.'

'But when you grow up,' I said, then faltered.

'Go on.'

'I mean, when you grow up, you get to have your life how you want, don't you?'

'Unless you get too screwed up beforehand. I mean, look at my mum. Do you think she's living the life she wants? She's miserable and makes other people miserable. Nobody would want that.'

I thought of Dad being so grumpy and silent all the time. 'I never thought about it like that.'

'Not wanting to depress you, or anything.'

'So what's the solution?' I said.

'Probably isn't one.'

'But maybe there is. Just, no one's thought of it yet.'

'So what is it, Einstein?'

I thought. 'Maybe you've got to eat thirty-one bananas in a row, then you get whatever you want out of life.'

'Yeah, but what if it's thirty-two?'

'Maybe you've got to keep on eating them till you almost explode, but don't, and then you can make a wish.'

'And what would you wish for?'

In the low light, with just Penny in the room, I felt I could tell her, but I hesitated, because I'd never said it to anyone before.

Then the door burst open and Joe flicked the light on.

'Oi, Computer Boy, get your arse downstairs and put the fish fingers on — oh, bloody 'ell.'

He stared at Penny, blinking, as though it was more likely he had a girl-shaped speck in his eye than there was a real one in the room. I realised, from the sound of the toilet flushing downstairs, that not only had Joe come home, but in one of those rare conjunctions, Dad had, too. I'd totally lost track of the time.

'Hello,' Penny said, as if to say, 'Give up blinking, I'm not going away.'

Joe shook his head once, to one side only, then retreated.

I listened as he went downstairs a few steps, paused, then took the rest at a rush. I heard him saying something to Dad in the room below. It was too muffled to hear what, but I could guess.

'Nice to make an impression,' Penny said.

I was beginning to feel the edge of a dawning panic, like I'd been caught stealing, and somewhere, in another room, people were discussing what to do with me.

'Shall we go down and I'll say hello to your dad?' Penny said. 'I might make him run away too. It's like I've discovered a new power.'

24

I led the way downstairs, holding onto the bannister because I felt any second I might take a tumble. Part of me wanted to. It would have been an easy way out.

At the living room door, I paused. There was no sound coming from the other side, but I knew Dad and Joe were there, waiting. This wasn't going to get any better by leaving it, so I opened the door and went through.

Dad stood solid and still like a lump of industrial iron, his back to the unlit gas fire in the corner. His face had all the expression of a concrete bollard. Joe was by him, gnawing a fingernail.

'Hi Dad,' I said, coming in further to give room for Penny. 'This is...' and my voice dried out.

Penny took over. 'Hello Mr Morrow. I'm Penny. I'm in the same class as Tim.'

'Hullo,' Dad said, and it was like he'd had to pull the word up from about a mile underground. It came out heavy and cold, like a bucket drawn from a deep, dark well. It wasn't exactly welcoming.

'Yeah,' Joe said quickly, and attacked his fingers with added urgency.

'Tim's been explaining about computers, which he certainly knows a lot about,' Penny said.

Dad said nothing to this. She might as well have told him I'd been demonstrating my morris dancing skills, or my way with a feather duster. His eyes moved slowly from Penny's face, down, to fix on her middle, as though all that remained was for her to go away.

Somehow, Penny kept cheerful and normal-seeming in the silence that followed. I felt I was battling this strange tug, like Dad was a black hole and I was being sucked towards him. There was part of me that felt it had to go and join him and Joe in their corner, leaving Penny to suffer our glares, and be banished from the house. But, by what felt like a physical effort, I resisted, and even brought a word out to break the silence. It was only, 'Well...' but it did the trick.

'Yeah,' Penny said. 'I'd better be going, but thanks for having me.'

Nobody said anything.

'Bye, then,' Penny said.

'Bye,' I said.

'Bye,' said Joe, then looked at Dad in a panic. Dad said nothing.

Penny let herself out. She shut the front door behind her with the lightest of latch-clicks, then headed past our living room window, smiling.

I felt a little firework burst of pride for her, and would have smiled too if I hadn't looked round to see Dad staring at me in the exact same way he'd been staring at Penny. It wasn't an angry look, nor a disappointed one, nor a sad one. It was a nothing look. Intense nothing, like three thousand miles of space compressed into two dark pupils. Joe's nail-biting had reached such a height, he almost had all ten fingers in his mouth.

I said, 'I'll put the grill on, then,' and went into the kitchen.

When I came back in, the TV was on and Dad and Joe were watching the end of Grange Hill.

Nobody said anything. I did the fish fingers and Dad did the chips, and somehow, in our tiny kitchen, we managed to completely avoid talking to, looking at, or even brushing against each other. When we sat down to eat, it was in utter silence, and it was only when we'd all finished, and were sitting with our plates on our laps listening to the news, that I glanced up and saw him looking at me.

The same look as before. It went on for almost a minute.

I looked back at my plate, up, and down again about five times.

What was he thinking? Was he expecting me to explain? Apologise? I wasn't going to, but I wish I knew. The thing I'd most been afraid of, with Penny, was what he'd say, but he wasn't saying anything. That was the one thing I hadn't thought of, and now I realised it was the worst thing of all. I felt cut off, like there was him and Joe, and then there was me. I'd always felt a bit like that, but now it was like it was confirmed, so there was no need for them to pretend anymore.

On the news it said Labour, at their party conference in Blackpool, had announced that if they got into power, they'd get rid of Britain's nuclear arsenal. Usually, this would have made Joe explode and would even have got a comment out of Dad. This time, nothing.

Finally, Dad took Joe's plate and stacked it onto his, then held them out to me. I stacked them onto mine, and put the knives and forks on top, and was just heading for the kitchen to start the washing up when Dad said, 'Not much of a girl.'

Joe said, 'Yeah, not much of a girl, eh, Dad?'

Once I'd done the dishes, I went up to my room and tried to work out why ELSIE had crashed, but couldn't concentrate. Downstairs, they were watching Top of the Pops, and I could hear Dad's usual rumbled comment at the end of each song, and Joe's too-quick, too-loud laugh in response. After that they watched Knight Rider.

It was unfair. If you'd been there, Mum, it wouldn't have been them against me. I wouldn't have been the one who was wrong. Sorry, but I felt a bit angry at you, then. I hope you weren't listening in at that moment. Anyway, it wasn't you I was angry at, really. It wasn't even Dad. It was everything. The world. The way it works. Like it's full of bugs, and no one cares enough to fix it, but we all have to live in it anyway.

I only realised I'd been hearing a tap at the window the third time it happened. At first I thought it was rain, but it was too sharp for rain. The third time, I poked my head between the curtains. It was getting properly dark now, but I knew who it was.

I opened my window.

'Hi,' Penny said.

'Hello.'

It was raining slightly, and she had an umbrella. She'd been throwing acorns to get my attention.

'Don't suppose I can come in, can I?'

'Um,' I said, wondering how to say it.

She shrugged. 'It's alright.'

Neither of us said anything for a bit.

Then she said, 'Do you want to come out, instead?'

'Round your house?' I said, unsure.

'No. Just out. Anywhere.'

'Um,' I said.

'It's just I've been a bit spooked.'

And then I thought, what am I worrying for? What do I care what Dad thinks or Joe thinks? I'm not going to take their side and punish myself.

'Hang on a sec,' I said. I shut the window and snuck downstairs to get my shoes and coat on. I closed the front door super-mega quietly, then joined Penny under her umbrella. Despite the rain, it felt tons better than being inside.

25

On the corner where Pritchard Gardens joins Fallow Lane, there's a little car repair garage. Or there used to be, because it went out of business a year ago, and now it's nothing but a patch of concrete, nettles and weeds behind a chain-link fence. But there's a low, crumbly brick wall round part of it, and Penny and me sat on that, both of us under her umbrella.

'Your dad doesn't say much,' Penny said.

'Nah. He's a bit...' But I didn't know the word for what he was, so I let that trail off.

'Has he always been like that, or just since... your mum?'

'Always a bit, but not as bad. Mum used to say silly things to get him out of it. She even tickled him once.'

'I can't imagine anyone tickling your dad.'

'Nah,' I said, trying to remember it. I realised I could picture it, but couldn't be sure if I was properly remembering it, or making it up. I find that more and more about memories of you, Mum.

A car passed, its headlamps making the rain into sharp yellow scratches.

'What do you mean you were spooked?' I said.

As we were close under the umbrella, Penny's shoulder was against mine and I felt it rise and fall as she sighed. 'Mum's back. And she's got her boyfriend with her. Caxton, apparently. They were both a bit drunk. Said hello then disappeared into her bedroom. Making a lot of noise.'

I wondered if that meant what I thought it meant, but didn't want to ask.

'So I made myself some dinner, and watched a bit of TV. Mum came out to grab a bottle of wine from the kitchen. She was laughing. Not in a nice way. More like she was trying to prove she was having a better time than I could ever have. Then she disappeared again.'

Another car passed, and Penny fell quiet till it had swished out of earshot.

'After that, I hung about in the living room, because I wanted to ask her how long this Caxton was staying. I was hoping she'd come out again. But the next one to come out was this Caxton. He came into the living room and sat down. He only had a dressing gown on. I mean, only. Sat there all sprawled. I kept my eyes dead fixed on the TV. He started saying these things.'

'What sort of things?'

She sucked squeakily on her lower lip. 'Suggestive remarks. I did my best to ignore him, but I was spooked. Then he got up, and for a moment I thought he was coming for me. But he staggered out, and said something about finding the loo.'

'What did you do?'

'I went to Mum's room. Said what he'd said.'

'And?'

'She said, "Well, it wouldn't be the end of the world, darling." Thought it was hilarious. Drunk as a skunk. So I got my shoes and coat on and left before he could come out again. I walked up and down for a bit, but had to talk to someone. Just to stop myself thinking about it.'

She gave me an apologetic look.

'That's awful,' I said.

Another car passed. The sound of its tyres on the wet road faded into the whisper of rain all around us, like the world was gently reminding us, under our umbrella, how much of it was out there.

'You can't go back,' I said.

'They're probably out for the count, now. Plus, I've got a lock on my door, and I'm going to use it. Tomorrow, or the day after, they'll have a blazing row and Mum'll kick him out, and that'll be that. It's happened before. With other, you know, boyfriends.'

She kicked her heels against the wall we were sitting on.

'I tell you what I wish sometimes,' she said. 'My dad told me, once, that when he got set up with his own house, and a proper family — you know, married and that — I could come and live with him. And it'd be like the family life I've never had. It'd make up for it all. I think about that whenever, you know, something like this happens.'

And part of me thought I'd really want that for her, just so she could be happy, which she deserved, but another part thought that I didn't want her to go and live in London, which was selfish of me, I know, but still.

She brushed a leaf off her knee. 'You never got to tell me what you wish.'

It didn't feel the same as it did before, when we were up in my room, but I'd started to say it then, so I might as well say it now. 'What I wish most is that I could know, definitely and for sure, that there wouldn't ever be a nuclear war.'

I could tell she'd been expecting something different.

'Does it bother you that much?' she said.

'Doesn't it bother you?'

'I don't think it's going to happen. I mean, Mum and me went to Greenham Common last year, you know, to help "Embrace the Base". But more because I'm against nuclear weapons than cos I think anyone would ever use them. I mean, if they did, what's there to worry about? We'd all be dead.'

'But we wouldn't,' I said. 'It'd be — the world, everything, after, would be just horrible. People dying, starving, or people with guns trying to take control. Fighting over cans of food, and no houses anymore, just ruins. Everyone having to struggle to survive. Just for themselves. And radiation everywhere. And it would be like that for ever. Or thousands of years, anyway. It wouldn't be like you could ever grow up out of it.'

We sat in silence for a bit. I wondered if I shouldn't have said all that, because it would be far better for Penny if she continued believing a nuclear war would simply kill every-one, then she wouldn't have to worry about all its horrible details like I do. I mean, if it was going to happen it would happen, and Penny worrying about it wouldn't make it any better. So why not let her live in ignorance till it did? I mean, if it did.

I glanced up, to see if there were any signs she'd started worrying, but she was looking at me curiously.

'Grow up out of it?' she said.

'Hm?'

'You said grow up out of it.'

'Um, yeah.'

'It's just... That, what you said, about the world after a nuclear war, it's all about a world that's nothing but fear, and without any sort of hope or love, isn't it?'

I shrugged, because as far as I was concerned it was about nothing but survival. Hope and, you know, had noth-ing to do with it.

'When you said "grow up out of it",' she said, 'it made it sound as if, well, you were living in it now. Or feel like you are.'

'But I'm not,' I said, trying not to sound annoyed she'd missed the point. 'It's what the world will be like after a nuclear war.'

She said, 'Mm,' and it was like she felt I was the one who hadn't got it, but she wasn't going to go on about it because it was obviously annoying me.

I wished I'd kept my mouth shut. Now it seemed she was annoyed at me because I'd sounded annoyed at her, but I really hadn't sounded *that* annoyed, so although the best thing would have been to apologise, doing that would only confirm that I'd been annoyed, whereas if I didn't apologise, I could at least pretend she'd misunderstood and that I hadn't been. I wasn't annoyed now, anyway. I was confused.

The rain started getting heavier, pattering on the umbrella like bubbles going off in a glass of cola.

'I'd better get back,' Penny said.

I realised I ought to apologise anyway, right now, in case the real reason she wanted to go home was she thought I was in a huff with her. Which I wasn't. But the more I thought about it, the more it seemed if I blurted out an apology for sounding annoyed, she'd think I'd been really annoyed, and I didn't want her to think that. This was getting so complicated!

We got off the wall.

'Shall I come with you as far as your house, so you've got the umbrella?' she said.

'It's just rain,' I said. 'It's not like it's radioactive.' I'd meant it to sound like a tension-breaking joke, but as soon as I said it, I wished I hadn't, because now it sounded like I was not only being sarcastic, but was going on about nuclear war an unhealthy amount.

'Bye then. Thanks for, you know. I don't feel so spooked now.'

She sounded totally normal. Perhaps I was imagining it all.

So I said, 'Bye,' and she walked off, and then I felt awful. I should have apologised. It would have been so easy. Just one word. But now she was gone, and suddenly I was sure she was upset with me.

I walked back home and snuck in as quietly as I'd snuck out. Dad was still watching TV, but Joe was upstairs, listening to Iron Maiden's chugga-da-chugging guitars.

That picture from Threads on Joe's door bothered me again, as I passed it. I kept thinking about Penny, and how quickly she'd ended the conversation. The more I replayed it in my head, the more upset she'd seemed, till I couldn't be sure what had really happened. It could have been the rain getting heavier that made her go home, but...

Damn.

I just don't understand anything.

26

Friday, I woke to the sound of rain being splashed against my window like someone was throwing it in handfuls. Wind was gusting in the street outside, cars were whooshing through puddles, Dad and Joe were up, Penny was upset with me, and I just wanted to stay in bed.

But what was the point.

I avoided Dad and Joe as they got ready for work, like a pilot fish among sharks. Once they were gone, I waited by the living room window, but Penny didn't show. I wondered if she'd nipped past earlier. Or gone a different route. Or was waiting round the corner, watching till I left. If a girl wanted to avoid you, she had lots of options.

I gave up waiting and set off.

The lights in our form room seemed flatly bright compared to the thick rainy dark outside.

Penny wasn't there.

'Micro Live tonight,' Patrick said as I sat down. (No hello's in the world of Patrick.)

'Eh?' I was trying to look at Kash without it looking like I was looking, to see if she was concerned Penny hadn't turned up. She was reading a book, so I couldn't tell.

'Don't you remember?' Patrick said. 'It's the new TV programme about computers. BBC2 tonight at 6. You're watching it at my house. Or have you got something to do for your dad again?'

'Oh, right, no,' I said. 'I mean, yeah. I mean, no.'

I was starting to feel guilty about all that self-pity earlier. It might not be that Penny was avoiding me. She might be ill. She might have caught a cold wandering in the rain last night. Or bronchitis, or flu, or, I don't know, all three. Or something might have happened at home. Something awful. What if her mum — or, no, what if that Caxton — well, I had no idea what if what, but if something *had* happened, something bad, I might be the only one who knew. The police might have to be told. This Caxton might be a real psycho, or Penny's mum might have started throwing roof tiles again.

'Apparently they're going to have a live bulletin board running for the duration of the programme,' Patrick was saying. 'We'll set my modem up, and you can help me get connected. They're going to be giving prizes to people who get through and leave a message, and I want to win.'

The bell went for the start of school, and Mr Slaughter came in with a 'Good morning' that everyone ignored.

He sat at his desk and went through the register. Once Patrick and me had answered our names, Patrick started whispering about how the superior baud rate of his modem ought to give him an edge in getting connected tonight, but I was listening for Penny's name. That would be the final confirmation. When Mr Slaughter came to it, he looked at Penny's empty chair, then at Kash, who gave a small shrug, then he took the lid off his red pen and made a careful O in the register.

So she wasn't going to be in.

It was something really bad. It could only be something really bad.

I had to say something. It didn't matter what Patrick would think, I had to. I was just wondering how to explain to Mr Slaughter how I knew what I thought I knew, when the door opened and in came Penny, breathless, wet and windswept. Her cheeks were quite rosy, too.

'Sorry — Mr — Slaughter,' she panted.

'That's okay, Penny,' he said, instantly forgiving as only an R.E. teacher could be. He uncapped his blue pen and changed that red O.

Patrick was still going on about his modem. Mostly, now, about how inherently superior it was compared to the equivalent products available for the ZX Spectrum. I watched Penny as she headed for her chair. What I wanted was for her to say something to Kash, some silly little joke, and then to laugh, or at least smile, so I could know everything was okay, and that something terrible hadn't happened at home. And then for her to glance at me. An it's-okay glance. An I'm-not-mad-at-you glance. Or just a hello glance, a glance that told me I existed. Even a frown. Or a scowl? I'd settle for a scowl. I mean, it was something to work on. She could even throw a roof tile at me, if she wanted.

But before any of that could happen, the bell went and everyone got up to go to assembly.

First lesson of the day was Biology, where we did an experiment with woodlice. We had a plastic dish with absorbent paper in the bottom, half of which we dampened with water. Then we put in eight woodlice, and covered them with a lid, half of which was see-through, half of which wasn't. This was placed at right-angles to the damp part of the absorbent paper. The idea was to see which the woodlice preferred: light and dry, light and damp, dark and dry, or dark and damp. After a bit, we lifted the lid and counted the woodlice in each quadrant.

Seven of ours were in the dark and damp area. One kept wandering in a circle near the middle, like he couldn't make up his mind.

'What an idiot,' Patrick said. 'Why doesn't it just do what it's supposed to?'

'Perhaps he's trying to find someone,' I said.

'Someone?' Patrick said. 'The Pope? Margaret Thatcher?'

'I mean, maybe he was in the middle of talking to his friend when we picked him up and put him in our dish.'

'His friend,' Patrick said, with a deadpan look.

'And maybe he said something he wished he hadn't said,

and now he wants to find his friend, just to make sure everything's okay between them.'

'Between woodlice.'

'But his friend's in another dish, so he can't reach her. I mean, him.'

'Tim, it's a woodlouse.' Patrick nudged our little wanderer into the damp, dark quadrant with the others.

I looked over at Penny. The trouble was, when we'd come into the Biology lab, she'd been so intent on talking to Kash — explaining why she'd been late, I suppose — that she hadn't noticed Mrs Flock standing with her arms crossed at the front of the class, waiting for her to be quiet. Penny realised, blushed, and apologised, and then of course had to make it look like she was giving extra special attention throughout the rest of the lesson, because Mrs Flock likes to give lines.

I wished she'd look my way. Just once.

I mean, I'd do her lines.

A hand grasped the top of my head and turned it back towards the dish.

'If your experiment's done, write up your conclusions,' Mrs Flock said.

Patrick said, 'Tim thinks woodlice have friends, and talk to each other.'

Mrs Flock examined our dish. 'Eight in the same quadrant. A little too neat, don't you think?'

'But that's where they're supposed to be.'

'They're living creatures, Patrick, not robots. Don't expect them to be where you expect them to be, observe where they go. After all, if you lot behaved as I expected you to behave, Tim here wouldn't have his attention on the other side of the Biology lab, and you wouldn't be nudging your experimental subjects into what you thought of as the correct quadrant. Start again and see where they end up a second time, then we can get them all back with their friends, can't we?'

Patrick looked at me like it was my fault, then covered our dish and gave it a shake.

This time, our results were a bit more scattered. Our wanderer had gone back to making little circles in the middle, though.

As I wrote up our results, I saw, through the corner of my eye, Patrick peering past me, trying to see what had caught my attention on the other side of the lab. I quickly gazed off in a random direction, like it was a new habit of mine, staring intently at remote corners of the Biology lab. I could feel Patrick studying me suspiciously, and for a moment felt like one more misbehaving part of the woodlouse experiment.

Then the bell went.

Next lesson was French, in the language lab. We had to hang around outside waiting for Mrs Norman, which should have given me the opportunity to catch a look from Penny, if only she and Kash hadn't been on the other side of the tightly-packed scrum of pupils all trying to get closest to the door so they could get the best booths. I craned my neck to see over everyone, but once James Barrack (our star football player, and nearly six foot tall) is in the way, there's no seeing anything.

Mrs Norman turned up red-nosed and clutching a hankie (as usual), meaning her last class had upset her and she'd been in the staff toilets recovering. She looked very much in need of the coming weekend. As we shuffled into the lab, I thought that, as me and Patrick were at the back of the scrum on one side, and Penny and Kash were at the back on the other, if I lingered a bit, I might end up beside her as we filed in. But when it came to it she and Kash had already been sucked in by the flow of pupils, and I ended up having to sit at the worst booth of all, right in front of Mrs Norman, meaning there'd be no glancing about to see where Penny was.

I spent the lesson asking how to find the nearest pâtisserie, boulangerie and tabac, all the while resolving that, if I ever did go to France, I'd stick to supermarkets, where you can buy everything in one go.

Où sont les bâtonnets de poisson?

Merci.

And then, because when the evil powers that rule this school were planning our timetables they knew I'd be spending Friday the 5th of October desperately trying to catch just a single glance from Penny, after French I had Computer Science, meaning Penny had Music, and we'd be at opposite ends of the school.

Scruffy Clyde handed back our essays on the future of computers and told us how much he hated them. I didn't care. As he droned on, I listened for that distant piano I'd heard last time, wondering if perhaps Penny might use it to send a message in morse code. I don't know morse code, and I doubt Penny does, but if she'd tapped out something that sounded like it, that would have been just as good. But perhaps she didn't care. Perhaps the obstacles that had been getting in the way all day had been deliberate. Perhaps she didn't want to give me a quick glance to say things were okay, because they weren't. Perhaps I'd been wrong about something bad happening at home, and she actually wanted to avoid me. Perhaps she really was upset with me. If only I could get a chance to say sorry!

When the bell went, I realised I had somehow got through an entire Computer Science lesson without once thinking of computers. Now it was lunch, and I trailed behind Patrick to the computer room, feeling not so much like I'd just heard the four minute warning, but more like a nuclear holocaust had been announced for sometime next week, and there was nothing to do about it but plod, glum and resigned, through my remaining days.

I didn't realise girls, as well as being telepathic, had the power to make you miserable.

27

The computer room was pretty much full when me and Patrick got there. This time, I was first through the door, so I was first to that single remaining computer. But once I got there, I didn't feel like doing any programming, and as Patrick would only spend the rest of lunch convincing me how important it was that he work on his graphics compression routine, I gave him the captain's seat, and sat there looking at rain clouds for a bit.

Then I had an idea.

'Need to go to the loo,' I said, and left.

Outside, I did a quick calculation. I reckoned I could have ten minutes wandering the school looking for Penny before Patrick started thinking I might be constipated or something.

First, I headed for our form room. The only kids there were the boys and girls who usually sit at the back. They're the most advanced in boy-girl relations, and generally spend their time making loud comments about each other and getting into arguments. Occasionally, a random pair will announce they're going out with each other, and hostilities will cease. For instance, when I came into the form room, Jason Salmon was sitting on Chrissie Makebook's lap, with his arms round her neck like he was trying not to fall off. It looked uncomfortable, but both seemed determined to see lunch break through like that. I didn't want to make it obvious I was looking for Penny, so I searched about under my seat, pretending I might have lost something earlier.

I was about to go when Simon Splint said, 'Give us a game of table rugby, Tim.'

'Um,' I said, trying to think of an excuse, but he was already dragging a desk free of the others and slapping down the necessary coins.

Table rugby is played with three coins. (Two-ps or ten-ps are best.) You start with them in a triangle formation, and move them from your end of the table to your opponent's end by shunting the coin closest to you between the two others, in a series of steps, till one falls off the table (and your opponent gets his go), or you manage to get it hanging enough off the opposite edge that you can flip it into the air and catch it. If you catch it, you get to go for a conversion, which involves throwing the coin using only your thumbs at goal posts made with your opponent's hands. I did my best to let Simon Splint win as quickly as possible.

Inevitably, because nothing else of interest was happening in their lives, our game became the focus of comments from the others.

Strange comments.

'He's not as good with those pennies as I thought he'd be.'

'Yeah, you'd of thought he'd of had loads of practice handling pennies.'

'Penny's what?'

'Perhaps we should ask him.'

I did my best to pretend I was too involved in the game to hear, but at least one cog in my brainbox was whizzing round like a flywheel, thinking, 'They can't mean... But what else can they mean..? In which case, how do they..? But how *can* they..? Got to get out of here!'

As soon as the game was over, I said, 'I just came in to look for my rubber. I thought I'd lost it.'

'Your rubber, eh? Penny's in for a treat,' Chrissie Makebook said, with a honking laugh that made Jason Salmon fall off her lap.

'I mean my eraser,' I said, and left before I could blush.

Outside, in the corridor, I paused.

My brain cog was still whizzing.

What had all that been about?

Some elaborate joke. That was it. They couldn't have meant what it sounded like they meant. How could they? They couldn't know anything, because (a) they just couldn't, and (b) there wasn't anything to know. Was there? Could they? If, that is, I'd understood what they were saying. Which I might not have. Because, with the kids who sat at the back, you could never tell. They had all sorts of slang and new ways of referring to things I didn't even know the proper words for. Everything, with them, was a reference to sex (at least, as far as I could tell) and to me it was all as confusing as computer terminology probably was to them.

So, it was all a joke.

Yeah.

They couldn't have been saying what I thought they'd been saying.

Yeah...

Next, I tried the dining room.

This was pretty crowded, it being lunchtime, and deafeningly noisy with clattering cutlery, forks squeaking on plates, chair legs grating on the floor, and about three hundred kids talking or shouting with their mouths full. A smog of mashed potato and custard hung over everything. But at least I could stand there looking round without anyone making comments.

Or so I thought.

Mr Witt, who I hadn't noticed lurking nearby on lunchtime guard duty, sidled up and said, 'Lost something?'

Mr Witt is one of those teachers who sees every moment in life as an opportunity to bring the many facets of his subject (he teaches Philosophy to sixth years) to scintillating life in the minds of us kids. For this reason, I do my best to avoid him. Plus, he wears a bow tie.

'I'm just looking for someone,' I said.

'Interesting, interesting,' he said, with a couple of head-thrusting nods, like he was about to do the funky chicken. 'You say you are looking for someone, yet here you are, in the one room that is, at this moment, the most *full* of someones in the entire school. Am I right?'

'Um...'

'So we could well say you have *found* someone, indeed have found many. Could we not?'

'Uh...'

'But of course,' he said, wrapping his arms round himself and tapping his mouth with the side of one long finger, 'they are not the *specific* someone you have in mind. To think that our wants could be so peculiar, even perverse, that, when presented with a room full of, shall we say, three hundred persons, we find all of them inadequate.'

'Um...' I hadn't been ready for that word, 'perverse', and was now wondering if it meant he'd seen right through me and knew I'd come here looking for Penny. I stared at him, suddenly sure he was going to denounce me, in front of the entire dining hall, for being a pervert, just because I wanted to make sure everything was okay between me and Penny.

But instead, all he said was, 'We humans are a finickity race, are we not?'

'Eh?'

'Finickity. Humans.' And he accompanied this with a pair of funky chicken nods.

'Um...' I waited for another bout of nonsense. None came, so I said, quickly, 'They're not here. The perv — I mean, the person I was looking for.' Then, for no reason, added, 'Thanks,' and left.

I got the feeling that, mega-brained as he no doubt is, Mr Witt gets really bored doing guard duty at lunchtime.

My next-best option was the library, but that was at the other end of school, and my ten minutes were nearly up.

The school bookshop was closer, so I thought I'd have a quick check there (it only takes a quick check, it's not much bigger than a broom cupboard), but as soon as I poked my head through the door, Mr Canterbrook, who mans it most lunchtimes, said, 'Come in, come in, they're only books, they won't bite.' So I felt I had to go in and make a show of looking around.

'Anything specific I can help you with?' Mr Canterbrook said.

I thought of making something up, but realised if he had it in stock, I might have to buy it, so I said, 'Actually, I was just looking for someone.'

He didn't look too offended. 'Alas, this is the last place to find someone. Everyone wants to be elsewhere, even when it's raining.'

'Sorry,' I said.

'No need to apologise, young man. Books are patient, youth is fleeting. Live for the moment! Seize the day! Read books about it later. Now, the person you're searching for — am I right — not a boy, but a, hmm?'

'Girl,' I said, feeling the edge of a blush.

'Well, then, books must indeed take second place. Youth may be fleeting, but love is as rare as a schoolboy's conscience.'

'Um, it's not, um,' I said, but found myself blushing even more, unable to say the word he'd used. For some reason, it was more difficult and dangerous than Mr Witt's 'perverse'.

Mr Canterbrook, not listening anyway, burst out with, 'But what am I saying? What am I saying! The Bard! Young man, the Bard!'

I took as much of a step back as I could in the cramped little bookshop, wondering if Mr Canterbrook had cracked. All these lunchtimes stuck in his little cupboard, alone, surrounded by nothing but books no one wanted to buy.

He brandished a paperback at me, like a ref with a red card.

'The very thing! Fate brought you here, young man, fate! The Bard has everything you need. It's all here, in this very book. Young love. Young love and tragedy—'

'Um, it's not—'

'This precious book of love, this unbound lover—'

'I don't want—'

'Borrow Cupid's wings and soar with them above a common bound!'

'I haven't got any money.'

'Oh well,' he said. He put it back. 'Thought I'd try.'

'Bye, then,' I said, before he could come out with something even more embarrassing.

'Farewell!'

Mr Canterbrook teaches Drama.

As I headed back toward the Science Block, I wondered, firstly, if all teachers became teachers because they were mad, or whether it was being a teacher that made them mad. And secondly, whether it was possible to go anywhere or do anything at all without people making comments about it.

I slowed down as I passed the cloakrooms. There were pupils hidden among the hung-up coats and sports bags, mostly older kids in pairs, wrapped around each other in even more advanced stages of boy-girl relations than Jason Salmon and Chrissie Makebook had yet managed. Not the sort of place to stop and stare, unless you wanted a slap in the face.

The thought that Penny might be there, that she might already have a boyfriend, or that she might fancy someone else, suddenly hit me, and it seemed so horrible, but so possible, that right then I'd have preferred a nuclear bomb blast. Did this mean Mr Canterbrook was right? Or the kids at the back in our form room, with all their hints? Did it mean it was, you know, Romeo and Juliet? Or, if Penny didn't like me anymore, and didn't want to even look at me, was it Romeo without Juliet, which was miles worse? I half thought about going back to the bookshop and buying that book from Mr Canterbrook, just so I could stand a chance of understanding it all. Maybe the Bard did know.

I found myself at the bottom of the Science Block stairwell. It had stopped raining, meaning there were now so many more places Penny might be. I could spend the rest of lunch wandering the school grounds and still not find her. I had this vision of myself as a woodlouse in a dish divided into four quadrants — Dad and Joe, Patrick, computers, nuclear war — and no Penny in any of them. (Not that I thought of her as a woodlouse. Only me.) And over it all, a giant hand trying to nudge me into the dampest, darkest, most radioactive quadrant. 'It's where you're supposed to be!'

I gave in. I went up the stairs to the computer room, ready with my excuses for why I'd been a little longer than ten minutes. But when I walked in, Patrick started explaining his latest coding trick as though I hadn't been gone. I couldn't be sure, but he might have been talking to himself anyway.

28

Right near the end of lunch, Chip, who'd been intently working on a huge flowchart covering several sheets of taped-together squared paper, looked up, like a deep sea creature surfacing for its once-a-week lungful of oxygen, and said, 'Tim, just the man I want to see.'

'Me?' I said.

'No, the other Tim who looks like you and is sitting in the same chair.'

I examined his squinty grimace for a second before deciding it was sixty percent likely to be a look of smug satisfaction at his own wit, not indigestion or anything like that, then went over. Patrick made some desperate noises, not wanting to be left out, but having to wait for his work to finish saving to floppy disk first.

Chip rummaged in his bag and produced a pair of battered paperbacks. He held them up towards me, one in each hand. (Was he in league with Mr Canterbrook? Had someone made this International Get Tim Reading Day without telling me?)

'Know what these are?'

'The Hitchhikers' Guide to the Galaxy, and Stranger in a Strange Land,' I said, feeling this had to be a trick because, I mean, I can read the titles off book covers.

Chip shook his head. 'The Bible. Old Testament' (raising Hitchhikers) 'and New' (raising Stranger). 'So here's the question. Have you read them?'

'I've seen the TV programme of that one,' I said, pointing at Hitchhikers.

'Close enough. Have this.' He handed me Stranger in a Strange Land.

'I've seen the TV programme, too,' Patrick said, trying to put his floppy disk in his disk box and his disk box in his bag at the same time as joining us.

'Good for you,' Chip said. He turned back to me. 'Read that, Tim, m'lad. Read it, and wonder.'

'Um, okay,' I said.

'Then hang onto it. I have a mission for you afterwards.'

'A mission?'

'Have I got a mission?' Patrick said.

'One mission at a time,' Chip said. He tapped the book in my hands. 'I can tell all I need to know about someone by what they think of these two books. All I need to know.'

'Is this a test?' I said.

'Not for you.'

'Is it for me, then?' Patrick said.

'Not for you, either. Now, that's enough questions. Isn't that the bell?'

Spookily, the bell went a half second later.

Chip turned back to his flowchart, and, taking up his stencil, started adding boxes and lines. Although Patrick and me had to be getting to our next lesson, I took a moment, while I was putting Chip's book in my bag, to see what the flowchart was all about. There was a rhombus with 'Gather data — likes, dislikes, etc.' written in it, a rectangle with 'Consult an expert' written in it, and a diamond decision box with 'Does she say yes?' written in it. I had no idea what it could be for. An adventure game, perhaps?

I was so lost in thinking about this new mystery, I forgot to look for Penny till we were all sitting down at our next lesson, which was Religious Education, and by then it was too late, because Penny was near the front of the class and to the left, and I was two rows back and to the right, so I could look at her, but she'd only be able to look at me by turning round, and she couldn't do that, because this lesson (as Mr Slaughter announced with much hand-rubbing delight) we were going to watch a film. It was called The

Cross and the Switchblade, and was about a priest working with gangs in New York.

Afterwards, Mr Slaughter did his earnest best to make sure we all understood the message of the film, which was that drugs were bad, and gang warfare was bad. R.E. is great, because it only ever teaches you dead obvious stuff. It's the one lesson in which you're actively not encouraged to think for yourself.

Once it was over, I faffed about as much as I could, putting my pens and things away, thinking surely this time Penny would glance, even accidentally, in my direction, but Mr Slaughter went up to her for a quiet, no doubt caring, word about why she'd been late that morning, and Patrick was getting impatient because the next lesson was Games and he wanted to be sure to claim our usual corner in the changing rooms. Although wedgies had gone out of fashion this year, there was always the risk some bored classmate from the more Neanderthal end of the spectrum would get nostalgic and revive the tradition with the help of one of the computer kids. It's easier to defend yourself in a corner.

Once we'd changed into our gym whites, Mr Dangerfield came in and said, 'Outdoor kits on, lads. It's not raining anymore.'

Patrick put his hand up. 'Mr Dangerfield? It's only just stopped raining, so won't the fields be muddy?'

'Very bright, Smith,' Mr Dangerfield said. (He calls everyone Smith but his star players, as though there's no point in remembering any of our names unless we're good at sports. I don't know what he'd do if he got a star player called Smith.)

'Shouldn't we be in the gym, then?'

'Girls have got the gym. Girls care about getting muddy. Do you want to join the girls or the men, Smith?'

Patrick knew better than to answer this. 'What are we

going to be doing, sir?'

'Rugby,' Mr Dangerfield said, with the sort of relish people reserve for phrases like 'ice cream' and 'Christmas'.

'But that's...'

'The muddiest of them all. Rugby and mud, Smith, rugby and mud. They'll make a man of you.'

Then he left us to get into our outdoor shirts and studded boots.

Once we'd clopped over the tarmac playground, Mr Dangerfield had us line up on the edge of the rugby field.

Patrick put his hand up again. 'Mr Dangerfield? Half the pitch is one big puddle.'

'You seem to be under the misapprehension, Smith, that we're out here to play croquet. We're not. This is a game of rugby, and in rugby, it's not the winning or losing that counts, it's the getting muddy. And if any of you lot isn't covered from head to foot by the end of the match, I'll throw you through that big puddle personally. Right?'

Patrick looked horrified.

'Right,' Mr Dangerfield barked. 'Two teams. Count off evens and odds. Odds turn your shirts inside out.'

Next thing I knew, Patrick had swapped to stand the other side of me, and I found myself counting odd, so I had to take my shirt off and turn it inside out in the cold. Then Mr Dangerfield blew his whistle and the game was on.

Rugby, for me, is mostly about avoiding the ball and wherever it's likely to be. And avoiding James Barrack, who as well as being our star football player, is our star rugby player too. Generally, I adopt a position marking, or guarding, or manning, or whatever the right word is, a corner of the pitch no one visits, with the occasional foray close enough to the main action to look like I'm not *actively* trying to keep away from it. Patrick does the same for the opposite side, which makes both our efforts seem more legitimate. We can always claim to be marking, or manning, or guarding, or whatever, each other. I've never done a rugby tackle in my life, and will be quite happy to get through school without attempting one. As for Mr Dangerfield's threat to throw anyone who wasn't muddy through the big puddle, Patrick would be in the same boat. Surely he wouldn't throw two of us?

It was only when things had got going that I noticed, despite what Mr Dangerfield had said about the girls using the gym, that they were in the tennis courts playing hockey. I was just wondering where Penny was, when I saw what I thought was her (they were a bit far away to be sure), standing near the back of the court, away from the main action. And was she looking in my direction?

If she was — and if it *was* Penny — then wasn't this what I'd been wishing would happen all day?

I started crossing to the other side of the pitch to get close enough to be sure. As I did, the girl — Penny, it had to be Penny — started to raise her hand. Was she about to wave? If she was—

Clonk!

I was hit by something as solid and heavy as a truck. The world turned upside down, and then I was sliding through an endless sea of mud and cold water. Even when I came to a stop, the world was still moving, though in some indefinable, clockwise-anticlockwise way, which made me realise it was only the inside of my head that was moving.

The white sky was blocked out by the head of Mr Dangerfield.

'You okay, Smith?'

In response, I blew a bubble of mud.

'Let's get you up.'

I was jerked up by the hand, to find myself standing, wobbly-leggedly, at the end of a ten foot skid. I followed the skid from its far point where I'd been standing to where

I was standing now, and noticed that it continued up the entire left side of my body.

'There you go, right as rain,' Mr Dangerfield said.

There was a heavy slap on my shoulder and James Barrack said, 'Alright, Smith?' Which explained the feeling of being hit by a truck. I must have been in his way when he was making for the try-line.

He jogged the ball back onto the pitch, saying, 'Does that count as a try, Tony?'

'That almost counts as a conversion, Mr Barrack.'

Not only does Mr Dangerfield call James Barrack 'Mr Barrack', but he lets James Barrack call him 'Tony'.

I glanced dazedly at the rest of the pitch, in time to catch sight of Patrick surreptitiously dipping his forearms in a nearby puddle, determined not to put Mr Dangerfield's threat to the test by being the only un-muddy person on the pitch.

Still dazed, I looked at the tennis courts.

And there was Penny, right up against the fence, and this time she did wave.

I did my best to wave back, though my right side (the side James Barrack had run into) felt a bit numb and reluctant to work properly. I'm sure there was a crack, or at least a click, when I bent my elbow.

Then Miss Hoop, the girls' Games teacher, blew her whistle and said something to Penny that made the rest of the girls laugh jeeringly, and after that she had to concentrate on the game.

Deciding I'd done all that could be expected from me for one Games lesson, I plonked myself in my usual corner of the pitch, and didn't budge from it till Mr Dangerfield blew his whistle and told us to get back in and have a shower. By this point, my left side was feeling a bit crusty, and my right was starting to tingle its way back to feeling.

Penny had waved at me, though. That made it worth it.

Everything was right with the world.

29

When we got to Patrick's house, I left my sports kit in its bag outside the front door. No one was going to nick it, and taking something that muddy into his spotlessly well-kept house would have been like bringing antimatter into contact with normal matter.

'Mum, my rugby kit's all muddy,' Patrick called as he opened the front door, meaning the puddle water on his cuffs.

He had no need to call. Mrs Luffley was there, in the cream-carpeted hallway, like she'd been waiting ever since Patrick left for school that morning. Her fingers twiddled, itching to take his bag, help him off with his coat, and change his shoes for the slippers waiting in the cupboard by the front door, but she knew Patrick didn't like her doing any of that, not when he had a friend round, anyway.

'Hello Tim,' she chirped, 'nice to see you.'

'Hello, Mrs Luffley.'

Patrick kicked off his shoes, dropped his bag and coat, and headed for the living room.

'Don't forget your slippers, dear,' his mum called, tidying up the things he'd dropped.

'Bring them in!'

'Just like his dad,' she said, with a what-can-you-do shake of the head.

She took my coat and schoolbag and hung them up, supervised the placing of my shoes on the shoe-rack by the door, then handed me a pair of Patrick's old slippers, which she'd told me were mine whenever I came round.

'We haven't seen you in a while,' she said, while I put them on.

'I've, um, had to do stuff for my dad.'

'Oh yes, I know,' she said, her voice suddenly full of concern. 'It must be hard for him, poor man, having to raise two boys on his own. You are good to help him out. If only his lord and master' (inclining her head toward the living room) 'did the same on occasion. Ha!'

On cue, Patrick called, 'Mum! Slippers!'

'Oh dear,' she sang, like a doorbell's ding-dong, and took him his slippers.

I followed her into the living room.

Patrick already had the TV on and was sitting in his dad's reclining chair, in the reclined position. He wiggled his toes and his mum put his slippers on for him.

'Now, you two, how about something to drink? Tim, something to drink?'

'I'll have a cherry SodaStream,' Patrick said.

'Tim?'

'I'll have the same, thanks, Mrs Luffley.'

'There might not be enough,' Patrick said, 'and it has to last till you go shopping.'

'I can always do a special trip,' his mum said, and she left the living room, saying, 'Now, two glasses.'

Patrick watched the TV, bored.

'It's only golf,' I said.

'They might have a trailer for Micro Live. They might give out the number for the bulletin board early.'

So we watched the golf. Mrs Luffley came in with our drinks, making sure there was a coaster in reach for both of us, then perched on the edge of a chair, hands clasped, looking at Patrick.

'Did you have a nice day, dear?' she said, after a bit.

'Mum,' he complained.

'Sorry,' Mrs Luffley sang, in the same way she'd sung 'Oh dear' earlier. She gave me a quick, conspiratorial smile, as if to say, 'What we put up with!' then continued gazing at Patrick.

After a minute of that, her eyes went a bit unfocused. She frowned. Her fingers did a nervous twiddle. Then she shook her head, smiled, got up and said, 'Your rugby kit, dear. I'll put it in the washer. What about yours, Tim? I'm sure it's muddy, too. It's no trouble.'

'Um, it's okay, Mrs Luffley.'

'Righto,' she said, and disappeared.

Patrick tutted, then sipped his drink and watched the golf.

I looked at the Radio Times.

'The golf's on till five,' I said.

He shrugged.

I sat back and thought what I could be doing. The thing I most wanted to be doing, right that moment, was walking home with Penny, down Pritchard Lane. I could ask why she'd been late to school that morning, and she could tell me, then we could laugh about what happened to me in Games. I could say how I'd spent all day wishing she'd look in my direction just so I knew she wasn't upset with me (I could say that, because this was in my head), and she'd say how she'd been trying to. Then we could forget it all and talk about pop music.

I came back to the real world and saw Patrick looking at me.

He looked away.

Then he looked back.

'Who were you waving at?' he said.

'What do you mean?' I knew exactly what he meant, but needed a moment to think.

'In rugby. James Barrack sent you flying, Mr Dangerfield helped you up, then you stood there looking at the girls playing hockey and waved at someone.'

'I was just testing my arm. It still feels a bit stiff.'

'Hm,' he said, like a mini sneeze.

I wasn't sure if that meant he believed me or not.

He continued watching the golf, which as far as I knew he wasn't the least bit interested in, and I watched him through the corner of my eye.

Why didn't I tell him? I mean, he was my friend, right? It wasn't as if I couldn't be friends with Patrick *and* Penny. They existed in separate compartments. In maths, they'd be two mutually exclusive sets.

I tried to imagine saying this to Patrick, and him going, 'Hey, yeah, that's great, I'm so happy for you.' And then a ginormous pig might land in the garden and start preening its feathers.

'And when you said you had stuff to do for your dad,' he said, '*did* you?'

'Yeah,' I said, trying to sound puzzled and hurt.

He went back to watching the golf, but was frowning now. 'Someone said they saw you walking back from town with Penny Poundley on Saturday. I heard them say it in class before you got in this morning.'

'Nah,' I said, then thought, why not admit a little bit of it? It can't hurt. 'I mean, I was in town, and she just started talking to me. She lives near me. At the end of Fallow Lane. That's all.'

I felt bad, saying it like that, and had to throw a glance at Patrick's living room window because of the sudden guilty feeling Penny might be standing there, listening. (Why would she be standing in Patrick's back garden, listening?)

'Do you fancy her, then?' Patrick asked sulkily.

'Course not,' I said, and then felt even more guilty. I tried to justify it by telling myself I'd only said it because Patrick had asked sulkily, and I didn't want to give in to him being sulky, so what I said didn't have to be the truth. I still felt bad, though.

'Does she fancy you?' he said.

'Don't be stupid.'

'She was looking at you in Biology.'

I felt a warm glow. 'Perhaps she thought I was an escaped woodlouse.'

Patrick didn't laugh. He said, 'And French.'

'I was right at the front. She was probably looking at Mrs Norman.'

Patrick fell into a huffy quiet.

We drank our drinks.

'Do you fancy anyone in class?' he said.

'No.'

'You've got to fancy someone.'

'Who do you fancy, then?'

'You can't ask till you've answered.'

'I did.'

'Well, if you're saying no one, I'm saying no one.'

We watched golf for a bit.

I finished my drink. Patrick sat with one more mouthful in his glass for a few minutes, then tutted moodily and finished it off.

As soon as he put it down, Mrs Luffley came in. 'Finished?'

She gathered up the glasses and coasters, then disappeared into the kitchen, la-la-la-ing.

Patrick sniffed moodily. Then he said, 'Let's go to my room and play Elite.'

Which meant him playing and me watching, but it had to be better than this.

30

Ten minutes before Micro Live came on, Patrick set up his modem, then we went downstairs. He perched on the edge of his dad's chair (in the un-reclined position) and called 'Mum! Mum!'

'Yes dear?' she sang, coming into the living room drying her hands on her apron.

'We need a notebook and pen.'

'Notebook and pen,' she said, thinking.

'Quick, Mum, it's about to start!'

'Oh dear.' She went into the hall and came back with the pad and pen they keep by the phone. 'Here you go.'

Patrick didn't take them. 'I need you to write down the number of the bulletin board as soon as they say it, then call it upstairs. I'm going to be ready, so I can get connected as soon as they say.'

'But I thought you wanted to watch—'

'I want to win, Mum!'

He left the room and ran upstairs.

'Oh dear,' Mrs Luffley said. She gave a musical sigh and sat where Patrick had been sitting. She fretted for a bit, then handed me the notepad and pen. 'You'd better write it down, Tim. I'm no good with technical things.'

'It's only a phone number, Mrs Luffley,' I said, taking the pad.

'I know, but I'll get in a tizz and get it wrong, and Patrick will be upset with me. I can't bear it when he's upset.'

'I'll do it,' I said.

'You are nice, Tim.' She fiddled with the hem of her apron. 'You really should come round more often. It's so nice to have someone nice around.'

I started to feel embarrassed, and wished they'd get on with announcing the number for the bulletin board.

'Patrick thinks the world of you, you know,' Mrs Luffley said. 'I know he might not act like it sometimes, but it means a lot to him to have you as a friend.'

Now I felt even more embarrassed. And guilty. I couldn't think of anything to say, so I shrugged.

'And when I think about your poor mother, and how you must miss her, and how unfair it all is,' she said, 'I just want to—' She smiled tearily. 'I just want to mother you myself,' she said, and gave a little laugh.

Now I really didn't know what to say. Patrick, and the TV programme, and the notepad and pen, went totally out of my head. I thought that, of all the things I miss about you being gone, Mum, it's having you there, as a person, in the same room as me, like Mrs Luffley was at that moment. Such a simple thing, but so impossible. And then I thought of Penny, and that came so suddenly on top of everything else I was a bit overwhelmed.

'Oh, it's his number,' Mrs Luffley said, putting her hands on her knees and sitting up very straight. I'm sure she held her breath till I'd written it down.

'Here,' I said, and gave her the number, and she rushed into the hall to call it up to Patrick.

On the TV they said that the bulletin board software they were using only allowed one person to connect at a time, and that if you got the engaged signal, you should hang up and try again. Patrick spent the entire fifty minutes of the show upstairs in his room, shouting 'It's still engaged!' in mounting frustration. Mrs Luffley sang to herself in the kitchen as she got dinner ready. I watched the programme on my own. When it finished, Mrs Luffley asked if I wanted to stay for dinner, but I said I'd better be getting back. I called 'Bye!' up the stairs to Patrick, but all I heard in return was, 'It's STILL engaged!'

I crossed the London Road and started down Pritchard

Lane. It was getting dark, and the streetlights hadn't come on yet, but at least if anyone tried to mug me, I could brain them with the cold, wet lump of my rugby kit.

I thought about Patrick and why I hadn't told him the truth about me and Penny. It all seemed too complicated. Whatever words I used wouldn't be right, but whatever I said, Patrick would latch onto and dissect, and come up with his own totally wrong way of seeing things. Then I thought about home, and Dad, and Joe, and that was complicated, too. Suddenly, the only thing that didn't seem complicated was Penny, which was completely the opposite of how things had been a week ago.

Was life all going to be like this? And if so, why didn't they teach you about it at school? A few hints might have been helpful.

'Hi, Tim,' Penny said, from the other side of the road.

'Hello,' I said, and felt a stab of guilt. 'You haven't been waiting for me all this time, have you?'

'It's been nearly three hours since school finished. Even I'm not that stupid.'

I still felt guilty, because she wasn't saying she hadn't waited at least some of that time. I said, 'I went to Patrick's. We'd arranged it ages ago. I forgot.'

'I saw you going in.'

And I knew that meant she'd at least been hoping I'd join her for our usual after-school walk.

'You're not still avoiding going home, are you?' I said.

'They had a major row this morning. Mum kicked him out. That was why I was late for school. Mum was upset, and I had to calm her down. She can be a bit of a danger to herself sometimes. She's been in her room all day, curtains closed. I came out because I wanted to... I don't know.' She looked at her shoes, then said, 'Actually, I was sort of hoping I might bump into you.'

Now my guilty-meter, which had been flickering about

in the red, went totally over to MAX, and probably bust a spring. She'd wanted to talk to someone, and I'd been at Patrick's watching TV. Now everything seemed complicated again.

I thought of something to make it better.

'Do you want to walk down the bumpy bit of Fallow Lane in the dark?'

31

Penny gave me a puzzled look, half smile, half frown, but said 'Okay.'

So we walked on, past where we'd usually turn up King George Way, to where Pritchard Lane ends at Fallow Lane. Here, Fallow Lane's just a bumpy track, nothing like the tarmacked, properly-pavemented road it is further up. It's lined on one side with a high iron fence, with a thick band of trees behind that (and behind that some fields belonging to a big house or farm you can't see). On the other side, there's the gardens of the houses on King George Way and, further up, the gardens of some of the houses on Prichard Gardens, including ours. Then the lane meets Pritchard Gardens and becomes a proper road. Between here and there the trees grow out over the iron fence, almost making it into a tunnel.

'It's pitch dark,' Penny said. You could see the corner where Fallow Lane met Pritchard Gardens far up ahead, lit by a streetlight, but you couldn't see anything else. It was like a huge sheet of black paper with a shiny 10p coin in the middle.

'That's the point,' I said. 'You walk down it in the total dark.'

Penny looked dubious. 'Is this something your brother would make you do, then leap out and scare you?'

'No, it's...' I didn't want to say it here. I wanted to say it further on, in the dark. So I said, 'It wasn't Joe.'

I'd just thought of something. You've probably thought of it already, haven't you, Mum? When we did this, you and me, we held hands, so we didn't get separated in the dark. I was just thinking if it could be done without that when Penny took mine and said, 'So I don't get lost.'

I suddenly felt responsible, and hoped I could remember where all the big puddles were, because there were a few you had to avoid. But my thoughts kept slipping to Penny's hand in mine, making it difficult to concentrate. I started to feel that heroic feeling again, and hoped this wasn't going to end with me making a fool of myself like last time, with the football.

'Let's go,' I said, before I could change my mind.

We took our first steps in silence. After a bit, I said, 'The whole point is, you know that, though it's dark, nothing bad's going to happen. You can see the light at the far end, and all you've got to do is take one step after another to get there. It's easy.'

'It really is dark,' said Penny, who I couldn't see at all, now. Her hand was still in mine. It felt strange to be the one doing the leading, the one saying not to be afraid and how simple it was.

I took another few steps and, now we were really in the dark, I said, 'It was my mum I used to do this with. We were out one evening, I can't remember why, and we came to the end of Fallow Lane, and she said we should walk down it, in the dark. Just suddenly. She'd do things like that sometimes.'

We took a few more steps.

I said, 'Because, I used to be scared of the dark. So Mum said, the best thing was to just walk into it. She even made it sound exciting. She said, once I'd done it, I'd know I *could* do it, and after that, I'd know I could do things even if I was scared of them. There's a huge puddle here somewhere.'

I felt the edge of the puddle with my foot and led Penny round it.

'Then,' I said, not thinking about where this was going, 'the second time we did it, we stopped halfway, and just stood there in the dark, to prove we could.'

'Stop, then,' Penny said.

We came to a halt.

'I think we let go of our hands,' I said.

Penny didn't let go of mine.

In the dark, you listen. We heard the traffic on the London Road echoing in the sky above us, and the occasional shout or laugh or sneeze from a house nearby. A bit of TV. A car chittering to a start. The high-pitched skwee of birds in the air, wheeling and catching insects. Then the traffic had a lull, and everything went quiet.

'It's like being in the dark, dark woods,' Penny said. 'I'm waiting for the howl of a wolf.'

'Shall we go on?'

'No. Not yet.' She gave my hand a squeeze.

Of course, there was another bit to this. The third time you and me did this, Mum, we stopped and you said, 'Now we have to tell each other a secret.' Because, you said, the dark lets you do that. It's a special place, it has its own rules. So I told you — what did I tell you? That I wasn't afraid of the dark anymore. Which wasn't really a secret, but you didn't mind. Then you told me what you told me. And that was a whole new thing to be scared of. We'd all been saying you'd get better, but you told me you might not. That was the secret. We couldn't say it anywhere but here, and couldn't talk about it again, but I had to know it, and you had to tell me, and here was the only place you could. And after that, you said, 'Bad things happen in fairy tales, too, but they still have happy endings.' And I don't know if that's true, Mum, but it's what you said, so I'll always remember it.

Anyway, I wanted to tell Penny a secret, too.

I could only think of one thing, and it was a bit odd, but I decided to say it anyway.

'Sometimes,' I said, 'I think about climbing onto the school roof. Just climbing up and lying there and forgetting everything.'

'Why the school roof?' she said.

'I used to have these dreams, every night, when I was really young. I'd climb out my bedroom window and fly from roof to roof, all over town. In the night air. It was so quiet and different. It was like the world was asleep, and I had it all to myself. But then, at the end, I'd forget how to fly, or be too tired, and I'd be stuck on a roof, and the fire brigade had to come and get me down. In my dream, I mean.'

'Nice,' Penny said.

'And I sometimes think, if I heard the four minute warning, you know, if they were going to drop a nuclear bomb on us, that's what I'd do. I'd climb onto the school roof. Just go up there, and let it happen. Much better than hiding in a shelter or something.'

I realised I was going on about nuclear war again, which wasn't what I'd wanted to do, so I shut up.

But Penny said, 'I always thought I'd go home. To my mum's studio. I used to play on the floor while she painted when I was much younger. But now... It'd be nicer if you were there, too.'

So she *did* think about nuclear war sometimes.

I thought that was it, but I could hear Penny breathing louder, like she was psyching herself up for something. She said, 'You know that time, when I hit Steph?'

'Yeah,' I said. How could anyone forget?

'As soon as I did it I wished I hadn't. Not because — I mean, I was really angry at her. Really angry. I wasn't going to say sorry, and I didn't. But all I could think was, it was what my mum would have done. And here I was, being like her. So I made the decision, right then, not to be like her. And it's difficult sometimes. But, well, I haven't hit anyone since, have I?'

She sniggered, then I sniggered, then we were silent again.

Somewhere, a dog yowled complainingly, like it had

stubbed its paw.

'Not quite the howl of a wolf,' Penny said.

We carried on.

After a bit, she said, 'What did you do at Patrick's?'

I told her about Micro Live, and Patrick's attempts to connect to the show's bulletin board. 'He's probably still at it now.'

'Does Patrick... I mean, have you... said anything, about me, to him?'

'Not really.' But of course I had. And now, what I'd said seemed really mean, like I'd been pretending I wasn't friends with her. So I tried to think about how it really was, and put that into words. I didn't want this to end with Penny upset with me, or even with me thinking she might be. I wasn't going to go through all that again. So I said, 'It's just... I don't know what to say without him... getting all jealous.'

Which was true. Amazing how suddenly uncomplicated it seemed! Perhaps it was being in the dark that helped. It made things easier to say.

'I don't mind,' Penny said. 'I know you like to keep things separate, in their own little boxes.'

And I thought, how can she know that? I wanted to ask, but was worried she might say it was telepathy again.

The 10p coin of the end of the lane was now as big as a hoop. We'd passed the backs of the houses on King George Way and were behind the last few houses on Pritchard Gardens. Our upper landing light was on, and I thought I saw Joe going into his room. Somehow, that made it seem all the more secret, me walking down Fallow Lane with Penny. And that made me realise, it wasn't that I didn't want Patrick to know. I didn't want the *world* to know. And I don't mean the people in it, I mean that big thing out there that makes the bad things happen. Because, for some reason, it seemed that if there was at least one person who didn't know about Penny and me, then the world wouldn't know, and if the world didn't know, we'd be safe.

I know it sounds silly, but it made perfect sense in the dark.

We came to the end of the bumpy part of Fallow Lane, and stood there for a bit.

'What are you doing tomorrow?' Penny said.

'Nothing.'

'Want to go to the cinema?'

'Yeah.'

'Come over about two, or something.'

'Okay.'

'See you, then.'

'See you.'

Then she giggled because I was still holding her hand.

So I let go, and she went up Fallow Lane, and I went home.

32

I woke up early on Saturday, and started reading the book Chip had lent me. It was about a young man raised by aliens on Mars. He knew only alien ways of living, and when he came to Earth he taught people a whole new way of looking at life. The stuff he taught seemed really convincing, till I put the book down and thought about it. Then I realised it would only work if, like him, you had Martian super-powers and didn't care if you got killed. There was a lot about sex and religion, too, but I had no way of knowing if he was right about those.

By lunchtime, I could hear the usual clanking and cursing from the garden that meant Joe was working on his bike. Dad had been out to buy a paper, and was reading it downstairs. I felt like staying in my room till two, then sneaking out to Penny's, but I didn't want to sit in the cinema with my tummy rumbling, so I should at least make myself a sandwich. Anyway, I needed my pocket money. Neither Dad nor Joe had said anything to me since Thursday, but it was silly avoiding them. Besides, what was the worst that could happen?

'Hi Dad,' I said, when I went downstairs.

He gave a grunt, but that was no different from usual. Maybe we'd gone back to normal. Or maybe it hadn't been as bad as I'd thought to start with. I mean, why should it be?

In the kitchen, I started making myself a sandwich.

Joe glanced up from the bike parts he'd laid out on the ground. 'Luncheon meat for me.'

'In the fridge,' I said.

'What you on about?'

'The luncheon meat,' I said. 'It's in the fridge.'

'Well put it in a sandwich, and I'll have it.'

'Put it in a sandwich yourself,' I said.

Joe pointed at me with a spanner. 'I'll put you in a sandwich in a minute. A spanner-head sandwich.'

'That doesn't even make sense.'

'Nor will your head, when I'm through with it.'

I took a big, deliberate bite out of my sandwich. 'Mm,' I said. 'Sandwich.'

'Git,' Joe said.

All that was normal, too.

I made Joe's sandwich and put it on a plate on the outer sill of the kitchen window.

'Here's your sandwich, then. Used teabags and mustard.'

'Ta.'

I continued to eat, watching him, till he put his spanner down and came for his sandwich.

'Joe?'

'What?'

'Do you hate me?'

'Course I do, you little runt. Next question.'

I rolled my eyes. 'Alright, does Dad hate me?'

'What you on about?'

'I mean, because of Penny.'

'Who?'

'You know. The girl I invited round on Thursday.'

'Oh.' He chewed his sandwich, and I thought he was waiting to get his mouth empty before answering. Then he took another bite.

'Joe!'

'What?'

'I asked you a question.'

'Which was?'

I tutted. 'Does Dad hate me because of Penny?' It sounded so stupid, having to say it twice.

'Let me ask you a question. Have you been seeing men following you about lately? Maybe dressed in white coats? Making notes on clipboards?'

'Joe, I'm serious.'

'Seriously deranged. Are you making tea?'

'No, I'm not making tea, you lazy sod!'

'Hey,' Dad said suddenly, making me jump. 'None of that. Make your brother some tea. I'll have one too.'

I wondered how long he'd been there, and what he'd heard, but before I could say anything, he went past the kitchen and into the bathroom. I put the kettle on and some tea bags in mugs. I thought about what to say when Dad emerged. It would be so much easier if I could just ask what I wanted to ask, and he'd answer. Dad, do you hate me for having Penny round, and do you think I've betrayed the family? It sounded so incredibly stupid. No one was going to say yes to that. But they might think it.

So how could I find out?

I realised I'd never had a serious conversation with Dad in my life. Nothing above the level of how to change a fuse, or what was for dinner.

He came out of the bathroom, so I said, 'Dad?'

And he said, 'You and Joe are cutting the hedge, front and back.'

'I'm going out at two,' I said. 'I need my pocket money to go to the cinema.' It was one-thirty now.

'Pocket money after the hedge.'

'But that's unfair! If I'd known, I could have done it earlier, but I'm going out at two. It's arranged. Dad?'

But he'd gone back into the living room.

'Go out some other time, then,' Joe said, coming in for his mug of tea. 'Eh, Dad?'

'But it's all arranged,' I said. 'For two.'

Joe smirked. 'He's going with his *girlfriend*.'

'She's not my *girlfriend*,' I said, with the same sneery tone.

'Why, she dumped you already?'

'No.'

'So you're saying she's a boy, and she's your *boyfriend*?'

'Shut up,' I said.

'Hey,' Dad said, from the living room.

I went through, with Joe following.

'All I'm saying,' I said, 'is if I'd known earlier, I'd have done it then, but now I've got to go out. I'll do my bit tomorrow.'

Joe said, 'In that case, your bit's all of it, because I'm not doing it on my own today, and I'm not doing any of it tomorrow.' I've never understood how Joe can get away with that, making up rules to suit himself, but he always does.

'Dad,' I said.

But Dad was reading the paper. He'd had his say, and that was that. Joe was smirking. It was all a game to him, and it didn't mean anything to Dad. I'd been wrong. It hadn't all gone back to normal. They were just doing this to be mean to me. They might even have planned it. And before I knew it, I was saying that, or something like it, and I don't remember the exact words, but the more they just sat there, Dad not looking at me, Joe smirking, the more angry I got, till I said the only thing that would make them actually listen to me.

I said, 'Well, Mum would have let me.'

Joe's smirk went sour. Dad calmly and deliberately folded his paper and looked at me. That stone-faced look.

'I'm going,' I said. I put my shoes and coat on in the hallway and left.

And once I was outside, walking to Penny's, I thought, 'That's done it.'

33

It was too early to go to Penny's, so I walked as slowly as I could up Fallow Lane. When I got to the end and found I hadn't walked slowly enough, I turned round to go back so I could walk up it again, but Penny appeared at her gate.

'I did say about two, not two on the dot,' she said. 'You can still come in if you're early.'

I went up to her. 'I just had an argument with my dad.'

'Major or minor?'

I didn't know there were degrees. 'Major, I think.'

'Did you throw anything?'

'No.'

'Did he throw anything?'

'He didn't even say anything.'

'Sounds pretty minor, to me.'

'I've never had an argument with my dad before.'

'That can make it feel major, even if it's minor. What was it about?'

'He said me and Joe had to cut the hedge. I said I was going out, and that it was arranged. He wouldn't listen.'

'Still sounds minor. I mean, nobody threatened to kill anybody did they?'

(Which made me wonder what sort of arguments she had with her mum.)

I said, 'No, but... I said some things.'

'What sort of things?'

'Well, it was only one thing. I said, "Mum would have let me."'

'And?'

'I left.'

'Did you slam the door?'

'No.'

'You can't have a major argument without slamming a door.'

'I had to put my shoes on.'

'Sometimes you have to put up with wet feet for the sake of a dramatic exit.'

I sighed. 'But I mentioned Mum.'

'That sort of thing happens.'

'But nobody mentions her, ever.'

Penny fiddled with the latch on Silversmith Cottage's gate. 'Are you saying no one, in your house, even in non-argument situations?'

'Nobody. Ever.'

'That's the most insane thing I ever heard. And I've heard my mum talking about art.'

'It's really bad,' I said, as what I'd said to Dad came back and hit me again, like a big rubber pendulum. There was no point trying to ignore it, because it was going to keep swinging back and hitting me from now on.

'I'll say it is. You need to talk about that sort of thing.'

'No,' I said, seeing she'd misunderstood, 'I mean, my saying what I said was really bad.'

'But that's so stupid. You can't not mention her. It's like, oh, there's a nuclear bomb in the corner of the room, but we can't mention it. In fact, with you, that's exactly what it's like.'

I didn't know what to say to that, so I said, 'The thing is, I haven't got my pocket money, so I can't go to the cinema.'

'I've got enough for both of us.'

'I can't ask you to—'

'You're not asking, I'm offering.'

'But...'

'But?'

I struggled. 'Isn't... I mean, don't I have to... I mean...'

'Are you trying to say that because this is a date, and you're the boy, you ought to pay?'

'Yeah...'

'Haven't you heard of Women's Lib?'

'I have, but I don't know the details.'

'Well, I'm paying for you to go to the cinema. That's the details.'

I stood there awkwardly for a bit. Then I said, 'Thanks.' Then I said, 'Is this really a date?'

We went inside for Penny to get her coat. I waited in the hallway while she knocked softly on her mum's bedroom door and told her where we were going. Apparently, her mum had been in there with the curtains closed since yesterday. Penny had taken her a cup of tea or two, but said she probably wouldn't emerge till tomorrow at the earliest. This, apparently, was normal.

It was only when we started walking into town that I realised I had no idea what was on at the cinema.

'Hadn't we better check?' I said. 'There might be nothing but 18-certificate films.'

'I already looked. There's an 18, a 15, and a PG.'

'What's the PG?'

'Only about the most perfect film for the two of us.'

'What do you mean?'

'Well, what would *your* most perfect film be about?'

'Computers,' I said. My two favourite films are War-Games and TRON, and both are about computers.

'And what would *my* most perfect film be about?'

'Um, pop music?'

(I was so glad to see I'd got that right.)

'So all we need is a film about computers that's got some great pop music in it, don't we?'

'Is there one?' I said, doubtfully.

'You don't think I asked you to the cinema on the off-chance, do you?'

As she refused to tell me any more, we discussed other films we'd seen this year. Both of us thought the new Indiana Jones film had been as good as the first, but that the latest Star Trek hadn't. Other than that, Penny really liked Splash (which I hadn't seen, it was about a mermaid) and Romancing the Stone (which I had seen, but hadn't liked, because I thought from the poster it was going to be like Indiana Jones but it wasn't), while I liked Greystoke: The Legend of Tarzan (which Penny hadn't seen) and The Karate Kid (Penny said she liked the old guy in it), and both of us thought Supergirl and BMX Bandits had been just okay.

We got so deep into that conversation, I forgot all about the film we were going to see, till we turned the corner in town and saw the names of this week's films above the cinema doors: Once Upon a Time in America (which was the 18 film), Moscow on the Hudson (which had the bloke from Mork & Mindy in it, but was a 15, so we couldn't see that), and Electric Dreams.

'Electric Dreams,' I said, savouring the title.

'Did you see the single on Top of the Pops the other night?'

'No. I was sort of hiding in my bedroom.'

'It's the greatest song ever. If the film's even half as good, it's going to be the best film of the year.'

So Penny bought us a ticket each, and a coke for her (I pretended I didn't want one, because she'd only have bought me one if she thought I did), then we climbed the stairs and found ourselves a place to sit.

I love the cinema. I love its reddish gloom before a film starts. I love its plush tilting seats that always numb your bum before the film's over. I love the moment the curtains part, even if it's just to show that Pearl & Dean thing then the ads for local restaurants and carpet shops. I even love the moment they show the certificate from the British Board of Film Censors (or Classification, as they seem to be now), because then you know the film's about to start.

Electric Dreams turned out to be pretty preposterous.

This man buys a home computer to help him design a new type of earthquake-resistant brick. Pretty soon he's hooked on computers and buys loads of gadgets for it, so it can control everything in his house. (I know this will probably happen one day, but the film didn't *say* it was set in the future.) Then he accidentally spills champagne on it, and suddenly his computer is not only super-intelligent, it also fancies the woman in the apartment below, who plays the cello. The man who owns the computer fancies her too, and all sorts of silliness occurs as he and his computer fight over her.

'Wasn't it great?' Penny said, as we came out afterwards.

'Yeah,' I said. I didn't want her to think she'd wasted her money.

'Could your computer do that?'

I decided to break it to her. 'I don't think any computer could. Not even the Cray X-MP, and that's the most powerful computer in the world.'

She didn't take it at all badly. She just said, 'And wasn't the music great?'

'Yeah.' I could at least agree with that. But I didn't think she'd grasped my earlier point, so I said, 'Really, though, if you spilled champagne on a computer, it would short out and die. Or, if you were lucky, you might *lose* functionality. You certainly wouldn't gain it. I mean, for that computer to have done what it did, it would have to be totally reprogrammed, and have additional memory chips installed. And that's just for starters.'

We were standing on the outside steps of the cinema now, and as I said all this, Penny started fiddling absentmindedly with the buttons on my coat.

'I wish I could play the cello, or something like that,' she said.

'And for a computer to actually write a pop song,' I said, 'it would have to have a really advanced music synthesiser module.'

'Or maybe the violin, as it's smaller,' Penny said. 'Don't you think?'

'Yeah,' I said. I guess it didn't matter how likely or unlikely the computer part of the film was. Still, the song at the end aside, it was no way the best film of the year. Penny was happy, though. She had a dazed, smiley look in her eyes, which might have been because of coming out of the dark cinema into the daylight, or might have been because we'd seen our first film together, and she was feeling a bit mushy.

She was still fiddling with my coat buttons.

I wondered if she was expecting me kiss her. I wasn't sure. If I was supposed to, I didn't want to do it on the steps of the cinema, with loads of people about. I mean, I'd probably head-butt her by accident, or get dizzy and fall down the steps, and maybe take her with me. I could just imagine us toppling onto the pavement, rolling under a passing bus, and getting squashed. I'd much rather have solid, level ground and a bit of seclusion for a first attempt.

I was just trying to guess what her thoughts on the matter might be, when her eyes focused over my shoulder, and she said, 'Hi, Patrick.'

I turned around.

Patrick was there.

He was standing on the cinema steps, too.

He looked at Penny, then at me, then at a point off in the distance. A point which seemed to be annoying him rather a lot.

'Hello Patrick,' I said.

'Hello,' he said, like he had a mouth full of superglue chewing gum.

Then he went up the steps and into the cinema.

'He's in for a treat,' Penny said.

I felt my world beginning to end.

34

All the way home I only half-listened to Penny. Luckily, she was happy babbling on about anything and everything, so it only needed me to say 'Yeah' every so often to keep things going. I was mostly thinking about Patrick. And when I wasn't thinking about Patrick I was thinking about Dad.

I didn't know what to do.

Actually, I knew there was nothing I could do.

What I didn't know was how to put up with the fact there was nothing I could do.

'Want to come in?' Penny said, when we got to her house.

'I'd better get back,' I said.

'You mean your dad. It'll be alright, you know. It's never as bad as it seems. Usually after an argument things are better. It's like a storm. It's noisy and scary, but it clears the air. As long as, you know, no one gets hit by lightning.'

'Yeah,' I said, meaning, maybe for the rest of the human race.

'Right, um, well...' Penny said.

She studied my left shoulder for a bit, then my right, and now I was sure she was expecting me to give her a kiss. This had been a date, after all. But I didn't want the first time I kissed her to be when my head was full of worries about what my dad was going to say when I got back, or what Patrick was going to be like on Monday, so I did my best to pretend I hadn't realised, and said, 'Bye, then.'

'Bye,' she said, with a little shrug. She didn't seem to mind too much.

I walked off down Fallow Lane.

Then I thought of going back, knocking on her door, and giving her a kiss anyway.

If I'd been in a film like Electric Dreams, I would have. But in the end, I thought about it too much — what would happen if Penny was in the middle of a coming-home argument with her mum, or if she was in the bathroom and her mum answered the door instead, or any number of other things — then realised I'd left it too long, so I went home.

Dad was out at the pub.

Joe told me as soon as I came in. He said it while sucking his finger.

'What are you doing?' I said.

'Found these in the pantry,' he said. 'Want some?' He held out the little tub of hundreds and thousands, now almost empty.

When I just stared at them, he put his wet finger in the tub, stirred it round till it was covered in multi-coloured sugary specks, then stuck it in his mouth and sucked.

'Bit stale,' he said.

He was watching TV, and I realised The Tripods was about to start, so I sat down. Patrick and me had been discussing The Tripods every Monday, episode by episode, mostly whether it was as good as Doctor Who or not. I wondered what would happen this Monday. (Of course, Patrick was at the cinema right now. But he usually got his dad to video record it. That way he could watch it twice, and be sure to win all the points in our discussions, if only by saying, 'Yeah, but I've seen it twice.' Which, of course, I couldn't do, because we didn't have a video recorder.)

Joe finished the hundreds and thousands, gave a little burp, then put the empty tub carefully to one side.

We watched TV for ten minutes, me waiting for Joe to say something about earlier.

He didn't, so I said, 'Did Dad say anything?'

'Yeah. He said, "Going to the pub."'

'I mean did he say anything about me?'

Joe shrugged and pulled a face, which could have meant anything.

I tutted.

Joe tutted back.

'Joe!'

'What?'

'You know.'

'I know what?'

I tried giving him an imploring look, but he just said, 'You making tea?'

'Okay,' I said, and went off to put the kettle on.

While it was boiling, I tried giving him a significant stare from the kitchen doorway, but he didn't even look my way.

I made the tea. I brought both our mugs in, and held his out. When he reached for it, I took it back.

'Joe,' I said.

'Oh, what?'

'Dad. And me. Earlier.'

'What about it?' Finally, his look showed he at least admitted it had happened.

'What did he say?'

'Nothing.'

'He must have said something.'

'He didn't say anything.'

'Well, what did he do?'

'What do you expect? He climbed Mount Kilimanjaro. He invented penicillin.'

'Joe!'

'He just sat there. I waited for him to say something. He didn't. So I went into the garden and got on with my bike. Okay?'

'Okay,' I said. I gave him his tea.

Joe said, 'Why did you have to...'

I knew what he was asking, but I sat there saying nothing to make him say it.

'...mention...'

I still said nothing.

'...Mum,' he said, mostly mouthing this last word.

'Well, why do you always take Dad's side?'

'Dad's side? What do you mean, you pilchard?'

'You always take Dad's side is what I mean.'

'There aren't any sides. We're a family. We're all on one side.'

'No we're not,' I said. 'It's always you and Dad against me. Always.'

Joe sipped his tea, then pulled a face. 'Did you put sugar in this?'

'No, I forgot.'

He held out the mug, so I took it back into the kitchen, put some sugar in it, stirred it, and brought it back.

Joe gave it a noisy slurp then carried on watching TV.

I thought I'd got as much out of him as I was going to get, so I was surprised when, near the end of The Tripods, he said, 'Anyway, she always liked you better.'

'What?'

'She spoiled you.'

'Mum?'

'No, the Queen. Who do you think?'

I thought about this. He might have been right. 'Sorry,' I said.

Joe said, 'You wally,' and threw a cushion at me.

I threw it back. He picked up two cushions and threw them both at me. I grabbed them, plus another, and threw all three. After that, we just held onto the cushions and battered each other round the head for a bit.

Then we sat watching Noel Edmond's Late Late Breakfast Show.

Halfway through, Joe said, 'You're still cutting the hedge on your own, tomorrow, though.'

35

One of my favourite games on the Spectrum is Atic Atac, which came out last year. It's pretty frenetic. You play a serf, a knight, or a wizard (your choice), trapped in a haunted house, and you have to find three keys to unlock the front door so you can escape. Meanwhile, all sorts of ghosties and ghoulies are trying to eat you. The longer you stay in any one room, the more appear, so it's best to keep moving.

I'm telling you this, Mum, because Sunday was like Atic Atac.

I was worried — mostly about what Patrick was going to say the next day at school, but also about Dad, who spent the morning in bed, then disappeared up the pub in the afternoon, so I still had no idea what he thought of Saturday's argument — and worries are like the spooks and skellingtons of Atic Atac. As long as you keep yourself busy, they don't bother you, but as soon as you pause, they crowd in and eat you up. The main difference is, you can't fling daggers, axes, or spell-bolts to get rid of them, like you can in Atic Atac.

To stop myself worrying, I did the garden hedge, front and back (as promised, Joe didn't help), then my homework, then I read some more of Chip's book, but mostly I played Atic Atac, which I thought was a nifty way of turning a situation being like another situation to practical use. It was like I *could* fling daggers, axes and spell-bolts at my worries to get rid of them.

Then Monday came, and I was worrying again. Playing Atic Atac before school didn't help. I wondered if it would be any better if I had a little axe to take in and fling at Patrick.

Maybe not.

Penny came by at the usual time, and was pretty perky

for a Monday. Her mum was up and about, and had even started painting again. I only half-listened. School, and the moment I'd finally have to talk to Patrick, was getting closer. With all my worrying, I'd thought about it so much, I had absolutely no idea what was going to happen. My mind was a scrawled-over, rubbed-out-a-hundred-times blank. I even found myself wishing the four-minute warning would sound, so I didn't have to go through with it.

Which, I suppose, is a bad sign.

When I came into the classroom, Patrick was in his usual place. (I'd wondered if he might have moved, just to make it clear he didn't want me sitting next to him, but he hadn't.) He looked up, saw it was me, then looked huffily at his desk.

It could have been worse. I'd even wondered, at one point, if he'd throw something at me the moment I came in. I'd say his old ZX Spectrum, only, with its rubber keys, it wasn't going to hurt anyone.

Penny went to sit by Kash, I sat by Patrick.

'Hi, Patrick,' I said.

He went: 'Hmph.'

I got a bit annoyed by that, so I pushed my face towards his and said, in an exaggerated way, 'Good morning Patrick.'

'Is it?' he said, still not looking at me. 'How can I tell? You say it's a good morning, but how can I believe you?'

'Uh, by looking out the window?'

(It was actually a bit cloudy, so not *technically* a good morning, but that wasn't the point.)

'Well, you lie about everything else,' Patrick said. 'I mean, your name might not even be Tim. It's probably Frank or Jim or something instead.'

This, I hadn't planned for. I'd expected Patrick to assault me with logical arguments and cutting denouncements, but instead he was just sounding a bit insane.

'Well don't call me Tim, then,' I said.

'I won't. I won't call you anything. I won't even talk to you.'

'Good.'

'Because it wouldn't matter if I did. I'd just hear lies, wouldn't I?'

'Yeah, but you're talking to me now, so you were lying when you said you wouldn't talk to me.'

'Well, I'll stop then.'

'Good.'

'Yeah.'

'You're still talking to me.'

'No I'm not.'

'Yes you are. You said "No I'm not".'

'I'm not talking to you, I'm talking to this nobody who keeps talking to me.'

'Well if it's a nobody, why are you talking back?'

'In the hope it shuts up and goes away.'

'Well, it's not going to.'

'Well, it's not going to,' Patrick repeated, in a silly voice, having run out of ideas.

So I said, 'Well, it's not going to,' mocking him mocking me.

And we could have gone on like that forever, if Mr Slaughter hadn't come in with the register.

'Good morning,' he said.

'See?' I said to Patrick.

We went to assembly, then to our first lesson, which was double Maths (they like to give you a good slap in the face to wake you up for the week ahead) and though we weren't talking to each other, Patrick and me still walked there together, and sat in our usual places next to each other. Fortunately, Maths doesn't require you to work together, so we didn't have to speak, but I noticed that Patrick put all his stuff — his pens, his mechanical pencil, his eraser, his protractor, his ruler and pair of compasses — on the far side of the desk, to make it clear I couldn't borrow them. Which I didn't need to. I had my own. He also leaned as much away from me as he could, and covered his work with his arm, to stop me copying it.

Like I ever did that!

(Okay, occasionally.)

I looked over at Penny, who was head to head with Kash. She glanced up and smiled. Patrick saw this, and gave me a look that could have curled a set square. Then he realised that by looking at me he was acknowledging my existence, so he stopped it and got on with his work.

After Maths, it was break time, when Patrick and me usually went to the canteen for him to buy an iced bun, and me to watch him eat it. (Unless I had some money, in which case I'd buy a rice crispy slice.) Just out of habit, we went there together and I sat down while Patrick bought his iced bun. He came over and sat next to me, and ate it as usual, both of us pretending the other didn't exist.

Then we went to our next lesson, which was English. We sat next to each other. And still didn't speak.

I know, Mum, I could have said sorry.

Technically, Patrick was right. I'd lied to him. But I wasn't going to admit it when he was being such a prat. Because then it would have been like saying he was totally right and I was totally wrong. Which, technically, he might have been, but...

Oh, you know what I mean!

So we kept going round with each other even though we weren't talking to each other, or acknowledging each other's existence. At lunch, we went to the computer room together. (This time it wasn't very busy. I got a Spectrum and Patrick got a BBC.) Patrick sat there, working loudly on his graphics compression routine, every so often saying things like, 'Ah, yes, got it!' or 'Of course!' as though to make me jealous of how much progress he was making, while I tinkered about doing nothing much, and thought that I could, by rights, go and find Penny and spend lunch with her, but I knew if I did that, it would be taking a fatal step in totally breaking my friendship with Patrick, which was somehow surviving through sheer force of habit, and I didn't want to be the one to take that last step, because that would make me totally *triply* wrong, and I *certainly* wasn't that.

So things went on like that for a while, till Chip said, ''Ere, Tim, m'lad. Have a word?'

36

'Don't talk to *him*,' Patrick said. 'You can't believe any-thing he says.'

Chip looked at Patrick, did a quick mental calculation, then decided to ignore him.

'So Tim, m'lad, have you read the book yet?'

'I'm about halfway.'

'Which means he probably hasn't even started,' Patrick said.

Chip looked again at Patrick (who'd gone back to typing loudly, with a lot of angry stabs at the delete key), then at me, and once more decided to ignore him.

'So, here's what I want you to do.'

'He won't do it,' Patrick said. 'He'll say he will, but he won't.'

'Right,' Chip said, 'is there something going on here I should know about?'

Obviously waiting for this, Patrick took a deep breath—

But Chip held up a hand and said, 'On second thoughts, I don't care. Tim—'

'He's a liar,' Patrick burst out. 'He lies. Nothing he says is true. Everything's lies.'

Chip considered this. He turned to me. 'Is that true?'

I opened my mouth, but Chip cut me off, too. 'No, don't answer that. Cos, if it is true, you'll say it isn't, and if it isn't true, you'll say it is, because only a complete liar says they never lie.' He wagged a finger thoughtfully. 'Now, there's a way to do this. It's one of those classic puzzles. One of you always lies and the other always tells the truth. So, I ask either one of you what the other would say, and take the reverse of that... No, hang on, that only counts if I actually give a damn. Right, back to the real world. Tim—'

Patrick, who seemed to have spent the last half minute gathering his breath for another outburst, came up with: 'He went out with a *girl*. To the *cinema*.'

'And these are crimes where you come from?' Chip said.

'Not—it—he—' Patrick said, with a series of wild gestures.

'Turn off, wait ten seconds, then turn on again,' Chip said. 'Sounds like you've got a glitch in your IO port.'

But I was feeling bad by this point, so I said, 'I'm sorry, Patrick. But there's nothing wrong with it. I mean, if I'd known you wanted to come, you could have come too.'

('Tell me you didn't mean that,' Chip muttered.)

'But you lied,' Patrick said, not looking at me.

'I said I'm sorry.' Saying it again was easy now I'd snuck the first one out.

Patrick gave a little sneer and a wiggle of the head. Then he said, 'Well.' Then he carried on typing.

Chip raised an eyebrow.

Peace had returned to the computer room.

'Right,' Chip said, 'this is what I want you to do.' He glanced at Patrick, but Patrick was typing more fluently now, with no stabs at the delete key. 'Once you've read it, shouldn't take you much longer, I want you to give it to that, um—' his hands fluttered '—friend of your, um, friend. You know, the, um, one with the dark hair. Right?'

I nodded, wondering where this was going.

'And I want you to tell *her*,' Chip said, 'to give it to her sister.'

Patrick tutted loudly from behind his computer monitor.

I ignored him. Chip, I think, didn't hear, because something strange was happening to his face. Chip's face, odd at the best of times, was having what I can only think of as the facial equivalent of an earthquake. A facequake. It was all jittery, like it couldn't decide whether to smile, frown, grimace, or gurn. Not that there's a huge difference between those expressions on Chip's ugly mug, but there was certainly a lot of movement involved. And he wasn't looking at me. He was looking anywhere but.

He said, too quickly, 'That okay? That good? Got it? Any questions?'

'No,' I said, too fascinated by what was going on with his face to think.

'Good.'

Then I said, 'Is she expecting it?'

'I thought you said you didn't have any questions.' He'd turned back to his computer, like he wanted to bury himself in that. 'Or is everything your friend over there said about you true?'

'I just—'

'No,' Chip said. 'She isn't. Give her the book to give to her sister, find out what the sister thinks, report back to me. Right?'

'Right,' I said.

'No more questions.'

I didn't know if that was a question or not, so I said, 'Right,' then went back to the ZX Spectrum I'd been using.

Ten minutes later, the bell went for afternoon lessons. Me and Patrick fell in beside each other, and though we didn't say anything to each other, we quite often don't anyway. The main difference was, this felt more like things were back to normal.

Which they weren't.

If a Martian had swooped down in his invisible UFO and (why, I've no idea) eavesdropped on Patrick and me as we walked home from school, he'd have thought things were back to how they'd always been. Patrick was explaining the superiority of the BBC Micro's implementation of Extended BASIC, with particular reference to the DEFPROC command, and I was doing my best to look like I cared, because I was grateful the day had been a lot less painful than I'd expected, and I had some excess guilt to burn off.

But the Martian would have been wrong.

The first sign was when we got to Patrick's house.

I thought, at this point, Patrick would have been glad to see the back of me for a bit, but instead he said, 'So do you want to come in? Have a cherry SodaStream?'

I should have realised, from the fact he was offering me one of his precious favourites, that something was up.

I said, 'Yeah, okay,' thinking it was a peace offering and I ought to go along with it.

Patrick looked smug, and it was only then I noticed Penny waiting at the end of Pritchard Lane, and realised Patrick had seen her, and had invited me in for that reason.

So I gave Penny a little shrug, and she gave one back to say she understood, and I joined Patrick.

'Mum,' he said, as he opened the front door, 'two cherry SodaStreams.'

I stepped inside, and immediately knew something was different. Mrs Luffley was usually there, ready to take our coats and shoes and provide us with slippers. But this time she wasn't. There wasn't even a busy noise coming from the kitchen.

Patrick had his shoes off and his coat half on the floor before he realised.

'Mum?'

Silence.

'Mum!'

'She might be in the loo,' I said.

'Don't be stupid. She knows I come home now.' He turned back to the house and shouted 'Mum!'

Then he pretty much screamed it. 'MUM!'

It was at this point I saw a small piece of paper on the floor with some neat handwriting on it. It must have been left on the little telephone table they have in the hall, and had blown off when we opened the front door.

'Patrick,' I said.

'Shut up!' he said, then carried on shouting, 'Mum! Mum!'

I tugged his sleeve.

'Get off!' he said.

'But—'

'I told you to shut up!' he said, right in my face.

'Patrick—'

He pushed me in the shoulder and said, 'Well, where is she?'

I said, 'Look, there's a note.'

He stared at it.

'What does it say?' I said, because he was still staring at it.

He picked it up and read it. 'She's had to go out. She'll be back soon.'

'See?' I said.

He glared at me.

I said, 'You didn't have to hit me.'

'I didn't hit you,' he said. 'And stop looking at me like that.'

I admit I was grinning, but it was all a bit stupid, wasn't it?

I stopped grinning, though, when Patrick said, 'It's alright for you. You don't have a mum. You're used to it.'

And before I knew it, I said, right back in his face, 'No it's not alright. And you don't get used to it. Ever.'

'Well why don't you go and cry on your girlfriend's shoulder, cos I don't care!'

I said, 'You're such a prat sometimes, Patrick.' Though I think I may have got the 'prat' and 'Patrick' mixed up and actually said, 'You're such a pat sometimes, Pratrick,' which, now I think about it, was even more insulting.

'Well at least I'm not some little girl's toy like you are.'

'Like you're your mummy's toy,' I said, then realised that was wrong, because it was the other way round. It had been a pathetic thing to say anyway, and didn't come close to how angry I felt. So, instead of letting Patrick have his go back at me, which I could see he was about to — probably some minor insult which would end the whole thing off — I pushed on and made things worse. I said, 'At least I'm not so self-centred I think the world revolves around me and nothing but me, and that I have to have the best of everything, and make sure everyone knows it. You're just jealous because I've got one thing, one little thing, you haven't got, and you can't stand it!'

Patrick flushed like I'd hit him, and shouted, 'Well you always thought you were better than me. Cos your mum's dead and you've got a brother, and now you've got a girl-friend. You think it makes you so *special*.'

And I said, 'You're an *arse*, Patrick,' which was about the strongest word I could think of right then.

And he said, 'Well you're the *arse* of *arses*.'

I'd have laughed at that if I hadn't been so angry. Arse of arses, indeed.

So then I slammed the door (I hadn't taken my shoes off, Penny had taught me that much) and I stalked off down his driveway. I was so angry I almost walked onto the London Road in front of a car. It honked me, and I gave it a glare, then I realised it was Mrs Luffley coming home, and it had been a hello-honk, not an angry one. (They ought to have different sounds, so you can tell.)

I half-waved, but couldn't smile, then crossed the road and almost ran down Pritchard Lane, to get out of the sight of Patrick, and his mum, and, really, everyone in the world.

37

First thing Friday morning, Joe burst into my room while I was still dozing and said, 'They've only blown up the bloody government! In Brighton!'

'Brighton?' I said, sitting up. Brighton is as far from us as London, but because it's not London (which you expect to get bombed by the IRA every so often), it seemed that much more scary.

'At their conference thingy. They were all in the same hotel. And they blew up the hotel!'

'Are they all dead?'

'No.'

'Is Maggie Thatcher dead?'

'No.'

'Do you think they'll cancel school?'

'Course not, you pilchard. Why should they cancel school?'

'There might be other bombs in other places.'

'Twit,' Joe said. 'Come and see it on the telly.' And he dashed back downstairs.

I got up. In my sleepy-headed way, it seemed pointless for anyone to blow up the government and for us to still have to go to school. But I knew that was only because school, at the moment, was a living misery. I was no longer friends with Patrick, but I still had to sit next to him because there weren't any other desks to sit at, and when I went to the computer room, he was there, too. Yesterday lunchtime, he'd got all chummy with some second years, and they'd sniggered when he made loud comments about the ZX Spectrum. (I later snuck over and typed 'I bought a BBC Micro' into his BBC Micro, then pressed ENTER, which made the computer come back with 'Mistake'. Which had seemed really witty at the time. Now, I just thought the whole thing was a bit pathetic.)

In the living room, Dad was on the edge of his seat, bowl of soggy cornflakes in one hand, spoon in the other, eyes fixed on the TV.

I got myself some Shreddies and joined him.

The TV showed images from early in the morning (the bomb had gone off at 2:54 a.m.) with firemen in yellow hard-hats and black jackets, ambulances arriving with flashing lights, people being carried out on stretchers, and a great jagged scar in the face of the hotel.

Dad patted my knee.

We sat there, not saying anything, and watched the same news report over and over.

It all felt curiously right. This was how I expected the world to be. I was only surprised there weren't more bombs going off, or bigger bombs, nuclear bombs, wiping out the whole south of England, not just a few rooms in a hotel on the coast.

I knew Dad and Joe felt the same. None of us said anything, but every so often Dad or Joe would nod, like they were agreeing, not with what the reporters said, but with the rubble, and the smoke, and the flashing emergency lights, and the shocked looks of the survivors. When the time came for the two of them to get ready for work, Joe threw some make-believe karate punches in the air, and he and Dad even had a quick wrestle over who should use the bathroom first. Dad won, of course, and Joe did some more karate kicks and punches while he waited, with accompanying Bruce Lee noises. When Dad came out, and was ready to leave, he stood behind me and watched the same news report through once more, before ruffling my hair (which he hasn't done since you were around, Mum) and going off to work.

Then Joe went, and I was on my own. It was an effort to turn off the TV.

I looked out the window at the kids on their way to

school, and the adults walking or driving to work, and was disappointed everything seemed so much the same. Surely things should be different. The world had shown its true face. People ought to be running, shouting, crying, or staring at the sky in fear. They ought to be carrying makeshift weapons, or first aid kits. Mums ought to be hugging their kids, not wanting to be parted from them, even for a day. There ought to be cars abandoned in the road and people boarding up their windows. The army should be driving through the streets in tanks.

But everything was the same.

Didn't they get it?

When Penny came by, she started talking about Top of the Pops the night before.

I said, 'Didn't you hear the news?'

'What news?'

'The bomb in Brighton.'

'Yeah, it's awful, isn't it? I mean, I don't exactly love the Conservatives, but I wouldn't want to blow them up. They're still sort of people.'

'But, what if it had been a nuclear bomb?'

'But it wasn't.'

'But what if it had been?'

'Okay, what if it had been?'

'Well, that would be — I mean, why *didn't* they make it a nuclear bomb?'

'Because that would be about a million billion times worse.'

'That's what I mean.'

She frowned. 'I don't get it.'

'I mean, what stopped them from making it worse? If they were going to plant a bomb, why didn't they plant the biggest bomb they could? Why — why doesn't the world, which has earthquakes and volcanoes and nuclear bombs, and all sorts of horrible diseases, just let them all out? What stops it? How can we just go to school each day when there's all these things that could happen, any moment?'

'I really think you worry too much, Tim.'

'No I don't,' I said. 'It's everyone else who doesn't worry enough.'

'Well, why are *you* going to school?'

'Well... because.'

'And that's why everyone else is. Because.'

'Because what?' I said, ignoring the fact it was my 'because'.

'Cos the alternative is to stay at home peeking out from behind the curtains, scared of all the things that might happen. I'm not saying they never will, but they don't happen much, and when they do, there's nothing you can do about it. So you might as well get on with your life and just, you know, hope it doesn't happen to you.'

'And you think that's alright?'

'Got any other ideas?'

'No,' I said.

'Well.'

We walked on for a bit. I spent a moment struggling to find the thing to say that would convince Penny I was right to worry about bombs and things. Then I thought maybe it was the proper thing, the manly thing, to do the worrying for both of us. To bear the burden. And that made me think of Dad, the way he seemed so heavy and silent sometimes, like he was made of lead. They use lead as shielding from radiation. Was Dad trying to shield me and Joe from knowing about the bad things?

If so, it wasn't working.

'So did you see Top of the Pops yesterday?' Penny said, making it clear she was in the non-worrying camp.

'Yeah.'

'Wasn't Sade cool?'

When we got to school, Penny sat by Kash, and I sat by Patrick. As usual, me and Patrick pretended each other didn't exist.

Mr Slaughter came in and took the register. Once that was done, there were still a few minutes before the bell, and I was only going to have to spend them in utter silence next to Patrick, so I thought, hey, I'm at school, and school is where they teach you things, so why don't I get them to teach me something I really want to know?

I got up and went to Mr Slaughter's desk.

'Mr Slaughter?'

'Yes, Tim?'

'I've got a question.'

'Go ahead.'

'It's about what happened this morning. The bomb in Brighton.'

'Ah, yes. Terrible. Terrible.'

'What I want to know is, if bad things like that happen, why don't they happen more often?'

Mr Slaughter visibly switched modes from form teacher to R.E. teacher, clasping his hands together as though about to pray, and peaking his eyebrows in a thoughtful manner.

'A good question, Tim. A very good question.'

I waited.

Mr Slaughter stared at his hands. I began to wonder if he was hoping the bell would save him from having to answer. Then he looked at me seriously and said, 'We have to re-member, those of us who have faith, that we are in God's hands, and God loves us.'

'But,' I said, '*some* bad things happen.'

'Indeed, and that is an important point.'

He considered his clasped hands a few moments more. He even tapped his index fingers together, as though wait-ing for an answer to come.

It came. 'It sometimes occurs that God sees fit to test us.

To test our faith.'

'And the bomb in Brighton was God doing that?'

'Not necessarily,' Mr Slaughter said. 'But possibly. I cannot, after all, claim to know His mind, now, can I?'

He beamed at me, as though we had both made our way through a very thorny conversation but come up trumps, and even ended with a joke.

'But,' I said (and tried to ignore the way his face fell), 'what about the people who were actually blown up? Was it a test of their faith, too? In which case, isn't it unfair they got tested so much more than the rest of us? And how can you tell God's not about to test *us* in the same way? And why does He have to do it with bombs, anyway? Can't He just look inside us?'

Mr Slaughter's smile turned a little tight. 'God tests our faith in Him because He loves us, Tim.'

I opened my mouth to ask about a dozen more questions, but the bell went.

Mr Slaughter, looking like he'd just been reprieved from one of God's more loving tests, said 'Do come to me again if you have further need of reassurance, Tim,' and was out the door before I could ask anything else.

Penny came up. 'What was that about?'

'I asked him about the bomb in Brighton.'

'God tests our faith because He loves us?' she said.

'Yeah, how did you know?'

She shrugged. 'I asked his advice about my mum, once.'

I went and got my bag. Patrick had already gone off to assembly, but after that would be waiting in his usual place, next to my usual place, in our first lesson of the day, Biology.

Patrick. Another of God's loving tests.

Biology lessons, too.

38

In the computer room at lunchtime, I faffed about doing nothing much on a ZX Spectrum (which people had been avoiding recently, because of Patrick's sarky comments, so in a way he'd helped me), till Chip, surfacing from a bout of coding, noticed me for the first time and said, 'Ah, Tim, finished the book yet?'

'Yeah, I have,' I said. I'd finished it the night before and put it in my schoolbag, but the morning's events had put it out of my head.

'And the, uh, mission?'

'I'll do it now.' It would get me away from any more snide remarks from Patrick.

'Good man,' Chip said, then turned back to his monitor with a painful-looking squint-and-pout combination which indicated total concentration.

I got my bag and went in search of Penny and Kash.

First I tried our form room. The usual bunch were there, on the back seats. This time, not wanting to get involved in another game of table rugby, I just poked my head in and looked. This got a few jeers from the girls, who started chanting, 'Find a penny, pick it up, all day long you'll have — a — good—' They paused, looked at one another, then said, '—luck.' And this, apparently, was hilarious, because they collapsed in giggles. I felt a blush coming on, so I left them to it. They'd obviously been planning to say something other than 'luck'.

I headed for the dining hall.

I'd just noticed Penny and Kash having their lunch at one of the tables (Penny saw me and waved), when Mr Witt, on lurking duty once more, said, 'Ah, the young man who's looking for someone.'

'Actually, I've just seen them,' I said, and was about to join them when I remembered Mr Witt taught Philosophy. If anyone ought to know things, he should.

'Mr Witt?' I said.

'That is I,' he replied, which should have told me straightaway this wasn't going to be an easy conversation.

'You know the bomb that went off this morning, in Brighton?'

'I know *of* it.'

I took that as a yes. 'Well, why didn't they make it worse? I mean, they could have put loads and loads of explosives in it, and really blown up the whole hotel, or even the whole of Brighton, couldn't they?'

'Assuming they had the resources.'

'And bad things in general, like earthquakes, and floods and things, and accidents, why don't they happen more often, or be worse when they do?'

'Hmm,' he said. He angled his head forward, as though to bury his chin in his neck, and regarded me from under his brow. 'First, we must define our terms. When you say "bad things", you are, of course, talking from a merely human perspective. To, for instance, the planet as a whole, earthquakes and floods and, as you say, "things", are not bad, *per se*, but merely part of the natural course of events, are they not? However, taking your question more in the spirit in which it was asked than the exact terms which you employed, what say we rephrase it thus: Why, when accidents occur — accidents including earthquakes, floods, and even bombs, for the purposes of this question — why, when these occur, is their impact not worse, from a purely anthropocentric point of view? Put thus, we find we may as well be asking why they are not less bad, or why they happen at all. Alternatively, if we broaden our definition of "accidents" not only to include acts of terrorism and natural disasters, but minor events out of our control, such as being drenched in a rain shower, or finding a piece of chewing gum stuck to one's shoe, we might say that all of life is nothing but a series of accidents, both good and bad, to use your own crude terminology, so we must, in fact, redefine and, indeed, refine, our terms further, if we are to provide a properly accurate wording to our question. Must we not?'

'Um...' I said.

Mr Witt, I could tell, was waiting for more than that.

So I said, 'But what's the answer?'

'But the answer to what?'

'To, um, why more bad things don't happen?'

'Young man,' he said, with a smile and a shake of the head, 'if I replied to so crude a question with as simple an answer as you are evidently expecting, I could hardly call myself qualified to teach Philosophy, now could I? Philosophy is about further defining our terms to better understand the questions we ask — to find, in fact, questions which *can* be asked. As for answers...' He shook his head with a pained expression.

'Um, thanks, then,' I said, and joined Kash and Penny, who had by now almost finished their lunch.

'Matching wits with Mr Witt?' Penny said, as I sat down.

'I tried asking him what I asked Mr Slaughter.'

'And?'

'He told me I should be asking a different question. At least, I think that's what he told me.'

Penny sighed. 'This is school, Tim. You don't come here to learn things. You come here to be educated.'

Kash looked at me studiously. 'What is the question you asked?'

'Why, if bad things like the bomb in Brighton are going to happen, they don't happen more often, or be worse when they do.'

Kash gave a short, sharp, 'Hm.' I couldn't tell if that was contempt or contemplation.

The truth was, Mum, I didn't quite know where I stood with Kash. I hadn't talked to her much, and I still remembered that warning glare I'd got from her back when she and Penny had come to the computer room and Penny had invited me round her house for the first time. It seemed so long ago, but that glare was still vivid in my memory. I had the vague feeling she disapproved of me, or was ready to disapprove at a moment's notice. She almost scared me as much as Penny's mum.

I took Chip's book out of my bag.

'Chip wanted me to give this to you, to give to your sister,' I said.

Kash took the book and turned it over.

'Chip?' she said.

'Mm.'

'The ugly guy in the computer room?'

'Yeah.'

'He asked you to give me this to give to my sister?'

'Yeah.'

'Why?'

'I don't know. Don't you?'

'Why should I know?'

'Um, I don't know. He just asked, that's all.'

Kash held the book like she was ready to drop it the moment it wriggled, and said, 'She has read it.'

'Oh,' I said.

'I have read it, too,' Kash said.

'What did you think? And what did your sister think?'

'Are you asking, or is it Chip who's asking?'

'Um, Chip,' I said. 'I mean, he asked me to ask what your sister thought. I asked what you thought.'

Kash nodded, as though to say, 'I'm glad we've got that settled.' Then she said, 'It is perverse.'

(That word again!)

She handed the book back.

'Um,' I said, 'is that what you think or what your sister thinks?'

'Both.'

'Shall I tell him she didn't like it, then?'

'Of course not!' She took the book back and mused over it some more. Then she turned to Penny, 'I know who Tim should ask. Mr Bosworth.'

'Should ask?' I said.

'Your question,' Kash said.

Penny broke into a grin. 'Of course!'

'He will be in the staff room,' Kash said.

'We can go there now,' Penny said.

'Mr Bosworth?' I said. 'But he teaches history.'

Kash said, 'And what is history but a list of disasters and bad things that happened? You have asked Mr Slaughter and Mr Witt, but they only have abstract ideas. You need to ask someone with concrete examples.'

Penny nodded at me encouragingly.

'Okay,' I said, still unsure. 'And shall I give Chip his book back?'

'No,' Kash said. 'I will go to my sister and give it to her, and she can go to the computer room and give it back herself.'

'He won't be expecting that,' I said.

'Exactly,' Kash said, and ate her last forkful of lunch with a smile. I'm not sure, but I think that was the first time I'd seen her smile. It wasn't much less scary than her glare.

I looked at Penny, not entirely sure what was going on. But Penny just gave me a grin that could have meant anything.

39

I tend to avoid the staff room as much as possible, and don't even like going near it. As far as I'm concerned, it's where teachers go to stop being teachers for a while, and the last thing they want is for pupils to come along and remind them that, sorry, they *are* still teachers, and there's no escaping it. This is why I think you need an absolutely watertight reason for going there, and I wasn't sure this was one.

Penny, however, seemed completely confident.

I've noticed this about her. She's confident about so many things. I'm only confident about computers, which are easy to be confident about, because they're nothing but facts. Everything about them can be looked up and checked, then tested in the privacy of your own bedroom where no one can see you make a total prat of yourself if you get it wrong. I don't know how to deal with things which aren't facts and can't be checked, but the more I think about it, the more I realise the world is made up of unfacty, uncheckable things. Things like people, and pop music, and the likelihood of getting through the day without being blown up by a nuclear bomb. Penny, however, is completely at ease with these things.

When we got there, it was Penny who knocked on the staff room door.

I said, in a panic, 'I don't know what to say.'

'Just say the same thing you said to Mr Slaughter and Mr Witt.'

'But I can't remember.' Suddenly, I couldn't. My mind had gone a defensive blank.

Mrs Norman answered the door. She had a tissue in her hand and looked teary, as usual. I wondered if the other teachers gave her as much of a hard time as her pupils did, then she sneezed and I realised she had a cold.

'Yes?' she said, between nose-squeezes with her tissue.

'Is Mr Bosworth there?'

'Oh, hang on.' She turned and called, 'Monty? Two for you.'

This is another thing I don't like about the staff room. Teachers calling each other by their first names. It doesn't seem right.

A moment later, Mr Bosworth appeared, brushing crumbs off the front of his waistcoat with one hand while holding a custard cream biscuit in the other.

'Penny Poundley and Timothy Morrow,' he said. 'Would you like a toffee?'

'Hello Mr Bosworth, thank you,' Penny said, taking a toffee from the bag as he offered it. 'Tim has a question he wants to ask.'

My hand hovered over the bag of toffees. There was only one left.

Mr Bosworth rustled the bag. 'Don't worry, young man. Plenty more where that came from. Pop it in your mouth and ask your question. Or, for the sake of clarity, the other way round.'

I took the toffee and said, quickly, before it went out of my head, 'It's about the bomb in Brighton, Mr Bosworth. Or not just that. About bad things, all sorts. You know, earthquakes, and floods and things. And bombs.'

'Ah,' said Mr Bosworth, gravely.

'I don't know if you know,' I said, 'because I asked Mr Slaughter, and he just said it was because God loves us, and I asked Mr Witt and he said I'd asked the wrong question, but what I want to know is—'

''Scuse me,' said a teacher I didn't know, and we all got out of his way so he could get into the staff room. (Another scary thing about the staff room. Teachers you don't know.)

'What I want to know is,' I continued, once he'd gone, 'is why, if bad things happen, they aren't much worse. Or they don't happen a lot more. Because it seems so many bad things *could* happen, or are waiting to happen, and I'm always thinking they're *bound* to happen, but they don't, except one every so often like this morning, and I don't know if it's just we're lucky, or what.' And then I realised what went to the heart of it, what I'd been wanting to say since I'd said all this to Penny on the way in to school. 'It just seems so unfair. I mean, life could be just, you know, really good, really—' (spit it out) '—nice, but these things come along, and it's like they're telling you how bad things could be instead.'

Which sounded a bit naff, but it was actually it, at last.

'Hmm,' said Mr Bosworth.

He put the empty toffee bag into his pocket, rummaged, and produced another.

'Boiled sweet?'

Penny, still chewing her toffee, shook her head.

I quickly popped my toffee into my mouth, and shook my head too.

Mr Bosworth gave himself a boiled sweet and looked thoughtful.

'History,' he said (though it was more like 'hishtory' because of the boiled sweet), 'is full of terrible things. Wars, famines, plagues, so on. It's easy to forget, looking at a list of important historical events, how much ordinary life went on in the meantime. People lived their lives while Napoleon ravaged Europe just as they did while the barbarian hordes savaged the Roman Empire. Ordinary lives, often filled with quietly wonderful events, unrecorded by history. May mornings, the call of a cuckoo, a first kiss. And while it is the major events, the terrible events, that most easily lend themselves to the study of history, it is these quietly wonderful events that make up our lives. Alas, there are bad things, too. We are all mortal. We all have at least one bad thing waiting for us. But that, young Tim, is already decided. Nothing we can do about it. It's the rest — the moments before and between — that we have our say in. So, do we pause to appreciate the glorious sunset, or pass on, telling ourselves it's merely an accident of the light? Do we go out of our way to study poetry, or listen to music, or do we tell ourselves such things cannot matter, because they cannot save us from death, or pain, or sadness? Do we stop ourselves from falling in love—' and for some reason at this point he gave Penny and me a particularly warm smile, and Penny giggled '—because ultimately it cannot matter? No. We do those things all the more, simply because it is the one thing we *can* do, as human beings, in the face of such an imposing, frightening, and baffling universe.'

He paused and jiggled his bag of boiled sweets.

'I fear, however, that my words cannot help you. This is an old man's view. Youth, being youth, is passionate, is concerned. It struggles — and rightly so — to set things right. But always against the tide. So, my advice is not to worry, young man, though I know you will. Useless advice, then. But, in the meantime, enjoy life all you can, for all it can offer. That way, when bad things do happen, and we can, alas, be sure they will, you will at least be able to shake your fist at them and say, "Yes, but I *lived*!"'

He straightened up and smiled. 'How did I do?'

'That was beautiful,' said Penny, beaming, and with a touch of the Mrs Norman about her eyes.

I wasn't as convinced. 'So you're saying there isn't an answer?'

'Alas, I am.' Mr Bosworth put his hand on my shoulder. 'Frightening, isn't it? But look at it this way. You have lived through a war already — the war in the Falklands — you have lived through civil strife and political unrest, which are the bread and butter of history. Yet you have survived. You have your life ahead of you, just coming into your hands. You have — am I right? — this young lady here —

am I?' (Penny blushed and looked at her shoes.) 'You have, in other words, the world — or as much of it as anyone is ever going to have. Live, young man, live! And — oh, have a boiled sweet.'

So I took a sweet, and Penny took a sweet, and Mr Bosworth went back into the staff room. I'm not sure, but I think I heard him singing in a low, resonant voice once the door had closed.

(That's another thing I don't like about the staff room. Teachers not acting like teachers should.)

'Wasn't that wonderful?' Penny said.

I said, 'Yeah,' but I wasn't entirely sure. I still didn't have my answer. Except to know there wasn't one.

'I wish Kash had been there.'

'Wouldn't she just have said he was talking nonsense?' I said. Though maybe that was more what *I* thought.

Penny shrugged. 'It was beautiful nonsense all the same.' She checked her watch. 'Seven minutes to the bell. I have to go to the, um, so, see you later.'

And off she went. I wondered what to do for seven minutes, then decided I ought to report the completion of my 'mission' to Chip. If he didn't know already.

The computer room was mostly empty, though Patrick was there (he looked up when I came in, saw it was me, then focused through me at the far wall). Chip was struggling with that massive flowchart of taped-together sheets of squared paper. Some of it had fallen apart and scattered on the floor, but he didn't seem to notice. He was shaking his head and following two separate paths with his right and left index fingers, muttering to himself as he did.

'Hi, Chip,' I said. 'I gave her the book to give to her sister.'

He said, 'Yeah,' like he was no longer sure I should have.

'She said her sister had read it.'

'Yeah.' Even more unsure.

'Apparently she said it was, um...' I still couldn't bring myself to say the word 'perverse'. It's not a word I've ever said before, and the computer room didn't seem like the place to start.

'Yeah,' Chip said again, resigned now. And then, though I was already close enough that only I could hear him, he beckoned me closer. 'She came up here.'

'Kash said she might.'

Chip swept a hand over his disintegrating flowchart. 'Now I don't know where I am. I didn't plan for it. You *can't* plan for it.'

'What is all this?' I said.

He slapped his hands on the enormous chart, laying it as flat as he could. 'This, my friend, is the fruit of weeks of thought and research. It was my master plan. Its logic was flawless, checked and re-checked and checked again. And now it's worthless.'

'Yeah, but, what is it? Or, was it?'

Chip glanced at Patrick, then dropped his voice even lower. 'It's how to ask a girl out. You know — a girl.'

I looked at it. Suddenly the boxes, diamonds, ellipses and rhombuses made sense. 'Gather data — likes, dislikes, etc.' That was what all this business with the 'mission' had been about. 'Does she say yes?' Obvious. And, 'Consult an expert'.

'Who was the expert?' I said.

Chip looked at me wonderingly. 'You.'

'Eh?'

'That was the point this whole thing took off. I mean, you're the one who had girls coming up to the computer room — a place girls just don't go. And I realised, then and there, this Tim, he's the one who knows. He's my expert.'

'But I'm not an expert!'

'But you got one. This Penny of yours.'

'Yeah, but... That was... I mean...' What was it? Luck? An accident? One of the good things that happen in the face of the bad? Suddenly, I realised just how amazing it was that she'd even started talking to me, let alone continued, and that we'd become friends. It had all seemed so natural, not amazing. But it was amazing. And natural. It was Penny who had made it so natural, not me. If it was up to me, it would have gone wrong any number of times and got nowhere. Perhaps Mr Bosworth had been right. What had he said? Quietly wonderful events. And that was what Penny was, wasn't she? An ongoing, quietly wonderful event.

'See?' Chip said, waving a hand over his forlorn-looking flowchart. 'Even you, the expert, don't know how it works.'

'So,' I said, 'when Kash's sister came up here, did she, I mean, did she say no, then?'

'There was no yes or no about it. She bypassed all that. She went straight to stage thirty-three, when I'd only mapped out as far as stage four. She — Tim, these girls, they can read your mind, did you know that?'

'Yeah. Actually, I did.'

'It just... defies... all logic.'

He sat, or collapsed is probably a better word for it, in his chair and tapped a few keys on his BBC Micro. 'It's not like computers, Tim.' He pressed enter, and the program he'd been working on began to scroll up the screen, lines and lines and lines of it. 'I know what every instruction does. I've got the whole thing up here, in me head. All the little bits, fitting together to make this one big thing. When I'm coding, it's like I'm standing in the middle of it, this whole new country I've discovered. I can see how it fits together. How it works *just right*. Like all these little Lego bricks, snapped into place. They add up, Tim. They add up. They're logical. And it's all just *right*.'

'Yeah,' I said, a bit breathlessly, because I knew exactly what he was talking about.

'And that's how the world should be,' he said. 'But it's not. It's messy. Things working against each other, not fitting together, going in opposite directions. In here' (he tapped his head) 'it's like clockwork. Out there, it's more like dodgem cars. If I could, I'd disappear up here. The only trouble is, Tim, there aren't any girls up here. Not, you know, real ones, anyway.'

And he sat there for a while, staring at the lines of code that were still scrolling past.

'Um,' I said, wondering if I should ask, 'what *is* stage thirty-three?'

He gave me the haunted look of a man who understood nothing anymore. 'We're going to the flicks this Saturday.' Then he turned to stare at his computer monitor and was still staring when the bell went.

After lunch we had R.E., and after R.E. we had Games.

I didn't care. The more I thought about it, the more I realised Mr Bosworth was right. There were loads of bad things waiting to happen in life — I could, and often did, think of hundreds a day. Nuclear wars, terrorist bombs, car accidents and illnesses, in all their varieties. But I didn't think of the good things, even when they were staring me in the face. And there was Penny, quite frequently staring me in the face.

I kept looking at the back of her head in R.E., and every time felt this flood of wonderfulness. I thought, 'She exists. Penny exists. In the world. The same world as me.' I wanted to tell someone, but of course the only person was Patrick, and though I felt I ought to, really, forgive him and make friends again, I didn't think telling him how wonderful it was to be in the same universe as Penny would quite do it for him.

At the end of R.E., Mr Slaughter gave me a nod and a wink, as though to say, 'I see our little talk has had its effect,' but I didn't care. I didn't even care when Mr Dangerfield, deciding it wasn't muddy enough for rugby, sent us on a cross country run. I ran it, and didn't even come in last.

Walking home, I chatted with Penny, wondering if I should tell her how wonderful she was, but then I thought surely she knew, and anyway, it would sound silly. She seemed as happy as me. She said that she and her mum were going to visit her grandfather on Sunday, but maybe we could go to town together on Saturday.

Home in my room, I fired up my ZX Spectrum and made a renewed effort to escape the goblin dungeons in The Hobbit. I actually managed it, though I immediately got stuck in the spider-haunted woods.

Dad came home early.

I called hello, just to let him know I was there.

After a bit, to my surprise, he came up.

'Tim,' he said.

'Hi, Dad.'

He came into my room.

'Been meaning to give you your pocket money. From last week. And a little bit extra, because it's late.'

'Cor, thanks, Dad.'

He lingered.

'So,' he said. 'This girl says you know a lot about computers.'

'Yeah,' I said.

'Wouldn't have thought there was much to know.'

'There is. Lots.'

'Well,' he said.

Suddenly I wanted to include him in it all. I mean, how good I was feeling at that moment. I wanted him to feel it, too. I wanted it all to go right between us. None of this not talking. So why not go straight to the heart of it?

'Dad?'

'Mm-hm?'

'I was wondering...' I kept looking at the screen, because this was difficult to say. 'I was wondering if there's a photo of — of Mum anywhere.'

Dad didn't say anything, so I pushed on.

'Cos we could put it up. In the living room, maybe. Just to, you know, because it's—'

'Don't—' he almost shouted, then forced his voice quieter '—push it.'

I stared at my computer screen and swallowed.

I could hear him moving about behind me, a lion in my tiny bedroom.

'It's,' he said, and it was like he was squeezing the words out from the bottom of a steel toothpaste tube, 'not — right.'

I didn't know if he meant what I'd said, or what happened to you, Mum. Or just everything.

I said, 'We don't have to—'

'You don't know,' he said, like he was trying not to shout it at me. 'And you can't — there's nothing—'

And then he left.

I heard him pause on the landing, breathing loudly, as though he was about to shout at me, or batter the walls, then he went downstairs.

I waited, listening.

I heard things clattering and bashing in the kitchen.

I just couldn't do anything, then, but sit and listen. Even when he finished his clattering and bashing and put the TV on.

When Joe came home, Dad gave him instructions about dinner, then went to the pub.

41

Next day, after breakfast (and before Dad got up), I went round Penny's. We watched Saturday Superstore on TV. Her mum appeared at ten o'clock and leant in the doorway, crunching toast. She had her paint-smeared dressing gown on, but at least with normal clothes underneath.

'Morning, you two,' she said.

'Good morning,' I said, and stopped myself before I started to say 'Mrs Poundley'. I still wasn't sure what to call her, and didn't want to attempt anything while she was blocking the only exit.

'Morning Mum,' Penny said, and looked very pleased her mum had included me in her good morning.

'Any plans for today?'

'Going up town later,' Penny said.

Her mum finished her toast and watched the TV. She even gave a half-amused laugh at Cheggers' antics with a rubber hammer. Then she said, 'Well, hang around a bit and you might have a cake. I'm going to bake something for tomorrow.' She said this as though it was a duty for all of us, the baking of cakes and the eating of them. Then she went into the kitchen.

Penny gave me a look that said 'See? She can be nice sometimes.'

Her mum came back with some warm fairy cakes three quarters of an hour later. They were a bit solid, but a cake is a cake, so I ate it, taking half in my first bite.

'What do you think of my efforts, then, Tim?'

I hadn't expected to be quizzed. My mouth was too dry and crumby to say anything legible. I tried, 'Mm, nice,' but it sounded more like, 'Mmf, knife.'

Penny and her mum thought this was hilarious.

Then Penny said she'd make some tea (which I desperately needed, to wash down the cake), and for a moment it was just me and her mum in the living room.

'Don't worry,' her mum said, lazily. 'I've never been great at cakes. Or mothery things generally. Maybe you guessed.' She patted her dressing gown pockets till she found her cigarettes. 'Have a nice time in town.' Then she went off to her studio.

Penny came back with our teas, grinning more than ever.

We were in the hallway getting ready to go when the phone rang.

Penny answered.

'Hello? Hello grandad.' She listened, looking solemn. 'Yes... Yes, I'll get her.'

She put down the phone and went to get her mum.

When she came back, she stood by me while her mum picked up the receiver and said, 'Hi,' in a rather short, unfriendly way, then listened.

I looked at Penny, wondering what was going on. Penny watched her mother, who just looked at her own finger, tapping with increasing impatience on the telephone table.

'Hm,' her mum said. Then, 'No.' Then, 'No.' Then she turned her back on us and said, 'I can't say I'm surprised.' Then, 'You know exactly what I mean.'

Penny looked at me. It was a look that said something was going wrong.

After a few more, increasingly testy, repetitions of 'You know exactly what I mean,' from her mum, Penny nodded at the front door, and we slipped out.

'What's happened?' I said.

At first, Penny just looked glum. We left Silversmith Cottage's garden and started down Fallow Lane.

'It's not fair,' she said.

We walked to the end of Fallow Lane and turned up the Hixfield Road towards town.

'He's cancelled,' she said. 'Again.'

'Your grandad?'

'He's always doing it.'

'Why?'

'It's a silly, stupid game.'

We walked on a bit more, then Penny sighed.

'It's always like this. We make plans to go up there, then at the last minute one or the other cancels. It's either Mum with her moods or grandad saying he's got something really important he just *has* to do. It's all a game. Which one cancels first, and with the stupidest reason. I don't know why they bother. And now Mum's going to be in a right mood again. It's not fair.'

She took hold of my sleeve. 'She was okay this morning. You saw her. She was okay. And that should have lasted all week. We'd only just got through the last one, and now this. It's not fair. I hate it.'

She let go of my sleeve and started chewing her thumb.

I said, 'Why do they make arrangements if they know they're just going to cancel?'

'I don't know. She was actually excited this time. I mean, she made cakes, and that's not exactly an everyday occurrence.'

'Good thing,' I said, rubbing my tummy, and was pleased to see her smile a bit.

She went back to looking glum, but more thoughtful-glum this time. 'Even when we do go up, they just argue. It's like arguing's how they get on, the only way they know of talking to each other. But at least it means they're together. You can see, between the arguments, that they sort of, I don't know, need to be together, just a bit. If they could just get together and shut up, they'd be okay. It's having to talk that does it. But when they're on the phone, it's only ever talk, and that's where everything goes wrong. Believe me, what you heard was just the beginning. They'll go on like that for about half an hour, till they're shouting at each other. Then it's a game of who makes the other hang up. And Mum'll be in a mood for days, now. I hate it. It's so unfair.'

Then she said, quietly, 'I don't want to end up like that. I'd rather die in a nuclear war.'

We walked in silence for a bit. As we came to town, Penny made an effort and shrugged the whole thing off. But it came back once we'd finished in town and were heading home.

'See you Monday,' she said, as we got to Silversmith Cottage's gate. She sounded like she knew she wasn't going to enjoy the rest of the weekend.

'We could do something tomorrow,' I said.

'Think I'd better stick around. Stop her doing herself an injury. Best if you don't come round, really.'

'Good luck,' I said, knowing how lame it sounded.

She shrugged but smiled, then went through the gate to her garden. She gave me a last-minute wave at the door, and disappeared.

I spent the rest of the day playing Terror-Daktil 4D. Life would be so much easier if all we had to deal with were monstrous, hungry dinosaurs.

42

Sunday, I started off feeling gloomy about everything.

Dad had taken to leaving the room if I came in and it was just me and him in it. Not obviously, but he always did it. I'd sit there silently counting, and never get to ten. Joe pretended not to notice, and to make sure he didn't have to, spent as much time as possible fiddling with his motorbike in the back garden. Then there was Patrick at school. And now there was Penny's mum, back to being the mad old woman of Fallow Lane again, making Penny unhappy.

I decided to load up ELSIE, who, as a computer psychiatrist, ought to know about these things.

```
"Hi, I'm Elsie, what's your problem?"
Dad's not talking to me.
"Are you saying no just to be negative?"
I didn't say no.
"You are being a bit negative."
```

Perhaps Penny was right about conversations with computers.

I played my Queen tape, paying particular attention to the songs It's a Hard Life and I Want to Break Free.

After that, I played Codename MAT for a bit, defending the solar system from Myon invaders. Then I remembered: half term! We had five more days of school, then it was half term. That meant a whole week of not having to sit next to Patrick. Even better, it meant a whole week of just me and Penny. We could do things like go on day trips. Up to London on the train, maybe. Or just stay here, in my house, because we'd have it all to ourselves, with Dad and Joe at work. Her mum could go as mad as she wanted.

Suddenly it didn't seem gloomy at all.

It was Penny. Penny made it okay. There could be a thousand million things wrong with the world, but as long as she was in it, it was okay. Thinking that gave me this weird, dizzy feeling, like I was standing on top of the highest building in the world.

There's no point telling you much about that week before half term, because it was as I've already said. Dad not talking to me, Joe pretending not to notice, Patrick at school. And Penny. Penny didn't seem as cheerful as usual, but she was dealing with her mad mum, so that was under-standable. I did my best to cheer her up, and it seemed to work. I thought it did, anyway. I mean, she'd dealt with her mad mum before, loads of times. How could this be any different?

Then all of a sudden it was Friday, and then it was the end of school on Friday, and then it was me and Penny walking home. Free. For a whole week. I was all excited now we'd finally got there. Penny wasn't as excited, and it was only as we started down Pritchard Lane that I realised she was probably thinking about having to spend the entire half term week locked in the house with her mum, because I hadn't mentioned any of my ideas about what we could do. I was just about to tell her when a car came up to the kerb beside us.

We kept walking, but it rolled on at the same pace.

Then the driver wound down his window and said, 'Fancy a milkshake?'

Penny stopped.

The driver had short, light-coloured hair, and a long face which was nearly all grin. I remember thinking the grin was familiar, but not the face.

Then the grin popped up on Penny's face, too, and she said, 'Daddy!'

'C'mere, Ape!' he said, and held out an arm. Penny ducked into it and hugged her dad through the car window.

(I thought, did he just call her an ape?)

'Daddy!' she said, again, like she had to make herself believe it.

'So, do you fancy a milkshake, or what?'

'But what are you doing here?'

'I came to ask if you wanted a milkshake, Ape.'

(There he was again, calling her an ape.)

She turned to me with dazed eyes and the biggest grin I'd ever seen on her face, like she'd been punched by a great big happy-making boxing glove.

Her dad said, 'Your friend can come too, if you want.'

I think he said it just to be polite, but Penny said, 'You will, won't you, Tim?'

'Only at the 'Appy Eater down the road,' her dad said. (He meant 'Happy Eater'.) 'Just a quick milkshake.' Like the small print to the offer.

I knew the answer had to be no. Penny would want to be with her dad, and her dad, I was sure, would want to be with her. But I was just about to say this when Penny either read it on my face or used those mind-reading powers I still wasn't sure she didn't have, and looked ready to be disappointed, so I could only shrug and say, 'Yeah, okay.'

'Fab!' Penny said, and danced over to the passenger side.

I got in the back.

'Seat belt on?' her dad said. 'Clunk-click and all that.'

Penny snapped hers into place and grinned at him, bouncing in the seat like an eager-to-go five year old.

I didn't have a seat belt.

'None in the back,' her dad said. 'You'll just 'ave to 'ang on.' (It was like the h-key on his inner keyboard had given up.)

He did a kerb-mounting turn, then proceeded at launch speed towards the junction with the London Road. For a moment I thought he was going to cross it without stopping, but he braked at the last minute, then edged forward, despite the oncoming traffic, muttering, 'Come on you buggers, let me go.' Then there was a gap and we were heading down the London Road (past Patrick's house, which I looked at, hoping he'd see me going by in a strange car and realise I had an interesting life), past the turning to the school, past the sign that told people coming the other way they were entering Eastead (and so, technically, we were leaving it, meaning this was a genuine trip somewhere), then into the car park of the Happy Eater, with its big orange Pac-Man sign (which was either pointing into its mouth asking to be fed, or trying to make itself sick afterwards, depending on your view). I realised that, though we often used to come here with you, Mum, for the occasional special Saturday meal, the last time I'd been was with Gramps, when he came down because of Dad not working, and that was ages ago.

'All safe and sound?' Penny's dad said.

Penny giggled, then had a bit of difficulty undoing her seatbelt. Her dad said, 'Pesky things!' and got into a comic struggle with the release button, which made Penny giggle even more.

After that, he looked over his shoulder at me. ''Ow about you, Tom?'

'Tim,' Penny said.

'Tim —Tom-Tim, Tim-Tom — oh, you 'aven't got a seat belt, 'ave you? Right, in we go. Those milkshakes won't wait. Well, they will. Still, it's not polite to keep them waiting.'

'Dad,' Penny said, in a what-are-you-like kind of way.

I trailed behind as we crossed the car park. Penny put her hands in her jacket pockets just as her dad reached out to take her hand in his. Getting her elbow, he said, 'Oops,' and she, thinking he was tapping her arm to get her attention said, 'Hmm?' Then she realised, said 'Oh,' and took his hand just as they went into the restaurant.

I knew I should have said no.

43

'Choose a table, Ape,' Penny's dad said. 'I'll be over in a sec.'

The place was pretty much empty, apart from a trucker making his way through a Real American Hamburger, and an old couple having tea in a corner. Penny chose a table by the window looking onto the London Road. I found myself wishing we'd come here, just me and her, for an end-of-school celebration. Maybe we could do it this coming half term week, pocket money permitting.

'Why does he keep calling you that?' I said, in a low voice, though her dad had disappeared into the bathroom and wasn't about to hear.

'Hape?' she said, with an 'h' her dad hadn't used. 'It's short for ha'penny. You know, half-penny. He's always called me that.' She smiled, embarrassed and happy in equal parts, then said, 'So, which do you want, chocolate, strawberry or banana?'

'Chocolate.'

'I'll have chocolate, too.'

'Does he often do this?' I said.

'No. I haven't heard from him since my birthday, actually. I haven't *seen* him for about a year before that.'

'Doesn't he live up in London?'

'Mm.'

'It's a long way to come for a milkshake.'

She shrugged, then started folding a paper napkin into increasingly smaller triangles.

'Do you like him?' she said.

'Don't know him,' I said. I knew she wanted me to say yes, but I didn't want to. Still, I knew I couldn't say no.

She tried not to look disappointed. 'I mean, first impressions.' Her napkin was now folded too many times to fold anymore, so she opened it up and stood it on the table, a mini pyramid. Her eyes still on that, she said, 'Don't you think he's funny?'

I struggled for a moment, but in the end couldn't say anything other than 'Yeah' without upsetting her. (Though to myself, I added, 'Funny-peculiar, not funny ha-ha.')

She gave me a grateful smile. Instantly, I realised I was being sulky and wished I wasn't. Maybe he was funny ha-ha. A bit.

Her look drifted over my shoulder and her smile went gooey again, so I knew her dad had re-emerged. He sat next to me, to be opposite her.

'So,' he said, 'milkshakes all round. No square milk-shakes for us.'

Penny giggled far more than that silly joke deserved, and I instantly changed my mind back. Funny peculiar it was.

The waitress came over, giving a little scribble in the corner of her notepad to check her pen was working.

'Ape?' Penny's dad said. No 'h' about it.

'Chocolate.'

'Chocolate milkshake for the young lady. Might as well have chocolate for me, too. And the young man will have..?'

'Strawberry,' I said. I know it's silly. I just didn't want to have what he was having.

I tried not to, then had to glance at Penny. She was giving me an odd look. For a moment I was sure she not only knew why I'd changed my mind, but could calculate the exact degree of sulk I was in to five decimal places, and how much it was really nothing but jealousy of her dad and the effect he so easily had on her, then she smiled, so maybe she simply thought I wanted strawberry instead. That, or she'd seen right through me but had forgiven me anyway, which made me feel even worse.

'Now, what's this, Ape?' her dad said. 'An empty spot on that jacket of yours? And, eh, what 'ave we here?' He put his hand in his pocket and came out with a great big round Top of the Pops badge. 'Is that about the right size? Or maybe this?' He put his other hand in his other pocket and came out with a Cheggers Plays Pop one.

'Thanks, Dad!' she said, and immediately set about pinning them on.

Her dad basked in it.

Our milkshakes arrived.

I remembered how much I hated strawberry.

He asked her about school, and she said it was okay. She asked him about work, and he said it was okay. He did a few impressions of the TV people he'd worked with and got us to guess who they were. I couldn't think of any of them. Penny gave me a look that said I wasn't trying. So, the next one, I said, 'Um, Mike Yarwood?'

She gave me even more of a look.

'So why *are* you here?' she asked, once he'd run out of silly voices.

He sucked up the last of his milkshake noisily, then kept doing it, gurgling the last few bubbles and giving Penny a googly-eyed look till she giggled. Then he said, 'Something to tell you. But in a bit.'

He meant when they'd got rid of me.

He glanced at his watch, as if to underline the point.

Penny finished her milkshake and said she had to go to the loo.

I tried to make the last inch of my milkshake last as long as possible, so I didn't have to talk to him. I sucked it all up, right down to the gritty, over-sweet dregs.

He seemed happy at first to pretend I wasn't there. Then, after a bit, realising he ought to make an effort, he said, 'In Penny's class, are you?'

'Yeah,' I said.

'Ah.'

And that was it.

Penny came back and sat down. 'One thing, Dad. Does Mum know you're here?'

'Not unless she's perfected 'er crystal ball technique,' he said, and mimed it with wibbly-wobbly fingers and spooky eyes.

Penny smiled, but also gave him a stop-it kind of look. 'But are you going to see her?'

'Could 'ave a word.'

Penny fiddled with a ketchup sachet. 'It's just, it might not be such a good idea right now. She's a bit, well, you know how she can get? She's not at her best at the moment.'

'She'll be fine,' he said.

Penny looked dubious.

'Fine,' he repeated, shaking his head.

We took off back up the London Road, Sweeney-style, and I was dropped outside my house.

I realised I hadn't had a chance to say anything to Penny about the coming week, what we could do, and so on.

I got out of the car and said, 'Thanks for the milkshake, Mr, um.' And although I knew he had to be called Poundley, I couldn't bring myself to say it, because of what had happened when I'd tried it with Penny's mum.

'Just call me Ian, uh, Tom, Tim, Tim-Tom.'

Then I barely had time to wave at Penny before he'd zoomed off down the road.

44

Waking up on the Saturday at the start of half term is like waking up to a whole new world. It's how life ought to be, every day, if only you could realise how amazing it is simply to be alive. And if you didn't have to go to school.

I lay in bed and made plans for the week ahead. Penny plans. Then I went downstairs and watched The Littlest Hobo, which is about a dog wandering across America solving people's problems (which in reality it would have as much chance of doing as ELSIE). Then I watched Saturday Superstore. I'd have preferred to be watching it at Penny's, but we hadn't been able to make arrangements the day before, because of her dad (who, I guessed, would be back in London by now), and I wasn't sure I could just turn up.

Anyway, we had days yet. We had a whole week.

I lingered and lounged most of the morning, then went to town. I walked past Penny's house slowly, willing her to come out. I even went up to the garden gate, thinking I might just go up to the door and knock, why not? The thing that stopped me seemed silly at the time. I saw a fragment of roof tile on one of the flagstones leading up to the front door, and that made me think of mad not-Mrs not-Poundley, and I got a bit scared of knocking on the door in case she answered, staple gun in one hand, pot of black paint in the other, so I went to town on my own.

I paused at the gate on the way back, too. That fragment of roof tile was still there. I told myself there were plenty of days in the half term week to see Penny, and went home. Besides, I had the new issue of Computer & Video Games to read.

Sunday, I decided to stop being a coward and go to Penny's and knock on the door. I took the latest C&VG with me, because there was an Electric Dreams competition where you could win a digital watch and a soundtrack album, so I thought Penny and me could enter and, if we won, I could have the watch and she could have the album. But I needed to know what American city the film had been set in, and was hoping Penny would have remembered, because I'd been too distracted thinking about the way the computer in the film worked, not where it was set.

That fragment of roof tile was still there, but I did my best to ignore it and walked up the path. There were a few more tile bits further on, which made me pause, and the stack of them by the door was, I could tell, shorter by a few.

I knocked lightly and waited.

Nothing.

My heart pounding, I knocked a bit louder.

Still nothing.

Perhaps they were out.

I went back up the path, and paused as I got to the gate, checking the windows for signs of life. No movement anywhere. Maybe Penny's grandad had phoned and re-arranged last weekend's visit. Maybe Penny's mum had cheered up and taken her out for a meal to make up for it all. Maybe her mum had been throwing roof tiles through sheer joy at being alive.

I went home and started a Manic Miner marathon that saw me finally conquering level seventeen, The Warehouse, with its massive block of crumbling floors and scissor-walking smiley robots who quite happily kill you.

I decided that, technically, half term didn't begin till Monday, so Monday was when me and Penny would start our week together.

Yeah, Monday.

I had a good feeling about Monday.

Monday, I had the house to myself. I listened to the Jimmy Young Show on the radio, which I only ever hear on school holidays or if I've got the day off because I'm not well. All the world's problems seem easy to deal with when Jimmy Young talks about them in his brisk, cheerful, sensible way, sprinkling them throughout with hits from the fifties onwards. I thought Penny was bound to come round, full of stories about where she'd been all weekend, but she didn't. After waiting as long as I could, I went to her house and knocked, but again nobody answered.

This was getting more worrying. Maybe I was just happening to go round when she and her mum were out? I left it an hour, then went round again. Then I left it another hour and went round again. Then I stayed home and worried. Maybe Penny's mum had been arrested for throwing roof tiles, and they'd arrested Penny too for, I don't know, aiding and abetting the throwing of roof tiles. Or maybe they were both in hospital, Penny with a knife-shaped fragment of tile lodged in her skull, her mum sitting by her bedside, riddled with guilt, while a machine went beep beep beep. Or maybe the evil boyfriend Caxton had returned, this time with a gun, and was holding them hostage. Should I stage a rescue? I could crash heroically through the glass roof of Penny's mum's studio, knocking out Caxton and saving the day. Or maybe I should phone the police. Then they could crash through the glass roof instead. They probably had the boots for it.

I didn't know what to do.

I couldn't ask Dad. I couldn't ask Joe. Even under normal conditions, I wouldn't have asked Patrick.

So I played Manic Miner again, and this time got through level eighteen, The Amoebatrons' Revenge.

Tuesday, I thought. Things will be different on Tuesday.

Tuesday started out rainy, so I put off going to Penny's, and concentrated on Manic Miner in the morning. I got through level nineteen, The Solar Power Generator, where if you stand still too long, you get zapped by this beam of super-concentrated solar energy. I glimpsed the final level.

Then I went round Penny's.

I knocked. I waited. I knocked. I went up to the living room window and peered through. Things looked normal. No bodies. No roof tiles. But no Penny, and no Penny's mum. Not even an unattended mug of tea.

I didn't know what to do.

I didn't know what to think.

I went home and, numbly, finished the final level of Manic Miner. I ought to have felt triumphant. This was one of the major achievements of my life, the sort of thing you had chiselled onto your tombstone. 'He finished Manic Miner, Tuesday 23rd October 1984.' But I felt more like what would be written was, 'Penny wasn't in', in big, heavy letters. And they might as well chisel it now, because all I wanted was to curl up in a nice, plush coffin and close the lid.

Once you finish Manic Miner, the game returns to the start screen and you just get the option of playing the whole thing over again. Which is sort of disappointing.

I watched daytime TV for the rest of the day, jumping up to peer out the window whenever anyone walked by, in case it was Penny.

It never was.

Wednesday, I was going to have to resolve this or go mad.

45

Nothing had changed at Silversmith Cottage as I opened its creaky garden gate and followed the flagstone path across the lawn to the front door. The broken bits of roof tile were still there. Everything was utterly silent. Why wasn't Penny playing her music? Or watching TV? Or shouting at her mum? Anything.

I lifted the door knocker and resolved to do a really loud knock.

I did three. Bang, bang, bang.

Then I waited three minutes by my digital watch.

Now what?

I went to the living room window and peered through. Nothing had changed. Penny's Smash Hits magazine, which had been on the sofa when I looked yesterday, was still there, open at the same page. It was like the place had been deserted. Like someone had dropped a mini-Neutron bomb. (A Neutron bomb, Mum, is a nuclear bomb that's specially designed to give out loads of radiation and not so much blast, so it kills loads of people, slowly and horribly, but doesn't damage buildings and property as much, which is why governments like the idea. Still, you wouldn't want to move in straightaway after one had gone off.)

I decided this was all impossible. Penny couldn't just disappear. However much I knew the world had loads of evil tricks up its sleeve, I was sure it didn't just make people vanish. It liked signs of destruction and devastation. It liked to show what it had done. It liked to leave its signature.

I started to walk round the house. I went clockwise, past the living room, so I'd get to Penny's room next. I knocked on the glass before peering through. I didn't want her thinking I was a Peeping Tom. But she wasn't there. Her bed was tidy, and her tapes were strewn over their little table with its ghetto blaster like always. All those pop posters on the walls, one with its corner hanging down. Surely Penny wouldn't let that happen. She'd stick it back up. Where was she?

I moved on. Next was her mum's room. The curtains were open, the bed was messy, but no one was there.

I moved on round the house till I came to her mum's studio. For a moment I just stared through its algae-spotted glass, at all the canvases ranged against the walls, and its mess of random objects.

Then I saw Penny's mum, sitting behind an easel, looking at me.

I almost bolted.

She raised a hand and beckoned. I froze. My feet, sensible things that they sometimes are, refused to move. When she realised I wasn't going to come in, she got up and opened the door that led from her studio to the garden.

'Come in, Tim.'

She didn't sound mad or angry. She wasn't carrying a staple gun or a roof tile. She was dressed normally. She seemed quite calm.

I said, 'Is Penny about?'

She went back to sit on the stool she'd been sitting on, in front of one of her three easels, the only one not covered by a cloth.

'She's gone.'

I came in, standing just inside the door without closing it.

'When will she be back?'

Penny's mum looked at me, then at the painting in front of her. 'Come here, Tim. I want your opinion.'

I went in, leaving the door open in case I had to run for it.

The painting was the one Penny had showed me when we'd come into her mum's studio that time. It was of a boy and girl, seen from behind, holding hands, the one where the girl looked a bit like Penny, and the boy looked a bit like me. But they were no longer standing in front of a big black space. Now they were standing in front of this magnificent, multicoloured mushroom cloud. It was pixellated, as though it had been drawn on a computer. And raining down from it, like a weird sort of radiation, were all these tiny little Space Invaders and Pac-Men, in sunset bands of red, orange, yellow and green.

'It's called Rites of Passage,' Penny's mum said, making me jump, because I'd forgotten she was there. 'Do you know what a rite of passage is?'

'Uh, no.'

'Back when we all lived in nice little tribes, when a boy or girl was old enough, they'd be taken from their family, to an isolated place. Sometimes it was a dark place, a cave or a hut. Sometimes it was out in the wilderness, far from the protection of the tribe. They'd pass through tests and trials. The details were different from tribe to tribe, for boys and girls, but the essence was always the same. They had to face demons and devils, the darkness of the world. They had to pass through death, and be reborn, an adult now, a child no more. Then they were welcomed back into the tribe, and taught the secret stories only the adults knew.'

She looked at me. If she was hoping for an intelligent comment, she wasn't getting one.

'We don't have that now,' she said. 'But we still have the need to be taught the secret of how to grow up, how to be a fully formed human being. Because the demons and devils come anyway. So we fight our way through our own rites of passage, not knowing them from nightmares or madness. And because they're unguided, they can often go unfinished, or go awry. And afterwards, who is there to teach us the secret stories that explain it all? That's what my broken fairy tales are about. Fairy tales are all that remain of our lost secret stories. They're about how to grow up and face the darkness. But what do we have now?'

I looked back helplessly, and shrugged.

'These computer games,' she said, putting a finger on one of the space invaders of the painting. 'They're like attempts at rites of passage. Journeys into the dark, facing demons. But they don't know what they're in search of, so they go round and round. And you're left to face the true darkness—' now she traced the mushroom cloud '—on your own, not part of a tribe, not part of anything. We're all on our own, like the ones who failed. Outcast, left to wander.'

Her finger drifted down to where the boy and girl were holdings hands. 'Unless you can find another like you, and make a tribe of two.'

We stood in silence for a bit, me breathless, not understanding, but somehow yes, understanding, though I could never explain it. But this wasn't what I wanted to know. I said, 'Where *is* Penny?'

'I scared her off. For good, this time.'

I looked at her almost desperately. 'I don't know what that means.'

She smiled a slight smile, somehow sadder than a non-smile.

'She came back on Friday with her father. It seems he's got married, to a normal young wife, and is expecting twins, of all things. He has a nice house of his own, now, and a nice family. He said Penny could go and live with him.'

'And — and is that what—?'

She smiled that sad smile again. 'I'm afraid that's when I started shouting and throwing things. I like to ruin things as much as possible. Perhaps, somewhere deep down, I thought it would be better for her to go. So I made them go.'

'Um, how — how long, um, for?'

She stared at her painting for a bit, then said, lightly, 'As I said. For good.'

46

I headed home, but didn't go there.

It doesn't feel like home anymore, so why should I?

Instead, I went down the bumpy part of Fallow Lane, even though it was during the day and it didn't mean anything. Last time I'd done this, it had been me and Penny, hand in hand, in the dark. Now it was just me, and I could see all the mud and puddles and rubbish that people had dumped.

I felt this ache, like someone was scooping a lump out of me with a sharp-edged spoon, then dumping it to one side and diving in for more. I'd never felt so scraped-out hollow.

I couldn't blame Penny. She wanted to be happy. Who didn't? And she'd been given a chance. Exactly what she'd wished for. I just wished — impossible wish — that there could be two of her, one to go away and be happy, and one I could have here, for me. Selfish. Silly. Impossible, anyway.

Fallow Lane met up with Pritchard Lane. I kept on down Fallow Lane. It got bumpier and narrower.

What could I do, Mum? What was there left to do? Everything had gone wrong except Penny, and now she'd gone, too.

It was the world that had done this. It knew what it was doing. Planned it, just to give me a glimpse, then taken it away. Great big hungry world. Great big drooling thing. Clawed with a million claws, mouthed with a thousand mouths. But subtle, too. Subtle like a man making a bomb, component by component, fitting it all together, letting the finished thing stand there sleek and silent, then pressing a little button, sending a tiny spark down a wire. And the spark is a signal to a computer. And the computer, stupid thing that it is, gets the signal and works out what to do. It goes, ah yes, signal 110 means turn on this light, signal 111 means blow up the world. And this is signal 111, so it blows up the world. Only, in this case, it's just *my* world. My personal world. Woomph. Gone. Smithereens and smoke.

I came to the London Road.

Traffic was whizzing by.

I didn't know where I was going, but I went there like I did.

I crossed the road, and took the turning toward the school. The school was of course closed, with chains on its gates. I walked past the gates, past the school building, to the hedge that runs along the sports field, then I ducked through the gap everyone uses as a short cut on cross country runs.

I still didn't think about what I was doing.

I followed the hedge round the sports field, looking at the school building, making sure, just in case the caretaker was there, but he wasn't. Then I walked round the back of the main building, where it was all so silent I could hear the echo of my feet as they tip-tapped on the tarmac.

I came to the bit where the gym block jutted out, and followed that round to the furthest corner, where there were trees behind me and no windows looking on. I knew this because I'd thought about it before. Never entirely seriously, but always knowing one day it *might* be serious, so I was ready.

At this corner, a black-painted metal drainpipe ran up the wall for three stories, then came to the roof.

I took hold of the drainpipe and tugged it.

It wasn't loose. It was a bit slippery, with its layers on layers of thick glossy paint, but if I gripped it with both hands, right round to the back, I felt secure.

There were brackets, every so often, holding it to the wall. Not as often as I'd have liked, but often enough to give me a breather where I could rest my feet. Three, no four, breathers.

I asked myself if there was anything I needed to do to

prepare myself, but couldn't think of anything. I gave one final thought to the ground beneath my feet, how hard it was, and how it might feel if I hit it with my head from a thirty foot fall. Then I gripped the drainpipe properly, and gave a little jump, clamping my feet round the pipe as hard as I could. Then I stopped there, thinking this is how it will be, all the way up. What I had to do (I knew, because I'd thought about it so many times) was do nothing but stare at the bricks in front of me, and at the pipe in front of me, and not think about up or down. Not think about how far I'd fall, or how far I still had to climb. Because if I thought about falling, I'd fall, and if I thought about how far I had to climb, I'd freeze, because it was so far.

Already I could feel a pain in my thighs and calves, and my knuckles were pressed into the sandpaper surface of the brick, skinning them whenever I gripped a bit tighter. But that was how it was going to be.

I straightened my legs a bit, and slipped my hands up a bit. Then I held onto the pipe and did a quick pull up of my legs, so I was back to how I had been, only that tiny bit further up.

My knees ached, already longing to be straightened out properly. But I wasn't going to be able to do that till I got to the top. But don't think of the top.

It was like a FOR-NEXT loop in BASIC. Do this thing, then do it again, and again and again and again. Twelve hundred thousand times, if necessary, each time identical. Then stop.

If a computer can do it, surely I can. If not, I can pretend I'm a computer.

I'd done one little step so far, one little shift upwards.

How silly I must have looked, a boy clinging to a drainpipe about a foot off the ground.

I thought, don't think of anything anymore, except: straighten legs, inch up hands, inch up legs, repeat.

Repeat.
Repeat.

47

I know what you're thinking, Mum.

What a stupid, stupid, stupid, stupid, stupid thing to do.

Plus a few more stupids.

The first time I looked down (I know I said I wouldn't, but I couldn't help it), I'd hardly got anywhere. I could have let go and dropped, and maybe hurt an ankle or grazed an elbow, but that would have been it. And I was tempted, because already the pain in my ankles was so bad, it was like someone had clamped a pair of fist-sized crocodile clips to them, and my arms were telling me they couldn't do this anymore, and the backs of my hands were raw from rubbing against the bricks. But one look down told me what a pathetic effort I'd made. If I dropped now, I'd hurt myself a little, limp home, go up to my bedroom, then sit there and — what? Think how everything was the same, and always would be? And Dad would come home, and Joe, and what was I going to do, say 'I almost climbed onto the school roof today'?

Almost. That meant nothing. It's like jumping up and down and saying you almost got to the moon.

So I inched up some more.

There's this thing that happens, that the world does. It gets you where you think everything's so bad that if it got any worse you couldn't go on. Then the bad gets worse and you find you can go on. Because what else is there to do?

Every inch I moved up, I hurt more. After I'd got over the first metal bracket holding the drainpipe to the wall, I had this jab of pain in my knee, so bad I thought my leg was going to shoot out straight, it so needed to be straight — straight, at that moment, felt like heaven — but it didn't. It trembled, all the way along, and I couldn't do anything for a bit. Then the trembling stopped, and I moved on.

When I got to the next bracket, I stopped. I couldn't get

my hands past it. Somehow, I can't remember how, I'd managed with the previous one, but now my shoulders felt as heavy as lead, and my arms wouldn't work. I stared at my hands, willing them to move. They didn't.

And so I looked down for the second time. I was still low enough on the drainpipe that if I let go, I could have got away with a broken leg, or perhaps a broken arm, or maybe a cracked rib or two. As long as I didn't land on my head, or break my back.

Then the ground lurched and swerved, and for a moment I thought this is it, I'm falling, but no, I was just dizzy.

I pulled myself close to the drainpipe, pressing its cold hard curve to my face. I opened my mouth and ran my teeth against it, as though I could grip onto it by biting it. I got splinters of paint in my mouth, and crunched them against my teeth with my tongue.

I thought, 'I'll stay here. Just stay here. I think I can do that. I'll stay here till half term's over and Monday comes around, and all the kids come back to school, and they find me here, clamped to the wall like a wodge of silly putty. Then they can get a teacher with a ladder to pull me off.'

And ask me why I did it.

And what would I say?

I did it because Penny went away?

But that wasn't it.

I did it because Dad wasn't talking to me. I did it because Dad was so angry, so clenched like a fist, he couldn't squeeze out words. I did it because he was telling me, with his every grunt and breath and look, that this was what the world did to you, if you gave it long enough. His not speaking to me wasn't because he was angry at me. It was because he was angry at everything, and trying *not* to be angry at me. Trying to hold it back, trying not to pass it on. Trying, at the last, to protect his family, his boys, from what the world is, what the world does. And on the verge of failing. Like a little boy clamped to a drainpipe, halfway up. (Too optimistic. Barely a third.)

I did it because of Joe. Stupid, blockhead Joe, clanking spanners and whistling the intro to Run To The Hills, revving his bike and listening to it purr, loving its every sleek line with such utter love. Because he'd said you'd always liked me more, Mum, and I wanted that to be made right, it *ought* to be made right, but it never would be, never ever in all the world.

I did it because of Patrick. Knowing Patrick was like battering your head against a soft brick wall. Dull thud after dull thud. But you couldn't hate him. You couldn't wish he was dead, or in pain, or alone, or unhappy. You couldn't wish that of anyone, could you? But he would be. The world would do it to him one day, because the world does it to everyone.

I did it because of Penny. Not because she'd gone away. She'd gone away to find that little bit of happiness she'd been owed for so long. I did it because she was owed so much more. Because she didn't know how much she was owed.

I did it because of you, Mum. Because of what the world did to you. It made you ill, and then kept at it, keeping you ill, keeping you ill, like it was squashing you under its thumb and twisting, squashing, squeezing, and you kept smiling and saying it was okay, till that one time in the dark of Fallow Lane you said it might not be, then it was back to smiling and saying it was okay, and then the world gave one twist too many even for you, and—

My hands moved, fluttering like a pair of broken birds, inching themselves up by their finger tips, to grip the top of the bracket, then slide over it. I was moving again. I didn't ache. No, I did. It was just I was nothing but pain now, so I couldn't tell what ached and what didn't, anymore. I pushed up, numb-headed, not relieved or grateful.

Just moving.

Up, I inched, like a boy-sized caterpillar. Every tiny movement of my legs or hands was a thing I had to think about, will into existence, fight against the rust of pain and weariness, till I felt like a seized-up junkyard thing groaning and grating its every movement, each one its last, its last, had to be the last, then there's one more, one more, one more. Every shift upwards got smaller and smaller, till I was moving in millimetres, till I couldn't tell I wasn't sliding down as much as I was moving up. The drainpipe was always the same. The sliding against my palms was the same. How could I tell which way I was moving?

There was only one way to tell, and that was to look down.

But I wasn't going to do that.

I'd wait till the next bracket. That would tell me I was moving up.

But what if I wasn't moving at all? What if my feet were sliding me down as much as my hands were sliding me up, and I was staying in place, between two brackets, never to reach either, like some stupid mechanical toy? I could be there forever. It already seemed like forever.

So I had to look down.

No, don't look down.

Just a glimpse. Just a quick—

I looked.

There was no ground. Only sky. A great, white blur, like the sharp-toothed grin of the world.

Then I fell.

48

The world was laid out below me, like I was a nuclear bomb hurtling towards the ground, having one last look at the everything that was, before I made it one great fiery nothing.

Actually, nuclear bombs explode before they hit the ground. Did you know that, Mum? They do that because it causes a lot more destruction, and kills a lot more people. The man who worked that out was called John Von Neumann, and he also worked out the basic structure of all modern computers, which is called the Von Neumann Architecture. I said there's loads of little connections between nuclear bombs and computers, didn't I? I almost wonder, sometimes, if it would be impossible to have one without the other, that I couldn't have the ZX Spectrum I love without the nuclear bombs I hate.

Funny how I had time to think about that as I fell towards the ground, isn't it?

Actually it isn't, because I wasn't falling.

It took me a moment to realise, but I was hanging, not falling.

Somehow, in the very beginnings of my fall, my hand had flailed up and caught — unmoving iron claw it now was — the gutter that ran along the edge of the roof.

I'd reached the top, but hadn't known it.

Now I was hanging off it.

I had an instant of relief, then the gutter creaked and started to sag.

It wasn't designed to hold the weight of a thirteen year old boy. They don't plan for these things when they build schools.

Suddenly, I don't know where from, I got this whip of energy, like some vital emergency button had been pressed, some switch marked 'This is REALLY IT YOU'RE GO-

ING TO DIE!', and I defied all the laws of physics to scramble up, grab the lip of the roof, and throw myself, I don't know how, onto the flat gravelly top.

I lay there.

I lay there, and my arms and legs and hands throbbed. At times I thought I was still clinging to the drainpipe, still climbing, and then that I was falling, and I'd jerk back to reality, and find I was on the roof, the flat roof, right near the edge, so I'd better not make any sudden movements.

I rolled (it was all I could do) away from the edge.

I had to roll through a puddle, but it got me away.

Then I lay there again, panting. My legs were straight at last. My arms could flop. I felt like I was made of broken bricks and shards of glass, something to be chucked in a skip and taken away.

Then everything went a bright, nuclear white.

Then it went black.

There was wetness on my face.

Single drops of rain were falling on me, each one a wake-up tap from a watery finger. One on the forehead, one on the nose. Then a wet splodge like a granny's kiss on the corner of my mouth. I opened my eyes, only to be poked in one by another rainy finger.

The world was nothing but sky. A great cauldron of black and grey coming slowly to the boil, streaked with veins of silver where the dying day showed through.

Or perhaps it was the moon.

How late was it?

I tried to lift my arm to check (my digital watch has a light, though I don't like to use it, because it eats up the battery like Hungry Horace), but my arm refused to move. I sent a signal through to my fingers — 'Wiggle if you're there!'— and they wiggled, but it hurt the back of my hand where the bricks had scraped it raw and the blood had dried.

I was stiff with hurt in every joint and muscle I had.

I decided to forget about my watch. It was definitely late, I knew that. Late enough for Dad and Joe to have realised something was wrong, unless they thought I was round Patrick's, or Penny's, not knowing I couldn't be at either. Soon they'd know, though. And what then?

It didn't matter. Nothing mattered. It was just me and the world now.

The clouds rolled by. On the ZX Spectrum, when the screen fills up, everything stops and you're asked 'scroll?', and you press 'y' for it to continue, 'n' for it to stop. The world doesn't ask, it just keeps on going, like it's saying it's got plenty more where this came from. And the same goes for the bad things. Always plenty more, always plenty more.

Every so often the wind would swoop down and nudge at me, like a great blunt paw, toying with this tiny thing that had strayed into its domain, wondering what it was, whether it was worth bothering with. Should it scoop me up and throw me into the mix of stormy clouds, to be chucked about by lightning bolts and thunder claps, then dropped, forgotten, broken on the ground?

It could have.

But it had other things to be doing. The peaceful sky of the day was turning into something wild and scary, a great mass of unquiet air hulking above me, shifting, moaning, spitting, like a dog snarling in its sleep. At night, the world could drop the pretence, rip off the mask, be the nighttime thing it was and always had been, like back in the days when primitives huddled in caves and shook to the sound of crashing thunder and moaning, screaming wind.

I was going to look this world — the real world, not the civilised thing we like to pretend it is — right in the face, and know it for what it is.

When you died, Mum, we hid in our shelter, me, Joe and Dad. Our world-proof shelter.

It didn't work.

And when Penny came along, I tried to bring her into it, shelter her from the world too.

But you can't hide from the world.

The world is where we are. We're in its belly already.

So I lay there with nothing between me and it, and thought: Go on, do your worst.

The sky blackened and thickened. The streaks of silver died away to hair-thin cracks. The odd raindrop still hit me in the face, each one ice cold, a numbing flick from a bully's finger. The wind whooshed and rattled and moaned and whistled and sang and growled. It swept on over me right up close, and sounded from way up high.

I'd had my warning, the world was saying. I should have been in bed.

Now it was going to get started.

And as the world filled with the dark of night, my head filled with all the dark thoughts I'd ever had. Dad, Penny, Patrick, nuclear war, and you, Mum. Everything. It was all boiling inside of me like the clouds were boiling above. I thought and thought and thought and thought, like I was trying to outdo the world for darkness. But you can't outdo the world. I thought myself to exhaustion. Not sleep. I couldn't sleep. Not with that vast, angry animal lashing about above me. I just couldn't think anymore. All my dark thoughts failed and I lay there, one more empty thing for the wind to whistle through, and the rain to fall on.

One more part of the world.

49

You almost know it all now, Mum. There's only one more thing to tell.

That night seemed to go on forever. It didn't matter to me. I'm not afraid of the dark (you saw to that), but I do remember thinking the world had really ended, and it would be nothing but darkness from now on, and if so, that was sort of disappointing. But what could I expect?

Then gradually, gradually, the sky was edged with the tiniest hint of grey. I didn't realise it at first because the clouds had gone, so there was nothing to see. But when I did, when I knew it was going to be a whole new day, I felt it was the most incredible thing ever. That might sound silly. It's the simplest thing, a new day, but right then it seemed impossibly wonderful. Just the fact that there was day, that there was life, that there was a world, made me think how amazing it all is. We're living on a speck of mud, rock and water, caught between a ball of nuclear fire and an ocean of freezing, spacey nothing. But somehow, we're alive. And not just alive, but *interestingly* alive. Yeah, we plot a million ways of destroying ourselves (why? it seemed so stupid as to put my climbing onto the school roof way in the shade), but we also do lots of little things that would be called miracles if only they didn't happen everyday. People had invented computers. And they didn't just make them do serious things like the household accounts (still don't know what those are, Mum), but they put games on them. Games, for people's enjoyment. Like they were so bubbling over with the thrill of being alive, they wanted to share it. I think people have written far more games than they've written programs for doing the household accounts. But not just that. People do all sorts of other things, too. They invented motorbikes for Joe, and a job for Dad, and they invented rugby, which I may not like to play, but all of a sudden it seemed a wonderful part of an amazing everything.

And Penny. Somehow, in the world, there was Penny.

The sun came up.

I wondered how I'd ever thought the world could only be horrible. It was nice, too. But most of all, it was incomprehensible. How did I ever think I could know enough about the world to say it was this or that? It's a million, trillion things, all rolled into one.

It's just so big.

And I am so happy to be alive.

Hello world!

I lay there and let the sun come up.

Then I wondered what I was going to do.

What *am* I going to do, Mum?

Here I am, on the school roof, and though I feel sort of wonderful, nothing makes sense. The only thing left is to climb back down (somehow!) to the ground, and return to normal life. But I don't want to. Penny's still gone. Dad's probably really, genuinely, shoutily angry at me now. Up here, I can feel my wonderful feelings, but that's all.

So I thought I'd tell you about it, Mum.

Today is Thursday 25th October.

My life might have just ended. Or it might have just begun.

I don't know.

And now you know everything there is to know.

So I'll just lie here.

There's this instruction in Machine Code called NOP. It stands for 'No Operation'. It's an actual instruction that tells the computer to do nothing. Weird isn't it?

But that's what I'm going to do.

Just NOP, up here.

I can't think of anything else to do.

Did someone just call my name?

50

Hi, Mum.

It's me again. Tim.

Not on the school roof this time. In fact, I've just got home from the school disco.

It's still 1984. Actually, it's only a week since I spoke to you last. In the meantime, I've managed to start reading that book. You know, the one about 1984. Turns out it's by George Orwell. (Penny's mum knew, and even had a copy.)

Anyway, I just wanted to tell you what's happened. Why I'm not on the roof anymore, and so on. There's a few things to tell.

First, about the roof.

I was lying there, NOP NOP NOP-ing, when I thought I heard my name.

I listened, and heard it again.

'Tim? Are you up there?'

It sounded like Penny, but that couldn't be right.

I sat up. My legs and arms didn't ache so much now, but were stiff and fragile like sun-bleached newspapers rolled up and made into stilts. I crawled to the edge of the roof and peered over.

Penny was looking up at me, shielding her eyes with one hand.

'Tim?' she said.

'Penny?' I said.

'Tim!' she said.

So I said, 'Penny!'

Then we looked at each other for a bit.

She said, 'I knew you'd be up there. Because of what you said that time on Fallow Lane. About where you'd go if there was a four-minute warning.'

'But why aren't you in London?'

'I'll tell you,' she said, 'but I'm not going to shout.'

'Okay,' I said.

There was a pause, then she said, 'Are you going to come down, or do I have to come up?'

'I'll come down.' I didn't want her to have to climb the drainpipe, too. From up here, I could see how stupidly dangerous it was. Which made me realise something. I said, 'Um, I don't know how, though.'

'Can't you drop down onto the main block, then from there onto the roof above reception, then onto the ground?'

I pictured what she was saying. If I crossed to the opposite corner of the gym block, the main block of the school was just one storey lower. Then the roof above reception was just one storey lower than that. Then the ground was only a one storey drop away.

'Isn't that how you got up?' Penny said.

'No. I climbed the drainpipe.'

'*This* drainpipe? All the way up *there*?'

'Yeah.'

'You idiot! You could have fallen!'

'I almost did. Twice.'

She gave a helpless-sounding little 'oh', which made me feel enormously guilty.

I said, 'I'll come down, then.'

'Be careful!'

I crawled back from the edge, and tried standing. My knees thought about giving way at first, but I staggered about till they got their strength back, then I crossed to the other corner of the gym block. I lowered myself over, and dropped to the roof of the main block. (I was now above the assembly hall. I briefly imagined crashing through the roof and landing on Mr Corking midway through one of his boring morning talks. That would get a cheer from everyone.) Then I crossed the main block and looked over the edge to see where reception was, thinking as I did how stupidly easy this was compared to the stupidly dangerous thing I'd done.

Penny gave a little wave from the ground.

I waved back, then lowered myself onto reception, and carefully (because my arms were getting a bit shaky now, and I was feeling weak) dropped from there to the ground.

As I landed I staggered, dizzily, but Penny took hold of me by the arms. She kept hold, and gave me a should-I-or-shouldn't-I look, which made me wonder if she was going to give me a slap, either to wake me up or because I'd done such a stupid thing. Instead, she kissed me. Just quickly. Suddenly her face was there, right up against mine, with a little warm touch at the lips and a tingle where our noses touched. Nothing like a raindrop at all. I looked startled, she looked worried, then I grinned, and she grinned.

She said, 'Your dad and brother are looking for you.'

'But how did *you* know?' I said.

'It's a bit of a story. Come on. Let's get out of the grounds. We're not supposed to be here.'

When we got to the sports field, Penny took my hand.

'I didn't mean to go up to London without telling you,' she said. 'It's just, when Dad got me home on Friday, Mum saw him coming up the path and was at the front door before we could knock. And he just blurted it all out. That he was married, and had a home, and had twins on the way, and that I could stay with him now. Mum went off like a sherbet dip. I mean, she started throwing things and shouting. It was like World War Three with roof tiles. We literally had to run to the car for cover. And Dad said, "Right, that's it," and drove off to London.'

We reached the gap in the hedge and squeezed through to the pavement.

Penny said, 'So, we got up there, and I met his wife, who I guess is my stepmother, and she's this lovely woman, but she was about to pop any moment, and didn't quite seem in the same world as the rest of us. Then Dad said he'd take me up to my room, because I was tired, and I went up there and slept. And it was only when I woke up next morning I saw it was a nursery. There were two cribs, each with a mobile hanging above it, and there were teddy bears painted on the walls.'

She shrugged. 'I knew it was all what I'd wished, loads of times. But those wishes had started when I was six or seven. And I'd stuck with them, because I never had to think about them being real. They were just this fairy tale I escaped into. Now it was real, I knew it wasn't right. I mean, for a start, though Dad's wife — my step-mum, I mean — was lovely, she was obviously just so happy about her coming event, and totally focused on that, and I can't blame her. But I knew I was only ever going to be an addition to the family, not a real part of it like they were. And Dad kept saying how it'd be alright, that the room would be mine, though the twins would have to sleep in it, too, but they were trying for a bigger house, and... And then, well, I knew this wasn't what I wanted anymore. What I wished for now was to get on with growing up, not going back to being a kid. Also, I knew I wanted you.'

I grinned like an idiot for a bit, and she seemed to like that.

'So, after a few days, I left him a note while he was at work, explaining it all. And I came back by train. I knew he'd only try and stop me, but I said I'd come and visit him, even stay for a bit, but it obviously wasn't going to work. So I got to Eastead, and I was going to go right round your house, but I knew I ought to see Mum first. And almost the first thing she said was your dad had been round to see if you were there, because you'd disappeared.'

She looked at me. 'Mum thinks your dad has a very interesting face. She wants to paint his portrait.'

I liked that, the idea of Dad's face hanging alongside the

monsters in Penny's mum's hallway.

Now it was my turn for explanations.

I thought about how to start. But the whole thing only made sense in one big lump, so I just dived in. I can't remember exactly what I said, but I don't need to say it again to you, Mum, because I've told you it all already.

By the time I finished, we were walking slowly up the London Road, and Penny was still holding my hand. (She'd given me a half-worried, half-telling-off look when she realised how badly the backs of my hands were scraped.)

Then this great growling thing screeched to a halt beside us and purred there like a self-satisfied tiger. It was Joe, actually riding his bike instead of taking it apart. He lifted his visor.

'There you are, you pilchard,' he said. 'You been with your girlfriend all this time?'

'No,' I said.

Penny said, 'He was on the school roof,' like it was this ordinary thing people did from time to time.

'Oh,' Joe said, then thought about it, then said, 'Oh,' again.

Then he added, 'Well, I'd better tell Dad you're okay.' And, with one more 'You pilchard', snapped his visor back down and roared off up the London Road.

It was only then I noticed we were opposite Patrick's house. Not only that, but Patrick was there, and his mum. They were unloading Sainsburys bags from the back of her car.

Mrs Luffley gave me a slightly sad little wave, which made me think she knew about me and Patrick. Patrick at first pretended not to see me. I waited till he looked, knowing he would, and waved.

He looked grumpy about it, but he waved back.

Penny swung my hand in hers, and we turned down Pritchard Lane.

I hadn't expected Dad to be home.

I came into the living room with Penny, and there he was, standing by the gas fire like before.

'Dad,' I said.

He said, 'Joe says you got up on the school roof.'

'Yeah,' I said. 'Um, sorry.'

He shook his head and frowned. 'Let's see.'

I went over, and showed him my hands. He turned them over, looking at the scraped backs, then he put his own hand on my shoulder.

'You hurt?'

'All over,' I said. 'But I didn't fall.'

'That was a mad thing to do,' he said, and I got ready to be told off. 'A right mad thing. But we know all about mad, don't we, you, me and Joe? Right bunch we are. Three blokes on their own. Bound to go a bit mad. You there, young Penny, you ought to know what you're getting into. But I've met your mother, and she's a mad one, too. Got to be mad in this world, haven't you? It's about the only way to stay sane.'

Then he looked at me, hand still on my shoulder, and said, 'Sorry, about...'

And I shrugged, and said, 'Nah.'

And he said, 'Since your... your mother...'

And I said, 'Nah,' again, and that was that.

He said, 'You know where the photo albums are, in the attic? Well, find a good one, of Mum, and we'll put it up.' Then he ruffled my hair and said, 'I'm off to work. There's five pounds, Tim, to keep you off the roof for the rest of the week. And look after this girl. She's a good one, I know. And you, girl, look after him. I'll get some fish fingers in for tea, and you're welcome to join us.'

And with that, he left.

I had something to eat (I was starving), then went up into the attic and got the photo albums down, and showed them all to Penny. For a bit, it was like looking at somebody else's past, then I started to remember, to feel it was mine. We found a good photo of you, Mum, and now it's in a frame on the mantlepiece.

(Joe found one of him doing a wheelie on his old Raleigh Chopper. He took the Threads picture off his door and pinned that up instead.)

The Wednesday after half term (which is today, Mum), there was an after-school disco. I don't usually go to discos, but this time, of course, there was Penny, so I did. We both rushed home to get changed. I just put on the sort of thing I wear most Saturdays, but Penny did the whole thing with makeup and big dangly earrings and a top that was all jagged flashes of bright colour, so she looked like a month's worth of Top of the Pops rolled into one.

We met up with Kash outside. Kash had pink and silver eyeshadow on, and looked ready to stare down anyone who might like to comment on it.

We went in, and soon they were playing Love On Your Side by the Thompson Twins, so Penny and me danced to that. Then they played Sweet Dreams, and as we were dancing, a robot shifted across the floor to do some moves nearby. It was only after a couple of minutes I realised it was Patrick.

'Hello, Patrick!' I shouted.

He gave me a robot wave, then moonwalked into the thumping dark.

Me and Penny went over to where Mr Witt was selling plastic cups of cola for 10p.

Kash was there.

I said, 'Me and Penny just saw Patrick dancing like a robot.'

Kash said, 'Penny and *I*,' which I thought was going to be the beginning of a sentence, till I realised she was correcting me. Then she said, 'Where did he go?'

I pointed at one of the darker corners of the hall.

'I am going to dance with him,' she said, and went off.

Penny and me — I mean *I* — drank our cokes.

Penny said, 'Is that your friend Chip?'

'Yeah.'

'And isn't that Kash's sister he's dancing with?'

'Yeah...'

We watched in a sort of awed silence as Chip made moves no normal dancing human should have made. Kash's sister, meanwhile, danced like the coolest creature on the planet. Together, it was like the battle of ancient, primeval forces, but somehow it worked.

Then they started playing Prince Charming by Adam Ant, and Penny wanted to dance to that, so we did.

Which, Mum, is my way of saying that's it. I can't think of anything more to say. The world hasn't been blown up in a nuclear war, and even Penny's mum has been sort of happy for a while. Dad, meanwhile, has decided to take up fishing, as he says it will (a) keep him out of the pub and (b) give us a change from fish fingers for tea every once in a while.

Joe told me the other day he's got a girlfriend. Or, he fancies this girl, and she's going to be his girlfriend, he just hasn't got round to telling her yet. He's also decided to take up photography, which must be why he had all those copies of Amateur Photographer in his room. (I knew there had to be a reason.)

So, that's it, Mum. Speak to you soon.

Maybe from the year 2000!

I feel a bit more positive about reaching it, now.

I wrote *hello world* as a 40th birthday present to myself. For a while, I'd had a vague feeling of mixed nostalgia and excitement about the 1980s, a decade that was increasingly starting to feel like a historical era, even though I'd lived through it. Researching the 1980s was partly about reviving memories, partly about new discoveries, and was wonderfully addictive. It's strange to remember how exciting it was to plug a 48k ZX Spectrum into a cathode ray television and have it print your name all over the screen in a range of fantastic colours. (Eight, anyway. Including black and white.) All the time I was doing this research, I kept adding any story or character ideas I had to a 'random ideas' file, and eventually Tim, Penny, and the others emerged, along with their story.

I was born (in Reading, England) in the same year as both Tim and Penny, and like them was 13 in 1984. Since then I've had the usual odd variety of jobs writers have, including vitamin packer, porter at a mushroom farm, computer programmer, technical support, and postman.

For more about me and the things I've written (or even, in one case, sung), visit my website at:

www.murrayewing.co.uk

www.ingramcontent.com/pod-product-compliance
Lightning Source LLC
Chambersburg PA
CBHW061026120726

47910CB00006B/2113